"There's no excuse for playing with fire."

Scott heard the hard edge in his voice but couldn't help it.

Evie crossed her arms as she continued to look across the bay. Probably waiting for the towboat so she could get out of here as soon as possible. She turned back to him. "Don't you ever play with fire?" she asked.

Scott felt her words like a punch. Felt the air drop ten degrees colder. "No," he said. He was sorry he'd tried to be nice.

"So those stories about firefighters being closet pyromaniacs are just rumors?"

Heat crept over his neck and ears like a burn.

"No one I know or have ever worked with," he said, clipping off the words with deadly deliberation, "would think it was fun to mess around with something that could kill."

He stopped himself before he said too much.

Dear Reader,

Thank you for visiting Starlight Point as you read *Meet Me on the Midway*. No matter the season, I believe it's always a good time for a summer romance!

This is the third of the Starlight Point Stories miniseries. The first book, *Under the Boardwalk*, follows the eldest of the Hamilton children the first summer he inherits Starlight Point. Jack Hamilton finds true love with Augusta after a roller-coaster romance. In the second book, *Carousel Nights*, middle child June Hamilton struggles with a tough choice: continuing her Broadway career or coming home to Starlight Point for good. This third book follows the youngest member of the family, Evie, as she finds her place at Starlight Point. Proving herself as more than just an accountant means she has to take risks with the family business. She also risks her heart with a man who stands in her way but sweeps her into a summer romance.

This is my ninth published novel, but I still fall in love with my characters every time. I hope you'll love spending time with Evie and Scott at Starlight Point. Thank you for reading my book, and please visit me at amiedenman.com, follow me on Twitter, @amiedenman, or send me an email at author@amiedenman.com.

Happy summer, wherever you are!

Amie Denman

HEARTWARMING

Meet Me on the Midway

—

Amie Denman

◆ HARLEQUIN® HEARTWARMING™

Recycling programs
for this product may
not exist in your area.

ISBN-13: 978-0-373-36817-4

Meet Me on the Midway

Copyright © 2016 by Amie Denman

Printed in U.S.A.

Amie Denman is the author of nine contemporary romances full of humor and heart. Born with an overdeveloped sense of curiosity, she's been known to chase fire trucks on her bicycle and eavesdrop on lovers' conversations. Amie lives in Ohio with her husband, two sons, a big yellow Labrador and two cats. She believes everything is fun, especially wedding cake, show tunes, roller coasters and falling in love.

Books by Amie Denman

Harlequin Heartwarming

Under the Boardwalk
Carousel Nights

Carina Press

Her Lucky Catch

Visit the Author Profile page
at Harlequin.com for more titles.

To my husband, with whom I fell in love many summers ago at an amusement park just like Starlight Point.

CHAPTER ONE

THIS SHOULD HAVE been my big day. Evie Hamilton wore a white linen dress and high-heeled sandals as she stood on the long sunny dock in the Starlight Point Marina. The project she'd dreamed up for her family's amusement park last summer and worked on all winter was scheduled to open today. The morning weather was perfect. Reporters lined a parallel dock, and a camera crew from the local news station waited. Starlight Point would be on the cover of the July issue of the *Roller Coaster Times*.

"You look like an advertisement for summer in that gorgeous dress," Evie's sister, June, said. "Why don't you toss your plain navy blue skirts and dress like this all the time? It's more dramatic."

"The role of the dramatic sister is already taken," Evie said. "And nothing is less practical than white linen. If it rains, I'm going to look like a naked waif."

"You might get a good offer," June said. She stood next to Evie and smiled and waved at the reporters.

Evie shook her head. "The only offer I want right now is the offer of a signature on our occupancy permit from the local fire inspector."

"It'll work out," her sister advised her. "Cut the ribbon and pretend the whole project is on time and boaters will be eating seafood at the restaurant for dinner."

"But they won't," Evie whispered. "The new fire inspector refused to sign our permit yesterday even though Jack met with him and pled our case."

"Should have gone yourself," June said. "You're much prettier than our brother."

"I couldn't. I was meeting with our construction super to see if there was a chance of fixing the supposed violations and widening the fire lane around the restaurant overnight."

June gave her sister a hug. The sun shone brightly on Starlight Point and happy screams from the roller coasters drifted across the newly renovated marina. Gleaming white powerboats tugged at their dock lines in the gentle breeze and the blue water of the bay sparkled.

New docks for seasonal and transient boaters stretched across the marina, but the gas lines running under the docks were currently dry. Because Starlight Point was right on Lake Huron, there was a new terminal for the ferry that made fifteen round trips a day to downtown Bayside. Just off the docks, a new restaurant and gift shop blended old-fashioned amusement park décor with modern conveniences. A shower house and comfort station for boaters completed the project.

It was all just as Evie imagined it would be. She'd convinced her brother and sister to go along with the plan based on her careful calculations of return on investment. Boaters would dock, fuel up, eat at the restaurant and stay overnight. While they were there, they would buy tickets to Starlight Point and scatter their cash over the amusement park with food and merchandise purchases. It was all part of Evie's plan to bump up revenues by improving accommodations.

But it wasn't going to return a dime of investment if they couldn't open in time for the summer boating season.

"It's wonderful," June said.

Evie loved her sister's optimism, but there

was no doubt who was the practical member of the family. "There's no fuel in the gas docks, the restaurant can't open for business, and even the shower house for boaters has a red sign taped to the window."

June shrugged. "Fake it. The reporters don't have to know the showers are dry and the ovens are cold. Everything looks perfect."

"I wish Inspector Gotcha would show up. I might take a swipe at him with my ribbon-cutting scissors." She brandished the oversize ceremonial scissors just for effect.

June laughed. "He's not going to show his face. He's probably two hundred years old and loves telling people to get off his lawn. I'm sure his lawn has a sprinkler system and a fire lane precisely twelve feet wide all around it."

Evie sighed. "I wish the previous fire inspector hadn't retired halfway through this project."

Jack Hamilton, suit coat flapping around his six-foot-four body, power walked up to them and put an arm around Evie and June. "How are my two favorite sisters?"

"We're your only sisters," Evie said. Although she and June were both tall, their brother cast a shadow over them in the late-morning sun.

"You'd still be my favorites if I had ten sisters."

Evie smiled. With hard work, she and her siblings had turned around a struggling amusement park and were finally hoping to see profits this year. And they would have if she hadn't sunk all their money into her big plans.

"Before the ceremony starts and we're swamped with adoring fans," June said, "I want to tell you both something."

"You're not flaking out and heading back to Broadway are you?" Jack asked.

"My Broadway days are over. You need me here to run all the live entertainment. Besides, what I want to tell you both is—"

"You're pregnant," Evie guessed.

"Yes!" June said, hugging her sister.

Jack shook his head and stretched long arms around his sisters. "I have no idea how you already knew that," he said in Evie's ear.

She shrugged. "I'm observant. When are you due?"

"January. It's early yet, but I had to tell you."

Emotion rushed through Evie like a roller

coaster cresting a hill. Jack's wife, Augusta, was due to deliver a daughter later this summer, and now June and Mel would soon have a baby to add to their family.

What did Evie have? Dozens of guests who'd shown up to witness the grand opening of the Starlight Point Marina.

She took a deep breath. "Showtime," she said. *It's going to be all show and no substance today.*

Evie walked to the end of the floating dock where a red ribbon stretched across three piers. Guests lined up on a parallel dock so they could have a good view, and her speech would easily carry across the thirty feet of water between them.

"Welcome to the grand opening of the Starlight Point Marina," she said. Quiet murmurs turned to applause and she smiled, flanked by her brother and sister.

"I'm Evie Hamilton, and it's my pleasure to share ownership of Starlight Point with my brother, Jack, and my sister, June Preston. The past several years have been amazing for our family-owned park, and we couldn't have done it without the support of the local community. Today we cut the ribbon on phase one of our planned capital improvement projects. When the marina project is totally complete, we will begin a massive renovation of the Lake Breeze Hotel. I won't tease you with details about that today, but I hope you'll come back this summer to a press conference where I'll be glad to share our plans."

If they are approved by Inspector Gotcha.

A cloud passed over the sun and temporarily shadowed the crowded docks. Evie glanced up. A line of rain clouds on the lake's horizon were far enough away. She and her siblings would have at least an hour to share refreshments and tours with the local media and invited guests before the rain hit.

Evie smiled brightly and brandished the pair of silver scissors for the waiting cameras. "The Starlight Point Marina is officially open!"

Except it wasn't…not until the fire inspector synchronized all his smoke detectors. She pictured an old man with a clipboard, a frown and a fire extinguisher hooked to his belt. Whatever his problem was, she could not let him stand in the way of the first project she'd taken on at Starlight Point.

If she wanted to play it safe, she'd hide in her office and tally the numbers in the accounting books. But she was more than a CPA. And she was ready to show her family she had more to offer than just accounting skills.

She cut the ribbon and watched the ends flutter to the water before seasonal employees on the docks reeled them in. This marina project would open. *Soon.* For today, she was taking June's advice and making nice with the press as long as the sun shone.

CAPTAIN SCOTT BENNETT idled the fire truck in the Starlight Point parking lot as he waited for the line of cars to pull out of the marina. Despite his refusal to issue an occupancy report for the marina buildings until a few fire-safety measures were taken, he'd seen no reason to prevent the grand opening ceremony from taking place. The Hamiltons had worked hard on the project and it was a nice addition to the resort.

Except for the fact that someone had treated the fire codes as if they were an afterthought. The realization made him feel ill.

He opened his eyes. Traffic had thinned, cars escaping for drier territory as the skies opened up in a drenching afternoon shower. He pulled onto the outer loop road to drive around the Starlight Point peninsula to the fire station located on the opposite side of the amusement park. In the off season, he might have driven straight across the peninsula, but it was the first day of June and the park was in full swing. No way would he open a gate and drive past the carousel and the hotdog stands. Unless it was a life-or-death situation.

Scott was new to the fire department at Starlight Point and he wondered how many life-and-death situations a mile-long peninsula filled with rides and food stands could have.

Right now, he focused on the road. The ancient windshield wipers on the fire truck smeared the raindrops and a missing piece of rubber left a streak. Scott made a mental note to change the blades before someone got in an accident due to poor visibility. Maybe he should also check the two ambulances, small pumper and pickup that made up the Starlight Point Fire Department fleet.

He squinted through the rain. A woman in a soaked white dress was walking along the outer loop despite the numerous signs prohibiting pedestrians. He activated the flashing lights on the fire truck and pulled as far to the side of the narrow road as possible.

He reached across and opened the passenger door.

"Get in," he said.

The woman was tall and slender. Her hair was probably blond when it was dry, but right now it hung down in dark streaks against her white dress. She held a pair of high-heeled shoes in one hand as she stepped onto the running board of the fire truck.

She leaned into his truck and looked over at him. Her huge smile was like a streak of sunshine and he temporarily forgot she was violating an important safety code. Not something he took lightly.

"I don't usually accept rides from strangers," she said.

He reached under the seat and pulled out a roll of shop towels. He tore off three and handed them to her.

"I don't usually pick up hitchhikers in the fire truck," he said. "But I can't allow you to walk along this road. It's dangerous."

Her focus dropped to the name tag on his uniform shirt.

A Starlight Point Fire Department patch was sewn on one shirtsleeve and the Maltese cross typical of fire departments across the country was sewn on the other. His navy blue button-down shirt tucked into navy blue pants was the uniform for the safety forces here. It wasn't much different from the one he wore on shift at the Bayside Fire Department. With two jobs, he lived in a uniform.

"Scott," she said. "You must be new this summer."

He watched her towel off her face and bare arms. It was a warm day, but goose bumps covered her skin.

"Seat belt," he said.

He reached over her, pulled the door shut, and then watched her click her safety belt. Switching off the emergency lights, he scrutinized the side mirrors for traffic as he pulled the truck onto the road.

"This is my first summer at the Point," he said. "Do you work here?"

She laughed.

He didn't think it was a silly question considering he'd found her walking along the outer road where pedestrians were forbidden for good reason. The road was barely wide enough for two cars. There was no shoulder on one side where it edged right up to the tall fence surrounding the amusement park. The other side had only stacked boulders between it and Lake Huron. There was no room for walkers or bikers.

"I've worked here for years," she said.

He glanced at her. "You don't look old enough for that to be true." He knew he sounded surly, but the rainy windshield was driving him nuts. There had better not be any more hitchhikers on this road. The thought of causing an accident made his gut feel hollow.

"I started very young. My name is Evie, by the way."

He looked at her again before turning back to the smeared windshield. Evie was an unusual name. He had just heard it somewhere else recently. *Where have I run across that name?*

"Why were you walking around the point?" he asked. "If you've worked here for years, you know that's prohibited."

She raised her hands over her head and fluffed her hair, running the long length of it through the remaining shop towel.

"Shortcut gone bad. I was going from the marina to the corporate office and thought I'd just dash across the road and through the gate behind the train yard. But it was locked. So I was walking up the road to the next gate."

"Why didn't you go through the guest entrance by the marina?"

"I didn't have a ticket," she said. She laughed again.

He had no idea why that was funny.

He tightened his grip on the wheel. "I can take you as far as the gate behind the Scrambler. That will get you close to the corporate office."

"Thank you."

Despite the wisdom of it, Scott rued the ten-mile-per-hour speed limit. He turned on the defroster, hoping to clear the windshield, which was now steaming on the inside from their breath. It was going to take at least another ten minutes on the slow crawl around the Point.

"How old is this truck?" Evie asked.

"Older than both of us."

"Maybe we should get a new one."

We? She said she'd worked here a long time. Maybe it was the royal *we*. Or maybe she was crazy. After all, he did pick her up walking in the rain in a see-through white dress.

He was trying not to look at the dress.

"New trucks are expensive," he said.

"How much?"

Okay, so we're going to discuss the price of fire trucks. Fine. He could talk about that all night. Or at least for the next nine minutes until he could unload his beautiful but strange passenger.

"In my opinion, Starlight Point should get a ladder truck. Something close to a hundred feet tall just in case of an accident on a coaster. It would also be good in case of a hotel fire. The center structure of the Lake Breeze is ten stories, so you'd need a hundred-foot ladder."

Evie nodded. "And how much does a ladder truck like that cost?"

"Easily half a million if you buy a new one."

His passenger laughed.

Doesn't she realize new trucks come with insurance savings and, more importantly, the potential to save lives?

"There's nothing funny about fire safety," he said.

Evie sighed. "So I've heard. Sadly, I don't have half a million bucks buried on the beach or hidden under the Silver Streak." She swiveled in her seat and faced him. "Can you believe some picky new fire inspector from

Bayside is giving us all kinds of grief on the marina project?"

Scott's insides felt like an ice-cube tray someone was shuffling to break up the cubes. And why was she saying *us* like she owned the place?

"Grief?" he asked.

"Fussy stuff. Signs, some valve, something about an electrical pancl, and a fire lane that's too narrow."

"Those sound like serious problems," he said.

Evie cranked her window down a few inches. Apparently she didn't care about the stray raindrops coming in since she was already soaked. Maybe it would help the steam problem they were having.

Anything would help right now.

"The previous fire inspector approved the whole plan," shc continucd. "Everything. I thought we were fine until the new guy crumpled up my dream project like last week's newspaper."

She rolled the window all the way down. Waved at people inside the fence. Waved at more people and called them by name.

Does my hitchhiking passenger know everyone at Starlight Point?

Scott slowed as he approached the hotel gate and came to a full stop when the police officer held up his hand.

The old man stepped onto the running board and leaned in the window. "Thought I saw you in there, Evie. Big day for you with your new marina opening." The officer patted Scott on the shoulder. "Take good care of my girl."

Scott pulled away and headed for the gate outside the Scrambler.

"How long did you say you'd worked here?" he asked.

"All my life. My parents owned Starlight Point until a few years ago when my father died. My brother and sister and I run it now."

Evie *Hamilton*. That was the name on the paperwork for the marina project. A project he'd stalled after uncovering fire code violations the previous inspector hadn't noticed or didn't care about.

"I'm Evie Hamilton," she said.

"I figured that out—now." He reached across and shook hands with her without taking his eyes off the road. "Scott Bennett."

"Nice to meet you. And thanks for the ride. I hope you like working here for the summer."

"Me, too."

"Are you full-time somewhere else?"

He wasn't ready to tell her all about his full-time job. Not while he was trapped in a truck with her. *Only a quarter of a mile to go.*

Evie leaned toward him and cocked her head, obviously waiting for an answer.

"What I mean is that most of our summer firefighters have other full-time jobs. I was just curious."

"I'm full-time for the City of Bayside."

Evie nodded. "I live in downtown Bayside. I just moved into my own place. Maybe I'll see you there. But I'm more likely to see you around here."

Scott nosed the truck up to the gate and put on the parking brake.

"Close as I can get."

"I know. I don't mind a short walk in the rain. I'm wet anyway." She picked up her shoes from the floor of the truck.

"You should put those on. You could step on something sharp."

She laughed. "Thanks for the safety tip. But putting wet feet in wet shoes is almost as lousy as feuding with the local fire inspector"

Evie opened her door and slid out. Gave

him a little wave. And slammed the door of the fire truck.

At least she left the window down so he could see in the side mirror as he backed slowly away from the corporate office where he knew he'd be about as welcome as a mosquito bite right now. As soon as Evie connected the dots and realized the fire inspector from Bayside who'd rained on her parade also worked part-time for her own company, he'd better be ready to hand in his employee badge.

Scott thought of his baby sister, twenty years old and working at Starlight Point for the summer. He had to keep this job if he wanted to keep watch over the only sister he had left.

CHAPTER TWO

EVIE TOOK OFF her name tag, dropped it in her purse and settled into her usual seat behind the ferry's tall wheelhouse. From the backward-facing seat, she could watch Starlight Point slip away. On the short trip from Starlight Point to Bayside, she was just another passenger. Not an owner of the amusement park that had been in her family since before she was born.

Evie loved Starlight Point like she loved her sister's smile, her brother's eyes, her mother's laugh and the memory of her father. But tonight she just wanted to enjoy the twenty-minute-ride home.

Home. The third-floor flat above Aunt Augusta's Downtown Bakery was still new to her. But she was starting to call it home. Too large a space for one person, the flat had two rooms—a spare bedroom and bathroom—that were completely empty. Her brother's house on the Old Road at the Point used to be a half-barren bachelor pad, but he'd traded houses with their mother. He was now living in their parents' house with his wife. Already the rooms were filling with the contraptions that seemed to go with babies, and the baby shower coming up would add even more.

Maybe her empty apartment wasn't so bad. It was quiet, organized…and the first place she'd ever lived alone.

Evie pulled off the band holding her hair back and ran her fingers through the long strands. She closed her eyes and leaned her head against the center island of the ferry, feeling the hum of the boat's motor. The bay was calm, the breeze light, the June evening warm. If her old blue sedan actually had any life left in it, she'd be missing this beautiful ride and making the daily drive in traffic to the Point.

After a twenty-minute trip, the ferry docked and Evie waited for the other passengers to leave. The moms and dads, friends and teenagers were in more of a hurry than she was. They headed for their cars parked in the wide downtown lot. She hoped they'd had a wonderful day at Starlight Point. Judging from their flushed cheeks and sleepy-eyed kids, it looked that way.

"Good night, Evie."

She turned. Smiled.

"See you tomorrow, Ken," she said to the retired navy officer who had ferried Starlight Point guests for at least a decade.

"I hope you never get your car fixed so I can keep seeing you every day," he said. "Although I could come take a look at it for you if you like. Can't be much different from a battleship."

Evie laughed. "I think it's just the battery. I'll get it fixed on my day off."

"Which is?"

"October something."

Ken smiled and propped a foot on the bench seat. He shoved his captain's hat back and gave Evie his full attention.

"Running that place over there," he said, gesturing at Starlight Point and the lights just starting to show against the twilight sky, "is no easy job. Especially for someone as young as you are."

If someone else had said the same thing, Evie might have bristled. But she'd known Ken for years and knew he wasn't judging her. She threw back her shoulders and tilted her chin up.

"I'm not young. Ask my feet. They'll tell you I'm fifty-seven."

Ken laughed. "When I was your age, the only thing I was good at running was my mouth. Although I learned pretty quick to keep it shut."

Evie stepped off the boat and tucked her purse under her arm. "Good night, Ken. See you on tomorrow's run."

"'Night."

Evie was several feet away when Ken's question stopped her.

"Got your new marina open for business? I wasn't able to come to the grand opening, but I saw the pictures of it in the paper a few days ago."

Evie's stomach sank like change thrown in a fountain.

"Almost," she said. "I'm just short of a few regulations and we'll be open before summer gets too far along."

Ken rolled his eyes. "Tell me about regulations. I was in the navy twenty-five years and hope I never see another piece of paperwork."

It was a beautiful evening, so she took the long way around to the front of her building, which housed her sister-in-law Augusta's bakery on the street level and condos on the second and third floors. From her third-floor window, she had a view of the bay and Starlight Point.

From a distance. Something she was just getting used to. Growing up, Evie had always wanted to be at the Point. She'd resented moving away, even a hundred miles, to attend college. Always there was a lingering fear that somehow Starlight Point would change while she was gone.

And it had. Her father's death near the end of her junior year had changed the Point forever. The life she had imagined for herself—working alongside her dad as his accountant and financial expert—disappeared. Instead she and her siblings inherited the park overnight because their mother handed it straight to the next generation. Growing up didn't seem like such a treat anymore.

It was a responsibility and she was taking it seriously.

On her walk, she passed the Bayside fire station where the four overhead doors were open to the warm evening air. Shiny trucks lined up. Waiting.

Sometimes Evie felt like she was waiting, too.

Right now she was waiting for a certain

fire inspector to get the burr out of his boots and approve her paperwork.

Maybe he's in there.

Evie paused on the sidewalk in front of the wide concrete apron. She knew the tiny office the former fire inspector used was just inside the front doors. She'd been there several times to meet with the former inspector, who'd initially approved her plans. All she had to do was go past the shiny red pumper truck and make a quick right.

She crossed the concrete with the stealth of a trespasser, tempted to glance around to see if anyone was looking. Not that she was committing a crime. She had business there. It was a public building. The doors were open.

When she stepped under the overhang and into the relative darkness of the station, she stopped. The interior smelled like rubber tires, engine oil and something that could only be described as *fire truck*. She'd spent time in the fire office at the Point when she was growing up, sitting on the engine's bumper and talking to the firefighters. But Starlight Point was only this quiet during the dead of winter.

"Hello?" she called. A call box was mounted to the inside wall with a note instructing people to press the red button in case of emergency. Getting her marina project back on track and getting her hotel renovation plans approved seemed like an emergency to her, but she was afraid of what might happen if she pressed that button. She pictured alarms, flashing lights and men racing for trucks while they threw on helmets and coats.

That would be too much excitement after a long day working at the Point, where she was in charge of resorts and safety. There, plenty of flashing lights, screaming people on the rides and millions of details competed for her attention. The quiet of the station calmed her mind, but only one thing would solve her problem.

Just as Evie laid her hand on the door to the office of the former fire inspector, a door to her left opened and a firefighter in navy blue from head to toe emerged. *Caught.*

The man glared at her as if she had burst into the bathroom while he was showering. Scott Bennett. After her ride in the fire truck with him a few days ago, she had made just enough inquiries to know the dark-eyed man who'd picked her up in the rain was also the one who'd picked apart her marina project.

And he'd obviously known who she was,

although he hadn't been brave enough to own up to it in the truck. Maybe he'd been hesitant because he was on her territory.

And she was on his right now.

"You're just the man I need to see," she said, attempting to force a cheerful tone.

Although it seemed impossible, his scowl deepened. "Is there a fire or other emergency?"

He sounded strangely hopeful. *These guys operate on adrenaline.* She would have to remember that.

"My marina needs your approval to open. The boating season is limited. I'm losing money every minute the docks and restaurant are closed. So, yes," she said. "It may not seem like an emergency to you, but it is to me."

Scott crossed his arms and looked down at her. Although Evie was five foot ten, Scott had her by several inches. With his broad shoulders and massive forearms, he seemed even larger. Perhaps it was the scowl.

Evie was not going to be intimidated, but honey might be more convincing than vinegar. The man was in the business of helping people, after all. *He isn't the enemy, right?*

And he had given her a ride in the fire truck on a rainy day.

But only because she was violating the No Pedestrians rule. And she owned that fire truck anyway.

Sigh. Honey. Not vinegar.

"Thank you for the ride a few days ago. Had I known you were the new fire inspector for the city, I would have invited you to my office to talk about our apparent violations."

"Real violations."

Maybe honey isn't strong enough.

"Enlighten me," Evie suggested.

Scott didn't move. Arms crossed, he stared her down as if willing her to get out of his fire station.

Evie expected to be arrested for trespassing at any minute. She imagined her mother, old dog in tow, showing up at the police station to bail her out.

"I have an office, too," he said. "You can come in."

Such a friendly invitation.

Evie stood her ground. She knew where his office was. He'd have to walk by her to get to it.

Scott carefully avoided touching her as he squeezed past to open his office door. Evie wanted to laugh out loud. She was making him uncomfortable. Of course she was.

He may think he had some pedantic fire codes on his side, but she had been operating under approval from the former inspector. And she was his employer—one of them— for the summer.

Scott flipped on a ceiling fluorescent light, and Evie glanced around the tiny space. Everything about the office said "former closet." She'd been in there twice before, recognized the empty, dustless square on the desk where the nameplate for the former inspector used to sit. So Scott didn't have his own nameplate declaring him the King of the Code. Perhaps she'd get him one if he ever made Employee of the Month at Starlight Point.

SCOTT LEFT THE OFFICE door open so he could listen for any calls that came in over the loudspeaker in the bay. He also felt better having an escape route in case Evie Hamilton was as ticked off as he guessed.

He gestured for her to sit in the orange plastic chair in front of his desk and retreated to take his own seat. And then he remembered the plastic chair was missing a leg. He'd discovered it by the trash bin out back and had intended to repair it in case he had visitors to his new office. There hadn't been any visitors in the short time he'd been the owner of the office, but if anyone sat in the chair right now, it would flip and toss the person onto the concrete floor.

He pivoted, swooped and caught Evie just as the chair started to tip. She gasped, dropped her purse, and the chair clattered to the floor. Scott held her around the waist as if they had just finished a passionate dance and he was dipping her for a kiss. Her blond hair swung freely and he could see the pulse beating wildly in her neck.

Surprise. Fight or flight. A natural reaction.

His heart rate was at sprint level, too, even though emergencies were part of his daily life.

He pulled her up and let go, keeping only one hand on her arm to make sure she was steady. The last thing he needed was someone getting hurt at the fire station. In his office.

"Take my chair," he said.

Before she could object, he reached over the desk and picked up his wooden chair. It was heavy, but he swung it up and planted it right behind his guest.

"Sit," he said. "I, uh, hope you're all right."

He bent and scooped the contents of her purse back into the bag. *Interesting.* Cell phone. Wallet-type thing. Hand sanitizer. Sunglasses. Two name tags, both black. One with her name and one that said Ford.

Who—or what—is Ford?

He handed her the bag. Instead of going behind his desk, he leaned on the filing cabinet next to it.

"Maybe I should come back another time," Evie said.

Her cheeks were flushed and she sat cautiously on the chair, probably afraid of another trap.

He had her off balance.

He was not going to admit he felt the same way. He took a long, slow breath, willing his heart to return to conversation mode. He shoved away from the cabinet and opened the top drawer.

"I have your file in here," he said. "The paper part, anyway. The application is on the computer." He gestured toward a dusty, black desktop computer that was probably old enough to buy them both a drink. Scott spread a construction diagram on the table. "Here's your problem," he said, pointing behind the shower house. "There's a huge cottonwood tree blocking the fire lane."

Evie spread long fingers over the drawing and leaned in to see it better in the dim lighting.

Her hair fell forward and Scott resisted the urge to touch it. When he'd picked her up in the fire truck, soaking wet, he'd guessed her hair would be this color if it were dry. He was right.

He had no idea why he cared about his boss's hair.

Except it was brushing the desk in his office.

"If I do something about the fire lane behind the shower house and restaurant, would you allow us to open them both?"

How easy did he want to make this for her? It was clear that Evie Hamilton had only one priority: open her marina area.

He had only one priority, too.

"Almost," he said. He tried to keep an even tone, but it was clear to him that Evie wanted to get past these obstacles the fastest way.

Obviously the loss of revenue was a motivating factor, but it seemed like there was something more going on to make her anxious enough to drop in at the fire station way past business hours. "You need evacuation signage in the restaurant and a check valve on the fuel line. And you're lacking clearance around the electrical panel that runs the whole building."

"I had maintenance order the check valve. They're installing it tomorrow."

"And the restaurant evacuation plan?"

Evie blew out a breath and sat back in the chair. "I thought the neon exit signs made the emergency evacuation route pretty obvious." She met his eyes and took a long, slow breath. "But I was wrong. Obviously. Maybe you could help me with the signs."

"Of course," he said. "That's my job."

Evie cocked her head and drilled him with a long stare. "How long have you had this job? I didn't even know Marty had retired until the day before my marina was supposed to open."

Scott shrugged. "He had some health problems and decided to hang it up. I was the only qualified guy here who wanted it."

And he'd been darn lucky to be in the right

place, right time. With a fire science degree in addition to all the required fire training, Scott was one of the few guys at the station who had the résumé for the job. Several of the older men had backed away slowly, hands up in defense when Marty tried to hand the position off to them. They hated paperwork and controversy.

Paperwork and a few terse words are nothing compared to the pain of burn scars from sloppily followed fire codes.

He had jumped at the job as if it were an arrow pointing toward his life's mission.

"What makes you qualified?" Evie asked.

Was that a polite question or an accusation? He didn't need to explain himself to anyone.

"What makes you qualified to run an amusement park?" he fired back.

Uh-oh. That was not how he'd intended to sound. His sister had warned him about his tone. She'd be punching him in the gut right now if she'd heard that.

Color rushed to Evie's face and she stood abruptly. "Please draw up emergency evacuation plans for the areas that need them and put them up. You can do it on company time the next shift you work at the Point."

"I'm there tomorrow for the afternoon shift."

"Good. Fine. Thank you," she said. "You can also check the fuel valve while you're working for me, and I'll notify you when the extra inches of clearance are added around the electrical box."

The way she said *inches* made it clear she didn't like making the change. Too bad. She would never have to find that panel in an emergency and shut it down while wearing fifteen pounds of gear and an air tank. That was his job.

"And the tree?" he asked.

"We'll see about that."

She picked up her purse and left his office without even a backward glance.

Scott followed her into the station and leaned on the ladder truck, watching her as she walked down the block and entered the front door of her building. She'd mentioned to him in the truck that she'd just moved to downtown Bayside.

Great. She's right under my nose.

He stood there long enough to see the lights go on in the third-story windows. His mind locked on the sprinkler and standpipe system in that block of buildings, the location of the fire department hookup, the available hydrants along the street.

He couldn't help it. Seeing danger every-where he looked was imprinted on him like a scar.

CHAPTER THREE

"TELL ME AGAIN why I should breathe," Jack Hamilton said.

"You have to," Evie replied, not even looking up from her desk across from her brother's. "Your body is smarter than you are."

Jack put his chin in his hands and stared at Evie. "You've always been the calm, rational member of the family, but you're spending money like it's your last day on earth."

"Maybe it is. The mother ship could be coming for me tomorrow. Maybe they need an accountant on their home planet."

Jack tapped a pen on his desk until the annoying noise got Evie to look up.

"I thought you didn't want to be an accountant anymore," he said. "That's why we hired someone to replace you and you're off building docks and knocking down our old hotel."

"I haven't knocked it down yet. I need permits."

Evie minimized her computer screen and gave Jack her full attention.

"I love numbers. Accounts. Spreadsheets. Love them." She sighed. "When I was younger, I thought those things would make me happy for life."

"But?"

"Dad died and left us Starlight Point. I want to be more than just a number cruncher. Accountants you can hire. What you need is a partner." She paused and grinned at him. "Especially since you'll be a family man before the summer is over."

Jack put his head on his desk.

"Don't be dramatic. You can come in here and cry about your sleepless nights. I'll pretend to be sympathetic. I'll even look the other way if you have puke on your tie."

"I believe you'd tell me if I had puke on my tie. I hope you would, anyway."

Evie laughed. "I would."

There was a knock on their office door.

"It's Mel," a voice called from the other side.

"You can only come in if you have doughnuts or good news," Jack yelled.

Mel Preston swept the door open. The head of maintenance at Starlight Point had married June Hamilton in a Christmas ceremony the previous winter. After the two of them had carried a torch for each other for more than a decade, Evie was much relieved when they'd finally given in to the flames. In her mind, it freed everyone up to get back to the business of running an amusement park. For her part, Evie had no intention of ever being such a ninny in the romance department. It killed on-the-job productivity.

"You don't have to knock, Mel," Evie said. "You're a member of the family."

"Still can't believe my good luck," he said. "I hope your sister never comes to her senses."

"She won't."

"What's up, Mel?" Jack asked. "Evie and I were in the middle of an important whining session."

"My brother's being a baby about having a baby in the middle of the summer."

"I can add to your problems if you need something more to cry about," Mel said.

"Do we have problems?" Jack asked.

"I think you should come see for yourself," Mel responded, his tone losing all its levity.

Jack and Evie jumped to their feet. "Ride problem? Someone hurt?"

Mel shook his head. "Someone's a pain in the rear."

Evie guessed who the pain in the rear was before Mel could explain.

"Is it the new fire inspector?"

Mel blew out a breath and made two fists. He tapped them together lightly. "Can't believe the guy has the nerve to wear one of our name tags while being our worst enemy."

Jack picked up his cell phone from his desk and shoved it in the interior pocket of his suit coat. "Where are we going?"

"Bennett's going through the employee dorm with a clipboard right now. He just got done raking one of my guys over the coals for parking in a fire lane while he did an emergency repair on the back of the Silver Streak. Yesterday we caught heck for using a torch near flammable materials. Guess the guy doesn't know that every single thing in the maintenance garage is flammable."

Mel's pickup waited just outside the employee gate near the corporate office. He was parked in the same place Scott had parked the fire truck when he dropped Evie off over a week ago on that rainy afternoon. That was before Evie realized who her chauffeur was.

Jack and Evie got in the truck and Mel

briefed them on the ten-minute drive around the outer loop to the employee dorms located close to the marina.

"Fact is, the guy's right about a few things," Mel said. "I hate admitting that."

Sandwiched between the two men in the truck, Evie saw the look that passed between her brother and his best friend of more than twenty years.

"We've talked about that dorm before," Mel continued. "It's eighty years old. The floors roll. The windows leak."

"We never promised our summer workers a palace," Jack said. "It's free housing."

Mel nodded.

"But?" Evie prompted.

"It's not the nicest. I wouldn't let my son stay there," Mel continued.

"Ross is six going on seven," Evie said.

"I know. He thinks it's fun camping out in the big box our new refrigerator came in. I mean I wouldn't let him stay there if he was a teenager working here."

"Why not?" Evie asked.

"It's not air-conditioned, the bathrooms stink and there are girls living right down the hall. Very dangerous."

Evie thought about the many times she'd

begged her parents to let her live in the dorms with the other summer employees. Although they'd owned Starlight Point, Virginia and Ford Hamilton had required their three children to work regular summer jobs in the park.

Evie had done time running the register in the airbrush art stand, scooping ice cream and sweeping trash off the midways. Her coworkers were her friends and they'd told her about all the fun they'd had off hours in the dorms after playing on the beach and going on rides.

Evie had joined her friends on some of their beach and park adventures, but she'd always been sorry to cross the lot to her parents' luxurious house on the Old Road abutting the Starlight Point parking lot on the lake side of the peninsula. Her parents had staunchly refused to allow her to bunk with the summer workers. Maybe she knew why now.

"When was the last time you were in the dorms?" Evie asked Mel as they drove.

"Yesterday," Mel said. "Power went out on the second floor because kids plugged in too much stuff and blew a fuse."

The three of them rode in silence on the low-speed road surrounding the Point.

"Dad was always afraid the summer employees were going to burn down that old barn someday," Jack said.

Evie blew out a breath. "Any idea what Inspector Gotcha is writing on his clipboard?"

She pictured him, dark eyes drawn together in a scowl, taping off the doors of the dorm by order of the fire inspector. Her pulse quickened. He wouldn't close the dorm, would he? Where would their employees go?

What if he found picky infractions as he had at the marina? Two of the three marina problems were already addressed and she had the asphalt truck on order to fix the fire lane. The giant old cottonwood tree that had shaded the marina area for a century was still an obstacle, but she was trying to find a way around it without sacrificing a piece of history.

Soon, her marina would open and she could move on to the hotel project.

If Scott approves my plans.

He had to approve them. Jack was panicking about the money she was investing in the capital improvement projects for the Point. The investment had to start paying off soon or they were all in trouble. Guilt nagged at her. How much was she motivated by planning the next century for Starlight Point and how much was her motivation driven by her own need to prove she was more than just an accountant and a little sister?

Like it or not, getting the exacting new fire inspector to endorse her plans was integral to the success of her project. Making an enemy of him over the employee housing wasn't wise, and Evie had a lingering feeling that Inspector Scott Bennett was going to make this the most difficult summer of her life anyway.

SCOTT WAS STUNNED. He knew the former inspector was too friendly with local businesses. Too sloppy. Let too many things slide. Maybe the guy had never seen someone die in a fire that could and should have been prevented.

He took a deep breath and focused on the fire escape at the employee dorm. A lawn chair blocked the door at the top and someone had parked a barbecue grill at the bottom. It mirrored what he'd found inside the dorm when he'd walked through all three floors.

Fire doors propped open. Cooking devices that were illegal and asking for trouble. Posters and fabric decorations covering the walls and draped over lighting fixtures. A shirt hanger dangling off a smoke detector.

The attic spanning the length of the building was filled with flammable junk, probably items left from years of summer employees. Old mattresses. A dresser. Cardboard boxes filled with who knew what. All kindling in the worst case scenario.

If it were a modern building, there would be fire walls dividing the attic to prevent the spread of flames. But it wasn't anywhere close to being modern. The employee dorm appeared to be almost as old as the Lake Breeze Hotel. The hotel was a different story, one he planned to dig his teeth into another day.

Scott lowered the tailgate on the fire department's pickup truck. He sat on the tailgate, dangling his legs. It was sunny and the breeze off the nearby lake cooled his heated mind. He began to write the list of corrections that had to be made immediately or he would be forced by a combination of the law and his own conscience to close the dorm.

A blue truck pulled up and three people

climbed out. Evie and Jack Hamilton and the head of maintenance, a man he'd already tangled with. Mel something.

Evie's long hair was pulled back tight from her face. Her green eyes flashed in the bright sunlight.

Her brother was much taller but his grim expression matched hers.

"I'm glad you're here," Scott said, resolved to deliver the true but unpleasant news without dancing around it. "We can begin the twenty-four-hour notification period required in the event of closure and condemnation by the fire inspector."

"Twenty-four hours?" Evie said. "Closure and condemnation?"

Her eyes were wide, mouth open in shock. Jack's face registered closer to murderous. Mel and Jack stood shoulder-to-shoulder behind Evie, as if they were her enforcers.

Interesting. She appeared to be the youngest of the three, but she was in charge. He had no idea how the Hamiltons operated. He knew there was another sister, but he hadn't met her yet.

"In the event of actual danger to life or property, I have the authority to close buildings, construction sites, parties and just about anything else," Scott said. "Michigan law."

"Is there actual danger here?" Evie asked. She stepped closer, her hip almost brushing the edge of the tailgate. Scott wished she wouldn't stand so close.

"This place is five seconds from going up in flames. I wouldn't sleep at night if I owned it or if anyone I cared about was staying in it."

He saw the glance exchanged between Evie, her brother and her maintenance man. None of them looked surprised.

What was wrong with these people? Were they too busy adding up their cash to make potentially lifesaving upgrades?

Evie held out her hand for his clipboard. Her expression softened just a little. Not a smile. But perhaps an admission that he wasn't the big bad wolf.

He handed her the clipboard and watched her read his neatly printed list of violations. She flipped to the next page and perused the diagram he'd drawn with marks indicating the locations of the infractions.

Her expression hardened as she read. Lines defined the set of her mouth. When she looked up at him, her eyes were narrowed, brows drawn together.

"These violations have nothing to do with the actual building," she said.

Scott shrugged. "True. It's the careless way your employees are living. Probably find the same things on a college campus."

"But you're holding us at fault and threatening to close our building."

Obviously.

"Yes," he said curtly. "It's your building." He took back his clipboard. "You," he said, pointing to her and Jack, "are responsible for the people living in your dorm, like it or not."

Evie slid onto the tailgate, only two feet away from him, swinging her long legs. Her skin was bare from her knee-length navy blue skirt to her low-heeled sandals. She had a small scar on the outside of her ankle and Scott was tempted to ask how she got it.

He shook off the thought and returned his attention to his clipboard.

"If we go through the dorm, knock on doors, educate our employees and remove hazards, would you be convinced to let this go?" Evie asked.

Scott glanced up at Jack and Mel, who

were towering over him, arms crossed over their chests.

"I wouldn't be letting it go," Scott said. "The problem would be solved. And that's what I want. It's what you should want, too. Assuming you care about the lives of your employees."

"Hey," Jack said. He uncrossed his arms and took a step forward. "I'm not going to stand here and let you imply I don't care about what happens around here. I care about every single thing that happens at Starlight Point. Maybe you don't want to work for a guy like me if you don't get that."

Evie bounced off the tailgate and took Jack and Mel by the upper arms. She walked away with both of them and had a low-volume conversation. Scott couldn't see their faces and was probably better off not knowing the direction their discussion took.

The two men got in the truck and left.

Evie turned around and walked straight up to Scott, stopping only when she was almost close enough to touch him. "If you're willing to go through the dorm with me and set things straight, I'm all yours."

CHAPTER FOUR

CRISIS AVERTED, EVIE THOUGHT. But when would the next one come? The daily life of Starlight Point was madness. A beautiful madness that ran through her veins like sunshine. And sometimes rain.

The employee dorms would remain open, but she had no doubt Scott Bennett would sweep through with his book of fire codes whenever he thought their guard was down. Following him through the dorm, floor by floor and room by room, made for the most exhausting morning she could remember. With every door they knocked on, her spirits sank because she dreaded the tangle of extension cords they'd find. Or the doors half blocked with furniture. Or the furtive hot plates. Ashtrays. Candles.

It was a disaster waiting to happen.

Scott was right about the reckless habits of summer staff. He was right about the vulnerable condition of the aged building. Of course he was. But there was something bubbling just under the surface of his determination that made her wonder what force drove him and when he would boil over.

She'd watched his smooth, confident stride as he authoritatively made his way down the halls of her building. His stern profile as he'd waited for doors to open. His mouth drawn in a tight line as he'd replaced a missing fire extinguisher in a hallway.

He'd be handsome if his dark eyes weren't tainted with anger and his square jaw weren't set quite so sternly. *But there's something about him...*

Evie's shoulders sagged as she passed through the marina gate and headed for her office. The sun shone brightly and the midway was dotted with lunchtime crowds.

"You need ice cream," Tosha called out, leaning over the counter of her stand. "No one as young as you should look so serious."

Evie stopped. Smiled politely. She liked Tosha, had grown up with the woman and her pink apron, and had even worked for her the summer she was fifteen. But why did everyone suddenly want to point out how young she was? At twenty-three, wasn't she old enough to get through a day without a well-meaning old friend trying to offer her an ice-cream cone as if she were a lost child? When Jack had taken over the park a few years ago at the age of twenty-seven, had people offered him lollipops and cookies?

Probably. His sweet tooth was notorious.

"Running Starlight Point is serious work," Evie said, keeping her tone level.

"Nonsense. Look around." Tosha swept an arm at the blue sky, which was only obstructed by graceful trees swaying and the cable cars gliding overhead. "Couldn't ask for anything more than this."

Evie stopped under the pink awning with an ice-cream cone painted on it. "Do you have mint chocolate chip?"

"Single or double?"

Evie glanced at the clock on the stand's wall and did the math. "If I have a double, it'll count for lunch, too. Saves me time in the long run."

Tosha laughed and shook the water drops off a silver ice-cream scooper. "You always were a practical girl, even when you were a kid. I remember you coming in here with dollar bills clutched in your little hands and figuring out the best deal for the money."

Evie laughed. "I think you always gave me more than I deserved."

"No," Tosha said. "You deserved every ounce."

Evie slid her hand into her pocket and pulled out a five-dollar bill.

"No way," Tosha said, handing a two-scoop cone across the counter. "This one's for luck."

"Do I need luck?"

"With all the big plans you have this summer, you need luck, time, good weather and ice cream. Not necessarily in that order."

Evie took a bite of the ice cream and lingered under the awning for a moment. Her eyes fell on a shiny red fire extinguisher mounted on the wall next to the side door of the stand, a giant reflective sticker pointing to it. And there was another reflective sticker on the door that said *Exit*.

Those signs are serious overkill.

Tosha noticed Evie's glance. "Like my new safety equipment?"

Evie nodded, reserving comment as she waited for what she knew Tosha would say next.

"I had a visit from the new fire inspector

who's trying to fill out his new boots by puffing himself up. I'm not the only one, either."

"Didn't you already have a fire extinguisher?" Evie asked.

Tosha shrugged. "Had a bucket of water. Worked for years."

"Well," Evie said. She hesitated, wondering if she should tell Tosha that Scott Bennett was the bane of her existence, too. Maybe not. It probably wouldn't help, anyway. "I hope you never have to use the bucket of water or the fire extinguisher. Thanks for the ice cream."

Tosha waved her away and Evie took a walk along the midway. When she was younger, she would walk hand-in-hand with her father and they would play Visitor. He would take off his name tag and they'd pretend it was their first visit to Starlight Point. As a child, Evie thought it was a fun game devised for her entertainment, but she had taken up the habit this summer and realized her father had a brilliant ulterior motive.

As she walked past the theater, she looked at it as if she had never seen it before. *Fresh eyes*. What if she didn't own the place? What would she notice? The heavy old marquee hanging over the theater entrance had been transformed during the winter. There were still flashing lights, but it was a computer screen that could be changed quickly to advertise shows, park events and times. No more black letters slid onto a white track.

Was it an improvement? Evie gazed at it. *Yes.* Her sister, June, would certainly think so. Coming home last summer and revitalizing both the theater buildings and their live shows had been June's achievement. And she hadn't slowed down. This year's shows in the Midway Theater and the Starlight Saloon in the Wonderful West would open in a few days. And they would be even more spectacular than last year's Broadway-themed performances. The new scrolling sign advertised a "Salute to Summer Extravaganza" with a promise of music and dance to celebrate the season.

June saw the fruits of her labor every day. Her music, choreography, costume choices and overall vision had made live shows more than an afterthought or just an extra offering at the point. Exit surveys from the previous year suggested there were guests who returned just to see the shows. June's effort and sacrifice had paid off. She had given up her career on Broadway to come home and be part of the family business, and she didn't appear to regret it for an instant.

What am I giving up if I devote my life to Starlight Point?

The carousel lurched into action with a burst of organ music, and Evie watched the horses blur past, going up and down on the same track they'd been on for decades. She glanced at the concrete beneath her feet. The same path she'd walked with her father for years.

There was no place else she wanted to be, but her path now was not the one she'd imagined as a girl.

SCOTT HANDED HIS SISTER Caroline a fifty-dollar bill. "That's for food. If you insist on being a security guard, you should bulk up a little."

Caroline laughed. Her slight build looked even slimmer in the all black uniform of the Starlight Point Police Department. Only twenty, she wasn't licensed to carry a gun. Yet. But she could still do foot patrol. Direct traffic. Keep an eye on the summer crowds.

"You're an excellent big brother," she said, snapping the crisp bill from his fingers before he could play keep-away. She slipped it into her pocket, picked up a plastic tray and cut in front of him in the cafeteria line. "I'll report to Mom that I'm keeping an eye on you and you're behaving very well."

Scott raised an eyebrow.

"You're still buying lunch today, right?" Caroline asked.

He nodded as he shoved a tray along the line at the employee cafeteria. "This is probably the only day this month we'll have the same schedule, so I can afford your grilled cheese and salad."

Scott took a cheeseburger and fries from under the warming lights, added a pudding parfait from the cooler and filled a paper cup from the soda machine. He paid for his sister's tray and his and followed her to a table by the window.

The employee cafeteria was industrial in furnishings, but the view from the wall of windows added a shot of beauty. Situated between the employee entrance along the beach and the backside of the Lake Breeze Hotel, the staff cafeteria and recreation center offered glimpses of Lake Huron through the trees. The cafeteria served inexpensive food for the minimum-wage summer workers who lived at the Point and counted on three meals a day.

"Are you still insisting on living in the employee dorm or have you decided to do the smart thing?" Scott asked. He took the radio off his belt and set it next to the tray.

"Living with my overprotective big brother in a bachelor pad in downtown Bayside is the smart thing?" Caroline took her radio off her belt and set it next to his, mimicking his action and smiling at him.

"Safer thing. I almost had to close the dorm a few days ago because of fire code violations."

"Of course you did," she said, smiling at him. "I was working at the time, but some of my friends reported a very grouchy fire inspector writing up violations and confiscating their extension cords."

Scott took a deep breath and reserved comment.

"If I lived with you, I'd have to find a way to work every day," Caroline said.

Scott chewed his burger and watched his sister squeeze dressing over her salad. "There's a ferry."

"Takes too long. Sometimes I might get called in on short notice if something exciting is happening."

Why does my sister have to be so difficult?

"Like a big fight or a gun-toting maniac," Caroline added, grinning at her brother.

"You know I hate this," he said.

"You hadn't mentioned it."

"If you lived in Bayside, you could use my truck. I walk to work in Bayside and take the ferry here. How about that?"

"Is that your final offer?"

"I've offered you everything I have."

Caroline reached for his pudding parfait and Scott snatched it. He snapped the plastic lid off and gave her one of the two spoons he'd picked up.

"You're the best," she said.

"And you," he said, sharing his dessert, "are driving me nuts."

She reached across the table and squeezed his hand. "Who do you think watches over me in college?"

Scott sucked in a breath. Caroline only had one year left before she graduated with a criminal justice degree. She was completing her police officer's training concurrently and, in less than a year, she would be putting her life on the line as a cop.

"You should get a dog," he said. "A nice German shepherd."

"I don't need a dog. I can take care of myself. This job will be great experience and, who knows, maybe I'll come back next year and work here so I can shoot you if you get on my nerves."

She dipped her finger into the whipped cream part of the parfait and dabbed a dollop on Scott's nose. "Or maybe you'll need me to protect you someday," she added.

Caroline glanced over at the drink machine where a tall blond woman was filling a soda cup. She waved and caught the woman's attention as she snapped a plastic lid on her cup.

How does Caroline know Evie Hamilton? And why is she coming over here?

"Evie," Caroline said as soon as she approached. "Sit with us."

Evie stopped next to the table but didn't pull out a chair. "I'm on my way to the Wonderful West to check on a guest complaint about the shooting gallery."

"Pacifists?" Caroline asked.

Evie laughed. "No. A matter of economy. It seems our machines are eating quarters at an alarming rate. Highway robbery."

Caroline smiled and pointed at her brother. "This is my brother, Scott."

Scott locked eyes with Evie and his pulse

throbbed in his neck. Her eyes were green like summer leaves. He had noticed them before.

"And this," Caroline continued, gesturing at Evie, "is Evie Hamilton. She owns the place so you have to be nice to her."

"We've met," Evie said, her expression neutral.

"Was he nice?" Caroline asked.

"No."

Evie thinks I wasn't nice? Was I supposed to be nice about slipshod safety?

"I'm not surprised," Caroline said. "He's been known to be too serious. Although the whipped cream on his nose makes him more approachable."

To his horror, Evie zeroed in on his nose while Caroline took a swipe at him with her napkin.

He had to change the subject.

"How did you two meet?" Scott asked.

"Self-defense training," Evie said. She pulled out the chair next to Caroline and sat on the edge. "I happened to sit in on the early season orientation for the police department because the safety forces here are under my jurisdiction."

So that was why she'd wanted to talk about

the price of fire trucks. And why she'd been the one to walk through the employee dorms with him. She was not only his boss as owner of the place, she was also in charge of the safety department. His department.

"I was about to take down a guy twice my size," Caroline said, "but I volunteered to spar with Evie because none of the other guys would touch her."

"I can't imagine why," Scott said. "Who wouldn't want to risk his job by tossing his boss to the mat?"

Not that he had much room to talk considering how difficult he was making things for Evie and the rest of the management at Starlight Point. *Sparring with Evie is not the smart way to keep my job.*

Caroline shrugged. "They were probably afraid of losing. Evie's tougher than she looks."

In build, Evie was much like his sister. Long, willowy limbs, delicate bones. He pictured one of the burly police officers grappling with her and it made him go cold, just like the feeling he got when he made the mistake of picturing his sister at work.

Evie laughed. "Let's just hope I'm tough

enough to handle kids who lost their allowance to the shooting gallery machines."

"I hope you have a bag of quarters in your purse," Caroline said.

"Even better. A preloaded card good for five hundred rounds of ammo. Their trigger fingers will wear out before they run out of bullets."

Evie took a sip of her soda and settled into the seat a little more.

"I'm curious," she said. "You two aren't from Bayside, are you?"

Caroline shook her head. "About an hour away. We used to come here sometimes, though. School field trips and a family trip once a summer."

"So how did you both end up working here?"

"Scott got a full-time job for the Bayside Fire Department over the winter. He's my only family in this area since our parents retired and moved to Arizona. They think Scott keeps an eye on me so they can be happy in the sunshine."

"Lucky for them," Evie commented.

"I was looking for a summer job and some of the guys in my police academy class told me about working security here. I thought it would be good experience. Maybe I'll come back and be a bonded officer next year."

"That sounds terrific," Evie said. "We could use a full-time female officer on our department. Do you live with your brother in Bayside?"

"No," Caroline said, sending Scott a crooked grin. "I live in the employee dorm by the marina."

"Really?" Evie turned a raised-eyebrow glance on Scott. "What do you think of the dorms?"

Scott wasn't sure if the question was directed toward him or his sister. Caroline saved him by jumping in.

"It's fun. Like living in a college dorm. But I don't want to say too much in front of " she jerked her head at Scott "—you know who. He already hates the fact that I'm living in the dorms instead of staying at his house where I'd be expected to brush my teeth and go to bed at nine o'clock every night."

Evie laughed. "During the summer, I'm lucky to be in bed by midnight."

No one said anything for a minute, the silence awkward in the loud cafeteria buzzing with conversations all around them.

He should say something. Ask her how her

day was going. Mention the weather. Ask her when the tree obstructing the fire lane at the marina restaurant was coming down.

"I heard we're expecting a record crowd this weekend," Caroline said. "I'm on toll booth and traffic duty on Saturday."

Evie laughed. "Good luck. Saturday mornings around ten are notorious. People have been driving for hours. They're hungry. The kids in the backseat are picking at each other. They hate the way our cones are set up. They don't want to pay for parking. It gets ugly." As she listed the problems, she ticked them off on her long fingers.

"I may ask to be reassigned."

"No way. We need someone rational at the toll booths when tempers flare," Evie said. Her smile turned serious. "But you have to be careful. We've had officers and traffic attendants hit by cars. It's a dangerous combination of orange cones, heat, anticipation and horsepower."

Scott pictured a station wagon mowing down his sister.

"Why can't you work in Kiddieland instead?" Scott groaned.

"Are you kidding?" Evie asked, meeting his eyes, a smile lighting her face. "You should see the stuff that goes down there. Parents fighting about the strollers, kids cutting in line for the motorcycles. And the crying. Holy smokes. The crying. I stay far away."

"Little kids give me the willies," Caroline said. "I'm never having any."

"You're not?" Scott asked. When had his sister decided that? Sure, she wasn't dating anyone—at least not anyone he knew of— but she wanted a family. Didn't she?

Did he? Maybe it was just an abstract idea right now...

"I'm going to try being an aunt first," Evie said. "When my brother's baby arrives this summer, I'll see how I do at that. Right now, I'm headed West for a showdown. See you later, if I live."

She picked up her drink, directed a tentative smile at Scott and wound through the tables on the way to the door. Scott watched her stop and exchange quick greetings with several staff members. She left the building and passed in front of the wall of windows, her long blond hair picking up the sun.

"She's so nice," Caroline said. "And lucky. I can't imagine owning this place. What a fun job."

"I'll bet it's harder than you think," Scott said. "And when did you decide you're never having kids?"

"Yesterday. When I was stuck on patrol at the entrance of the kiddie coaster." She shook her head and forked some lettuce. "It was horrific."

CHAPTER FIVE

"DOES THE TREE have to go?" Evie asked. She shaded her eyes and looked up at the century-old cottonwood that guarded the new marina restaurant building, hanging over it from behind like a protective parent.

"You need a wider fire lane," Scott said. "The tree is too close. It could block trucks and be a hazard." He shrugged. "It's just a tree, right?"

"Yes," Evie said.

Scott drew his eyebrows together and scowled at her. *Why does he have to be so grouchy about it?*

"I don't see why this is a problem," he said.

"I love that tree. It's visible all the way across the parking lot from my house." She paused. "My former house."

"And?"

"And it's part of the skyline. Skyline that is not just roller coasters and rides." She squared her shoulders. "I have happy memories of that tree, okay?"

"Okay."

Before the restaurant was constructed over the past winter, boaters, day visitors and employees in the nearby dorm had come here for picnics. There was even a storage area for coolers and a dozen picnic tables. Sometimes on summer days when Jack, June and Evie were growing up, their mother would pack a cooler and the family had lunch in the shade of the tree. No matter how hot and sunny the weather was, it was cool and shady under the tree.

She could picture Jack swinging his long awkward legs over the bench. Her sister, June, kicking Jack under the table. Her mother handing out sandwiches, each of the plastic bags marked with a sticker denoting its intended recipient. Evie's stickers were green, to match her eyes her father said. She pictured her dad taking off his suit jacket and cracking open a soda from the cooler. He'd always stay long enough to eat and talk for a few minutes, but then it was back to work.

Evie had longed for the day when she'd go to work with him.

The family picnics probably only happened three times a summer, but in Evie's childhood memories, it seemed more often. Her father was gone now. And the picnic tables, too. But the tree remained. A tree that had been on the peninsula before all the swirling rides and flashing lights. It was a piece of history.

"Sometimes," Scott said, interrupting her thoughts, "you have to let go of the past."

If he had said it in a negative or even practical tone, she might have bristled. But his words were quiet, as if they were unintentionally spoken aloud. As if he'd meant them for himself.

She glanced at his face. His cheeks and neck were red. The tips of his ears, visible under his close-cropped hair, were pink.

Interesting. What was in his past that made him color up?

"So what are we doing here?" Scott asked gruffly. The moment of vulnerability was clearly over and he wanted answers. But Evie wasn't going to be rushed or bullied. He was on the clock at *her* park. On *her* time.

"We used to have family picnics under this tree," she said softly, a part of her still unwilling to give up without a fight.

She had no idea why she was sharing that

detail with a man whose next question was probably going to be whether they had a fire extinguisher in their picnic basket.

Scott leaned against the rough bark of the wide trunk, waiting for her decision.

Evie let out a long breath and turned her head from side to side, taking in a wide-angle view of the marina. Even with changes, some obvious, some subtle, Starlight Point was still her family's history. Perhaps she would institute a family lunch with her siblings and her mom at least once a month at the new restaurant. Without a tree shading them, but still a meal together.

Sometimes Evie wished she could stop time and keep everything as it was, but at other times she could hardly wait to see her plans in action. The future of Starlight Point didn't always mean sacrificing the past...but sometimes that had to happen.

"Since it stands in the way of progress," she said, willing herself to be the practical columns-and-numbers person everyone thought she was, "I guess we cut it down."

Mel Preston pulled up in his work truck and joined them under the tree. He studied Evie's face and shoved his hands in his pockets. Rocking back on the heels of his work boots, he looked up at the spreading branches of the old cottonwood.

"Did you work out a way to keep this old tree?" Mel asked.

Scott crossed his arms and said nothing.

Evie could feel the tension between the two men, but that was silly. *It's just a tree.*

She shook her head. "The tree has to go." She swallowed. The sympathy in Mel's eyes almost undid her resolve. Mel had been at Starlight Point a long time. He understood.

"Will you call the tree service and make arrangements today?" Evie asked.

Mel nodded. "I'm sorry, Evie. Ever since your father passed, your family has had to make one tough decision after another. But look how far you've come."

Evie put a hand on Mel's shoulder. "Thanks. Some decisions have been a lot easier than others. I keep reminding myself it's just a tree."

"I kissed your sister under this tree almost ten years ago," Mel said.

Scott tucked his clipboard under his arm and stalked off. He entered the back door of the restaurant.

Evie laughed. "I guess he doesn't want to

hear about family memories or kissing. It's all by the book for him."

"Then I'd guess he isn't having any fun," Mel said.

Evie smiled at her brother-in-law. "You should take home some of the wood when we cut this tree down. You could make a bench for your front porch and kiss my sister on it the rest of your life."

"That's not a bad idea."

"I'm full of ideas," Evie said. "At least, I try to be. As soon as this project opens and starts putting money back into the bank account, I'll know how much I can afford on my hotel renovation."

"I thought you had the whole thing planned out?"

She nodded. "Parts of it. Most of it, I guess. But there's a wish list. We came in slightly under budget on the docks and restaurant here, but I'm afraid renovating a century-old hotel is going to present surprises."

Her construction superintendent had already warned her about the mysteries lurking in a hotel built when automobiles were a new invention. Was she making a huge mistake? Gambling on a possible payoff and a hopeful outcome just as her father had?

"First things first," Mel said. "We've got two weeks until the July Fourth weekend, right?"

"Yes."

"We'll get this tree down, open up the fire lane and finish moving the wall that's too close to the electrical panel. The signs in the restaurant got done last week."

"Thanks, Mel. It's nice to have the head of maintenance officially in the family."

"You need all the friends you can get."

Scott came out of the restaurant and balanced his clipboard on the hood of the fire department's pickup truck.

"Should we go make nice?" Mel asked.

Evie shrugged. "We could ignore him so he'll be more productive on the job. He's on the clock."

"Which makes it twice as irritating when he writes up violations while he's on your payroll."

"Maybe. But I'm still trying to stay on his good side because I need him to sign off on my hotel plans. And sooner rather than later."

"What's the rush?" Mel asked. He kept his voice low as they both watched Scott write up his notes.

Evie could guess what he was putting

down. Inside that door, an electrical panel still sat too close to an interior wall. By only a few inches, but the inspector apparently considered it too close.

"There's a tight time frame," Evie explained. "Especially since we can never count on what kind of winter we're going to have here. Remember last year?"

The marina project had faced numerous delays because of crippling snowstorms and record-breaking low temperatures. Windchills below zero and snow higher than the bumper of a truck made lousy conditions for working outside and staying on schedule. The hotel project was three times the size of the marina project, and weather-related delays could mean it would fail to open on time. And each day it was closed meant lost revenue. "Demo on the old wings has to start mid-August so we can prepare the ground and pour the concrete foundation before freezing weather slows us down. Even following the tight schedule Dan put together for us, we'll barely make opening weekend next May."

Scott turned his attention to the fire hydrant behind the restaurant and then propped his clipboard against the wall, making notes.

Even though they were only fifteen feet away, he ignored Evie and Mel. When Mel made a low grunting sound like an angry animal, Evie laid a hand on his arm.

"I'll go talk to him," Evie said. "If we can work together, maybe we can get the restaurant open and start making money instead of losing it. And I think the gas lines for the docks are ready to open as soon as tomorrow if I get him to sign the permit."

"Good luck," Mel said. He got in his blue maintenance pickup and pulled onto the outer loop.

Evie walked over and leaned against the wall where Scott was still writing with a felt-tipped pen.

"Did you see the new fuel line valve?" she asked.

Scott nodded. Continued writing.

"I'm hoping you'll sign the permit so we can start selling gas to boaters right away."

"Signed it this morning," he said without looking up.

Whew. Her relief was stronger than her irritation at his definite lack of people skills. She wasn't asking him to dance. She needed his official blessing for her project—a project that would provide jobs for dozens of locals waiting to start work in the marina. She'd tried to put their skills to use in other areas of the resort but it still made for an unnecessary strain on payroll.

"And I'm sure you noticed the wall is being moved inside," Evie added. Might as well get it all out there.

"Uh-huh."

Fine. I'll do all the talking. She really wanted to snatch his pen and his clipboard and toss them into the lake.

"I appreciate the very clear signage you installed in the restaurant," she said. "If there's ever a fire in there, I'm sure all our guests will find their way out."

"That's the idea." Scott capped his pen, slid it into his chest pocket and tucked the clipboard under one arm. He looked at her, waiting.

At least he made eye contact. Was it courtesy? Was he only being remotely congenial because she was his boss? How she would love to test that theory by firing him. But she hated to do that to his sister, Caroline, who had apparently gotten all the friendly genes in the family.

Maybe now was the time to mention her next project and invite him to look at the plans early so there would be no surprises. Maybe they could be friends, not enemies.

She risked a glance at his face. A deep vertical line cut a groove between his eyebrows as if frowning was his natural expression. *Perhaps not friends.* Where was the slightly warmer version of Scott she'd seen as he shared lunch with his sister?

Clearly not evident while he was in Chief Inspector mode.

Still, it couldn't hurt to plant a seed about her hotel plans. Evic opened her mouth to tell him she wanted to ask his advice on an upcoming project, but she didn't get the chance. The radio on his hip beeped and Scott pulled it against his ear in one swift movement as if he'd done it a thousand times. His dark eyes remained on Evie as he listened.

"Dispatch to SP Fire. Possible MI, Space Race queue lines."

Abruptly shifting his attention away from her, Scott raced to his truck, tossed his clipboard through the window, grabbed a large zippered bag and started running.

Evie took off after him, barely keeping pace as they headed for the park entrance at the marina gate. "What's an MI?" she asked as she ran alongside.

"Heart attack," Scott said. He keyed his radio and talked as he ran. Evie overheard him discussing whether or not to drive an ambulance onto the midway.

Heart attack. The same thing that had robbed her family of her father three years ago. She prayed the dispatcher was mistaken.

"The park is open," she said, huffing out the words as she ran. "You can only do that if it's life or death."

"I'll make that decision," he said.

Evie was about to say something in response such as "I own the freaking park, maybe I'll make the decision," but Scott cut her a swift glance as he dashed past the summer employee at the gate.

"When we get there."

Maybe he was right. That's why she had him and the other firefighters on staff night and day.

Emotion raced through her as she ran with Scott past the bumper cars and through Kiddieland to the Space Race roller coaster. The coaster itself had been at Starlight Point for over twenty years and initially had enjoyed limited success. Too scary for little kids, not terrifying enough for teenagers or thrillseekers. To make it more interesting, the ride had been enclosed about a decade ago. The coaster now had strobe lights and special effects, making it feel like a rocketing ride through the blackness of space.

Everything about the ride was dark. Even the queue lines snaking back and forth inside the large steel structure had limited light.

Scott reached the entrance to the ride first and paused to talk to the operator guarding the turnstile and checking the heights of hopeful kids. Evie saw the summer worker gesture inside and explain something to Scott. He raced ahead into the building and Evie followed, willing her eyes to adjust to the sudden darkness.

Her breath came in jagged gasps, and she was glad she didn't have to carry the large first-aid bag Scott had with him. She wondered what went through his mind on the way to an emergency.

They wound through the queue lines, bumping against the silver rails and jostling people. Evie wished someone had thought to turn on the emergency lighting. Searching in the dark in a crowded venue for a person having a heart attack was torture. Minutes could mean the difference between life and death. Why had no one turned on the lights?

She shouted to the worker at the door to hit the emergency lights, but it was noisy and the girl didn't hear. Evie considered running back and doing it herself, but she didn't want to leave Scott alone to face whatever they found. She squinted her eyes and tried to focus.

"Where is he?" Scott said aloud. "Fire department!" he shouted. "Anyone know who called us?"

A summer worker ran from the other direction and met them under a replica of a planet.

"I called it in," the kid said. "A man was clutching his chest and gasping, his wife was crying. But they disappeared. I swear."

Evie felt sorry for the teenager. He was clearly shocked by what he'd seen.

"Why didn't you stay with them?" Scott growled. The employee shrank back, looking desperately around, holding up his phone with the flashlight app.

A little boy who appeared to be about ten stepped out of the line, tugged at Evie's arm and pointed. "I know where they went," he said. "I saw some people go through there." He gestured toward an emergency exit that would open onto the beach side of the structure if her orientation wasn't a complete disaster.

Without hesitation, Scott climbed over the silver rail and headed for the emergency exit. Evie stayed right behind him, clambering through the waiting guests, cell phone in hand, wishing she knew what awaited them on the other side of the door.

Scott burst outside with Evie at his heels. The bright sunshine reflecting off the sand and water blinded them temporarily. Scott was the first to recover. He whirled and dropped to his knees next to the man on the ground.

Evie gasped. The man was about fifty years old. Overweight but not obese. Ghastly gray. Sweating. Clutching his chest. A woman sat on the ground next to him, sobbing. Two preteen children stood behind their mother, their faces tearstained and panicked.

Scott zipped open his bag and pulled out oxygen tubing. He turned briefly and handed his radio to Evie. "Call it in, give our exact location and get me an ambulance. Now."

She dropped her cell phone and took the radio. With trembling fingers, she pressed the button on the side. In all her years at Starlight Point, she'd never had to use a radio in an emergency.

"Dispatch, this is Evie Hamilton."

"Go ahead, Evie," a woman said. Evie knew the voice. Louise Higgins had worked dispatch at Starlight Point for years. There was curiosity in her familiar voice.

"I need an ambulance on the beach side of the Space Race."

"Is this the same call, the possible MI?" the dispatcher asked.

"Yes. Definitely an MI. Beach side emergency exit. Space Race." Repeating the exact location made her feel better. As if it could bring help faster.

And they needed it.

The man was apologizing, clutching the hands of his wife and kids and telling them he was sorry for every unkind word he'd ever said.

He clearly believed he was dying.

"Tell them to drive the ambulance right down the midway," Evie told the dispatcher. "Whatever it takes."

CHAPTER SIX

SCOTT HAD SEEN this same thing a dozen times in his years as a firefighter paramedic. It was serious, but the man had a shot at living if they got him to the hospital. *Where is that ambulance?* He'd heard Evie call it in, noticed her trembling voice but clear directions. Maybe there was a reason she was the Hamilton in charge of safety forces. Or maybe she'd lost the draw in the family lottery.

He put a mask on the victim and loaded him with oxygen. Monitored his vital signs. Listened for an approaching ambulance. Getting the man to the hospital before he went into full cardiac arrest was his only hope.

It would be a lot easier to hear the victim's heartbeat through the stethoscope if the wife wasn't sitting there crying. Blaming herself. And the kids… They looked like they were soon going to need medical attention themselves.

Scott laid his hand on the wife's arm.

"Trust me," he said, "we'll get your husband to the hospital and there's a great cardiologist on staff there. They'll take care of him."

The woman nodded, eyes locked on Scott as if he could single-handedly determine the fate of her husband.

"I need you to do something for me," he said. "Breathe slowly and deliberately, and get your husband to do the same thing. Count two seconds in, two seconds out. Do this together and it will help all of us."

She nodded. Turned her attention to her husband and counted slowly, breathing in and out.

"Good job. You're doing great," Scott said. He turned to the kids. Wished he could think of something for them to do.

Where is that ambulance?

"What can I do?" Evie asked, leaning over him so that her long blond hair fell across his shoulder. She placed a hand there and he could feel her breath on his neck.

It was oddly reassuring to have her beside him.

"Radio Dispatch and get an ETA on the squad."

He assumed she'd straightened and moved away because her touch, her hair, her warm breath, were all gone. He heard her talking with the dispatcher on the radio.

A police officer raced up and dropped down next to Scott. "I'm a first responder," he said. "Trained in CPR."

"Good. Stand by. But I hope I won't need your help."

The officer glanced at the access road leading to the ride. "Here's the squad."

Scott let out a breath, relief rushing through him. He had to get this victim to the hospital to improve his chances of recovery, to relieve his family of the agony they were suffering. And there was another reason. He took a quick look at Evie and didn't like the expression on her face. Shock. Fear. Grief? He had no idea if she'd ever witnessed something as terrifying as this, but it was obvious she wasn't taking it lightly.

She would need someone to talk to when this was over. At the fire station, the team did their own form of group therapy after calls that were ugly. A heart attack like this was, sadly, quite common. But they needed the camaraderie, the dark humor, the friendships born of hardship.

The squad pulled up and Scott's shift partner jumped out and opened both back doors.

He rolled a gurney over without asking. Together, Scott and his partner loaded the victim.

"Can we come along?" the man's wife asked. "We're not from around here. I have no idea where the hospital is."

Evie stepped close. "I've arranged a ride for you and your kids."

Scott hoped Evie was not driving. The vulnerable look he'd seen on her face a minute ago was now replaced with a professional expression, but he wondered about her. Worried about her.

"We have a company car waiting right outside the gate," she continued.

When had she arranged that? Must have been when she was talking to the dispatcher. She thought ahead. He respected that.

Scott climbed into the back of the ambulance and signaled his partner to start driving. He hoped the precious minutes they'd wasted locating the man and getting an ambulance hadn't jeopardized his chances for survival.

That was something he needed to discuss with the head of safety at Starlight Point.

THAT EVENING EVIE sat on a bench in front of the train station at Starlight Point. Guests breezed past her on their way to several more hours of fun before the park closed for the night. A few families lined up for the old-fashioned steam train that would take them on a circular tour of the peninsula and entertain them with a staged shoot-out along the tracks in the Wonderful West. Despite its sedate speed, the train had the highest passenger count of all the rides at Starlight Point, probably because of the large number of people it could accommodate at one time.

Evie wasn't boarding the train tonight. She was thinking about her ride to the hospital earlier in the day with the family of the heart attack victim. One of the security guards had driven the "courtesy car," a large sedan they used for minor things like delivering guests back to their hotels when their own cars wouldn't start.

On the way to the Bayside Hospital, Evie had gotten a description of the heart attack victim's car and a set of keys so that she could arrange to have the family's vehicle driven to them later in the day. Given the man's condition, Evie was not surprised when she'd heard he had been transferred to one of the larger hospitals in the area with a cardiac intensive care unit.

As she'd tried to offer comfort and support to the family, she'd thought about Scott alone in the back of the ambulance, doing what he could to save the man's life. She remembered the compassion he had shown to the man's wife and family. It was a side of him she had not seen before. Knowing him, he'd done everything according to the book, even though there was nothing textbook about the situation.

Everything had taken too long. Locating the victim. Getting an ambulance to him. As a one-third owner of Starlight Point, she wanted to make her mark by capital improvement projects like the marina and hotel, but she was also the overseer of the safety department. And therefore responsible for the lives and safety of her guests. A heavy weight settled on her shoulders, stealing the air from her lungs.

They had to do better. And she couldn't do it alone. Tomorrow, she would sit down with the Starlight Point fire chief, Link Harlan, and review their emergency response plans.

Evie closed her eyes and listened to the familiar sounds. The whistle of the train as it left the station. A child laughing. People screaming on roller coasters. Music. A games employee on a microphone trying to draw people into the weight guessing contest.

I hate those games encouraging people to throw away their money. They'd be better off spending five bucks on a hot dog and fries.

If only all decisions were a clear either-or choice. It would be so simple.

She breathed in the smells of Starlight Point. The lake, the food, sunscreen, the flowers planted aesthetically behind her bench. She loved it here at the junction where the midway split into two sections. The main part near the entrance was lined with shops and restaurants on both sides, but the train station marked a dividing point. If guests veered down one path, they would go past roller coasters on their way to the Wonderful West. If they chose the other path, they would have a quiet walk down the Western Trail.

This bench had been her father's favorite place to take a break. He'd said it was the heart of Starlight Point, a spot where he could see the front gates in the distance, hear the train behind him and watch families stream past.

Evie closed her eyes, wishing her father was there next to her on the bench—even for just a moment so she could pretend she was a little girl again and the Point was magical.

"Funny place for a nap," a man's voice said, interrupting her childhood flashback.

Evie opened her eyes. Scott Bennett sat next to her on the bench. He wore a green T-shirt and shorts. Sneakers. A black backpack rested next to him on the ground. He looked like an average resort guest hoping for summer fun.

Except that he was far more attractive than the average male. Dark hair and eyes, broad shoulders and muscular arms exposed by the T-shirt.

"What are you doing here?" Evie asked. She didn't mean to sound rude, but he'd surprised her. In several ways.

"I work here."

She smiled. "I know."

"My shift ended a few minutes ago and I'm headed for the ferry dock."

She glanced at his T-shirt and shorts.

"I changed at the station," he said. "I like to take the long way, walk up the Western Trail and relax. Sometimes I get junk food. Sometimes I call it dinner if we've had a busy shift."

"And you like to be undercover," she said.

"So people don't stop you and ask you to put out fires or remove splinters."

He cracked a small smile. "Do you ever go undercover so people don't ask you to hand out free tickets or keep the park open later?"

"I'm doing it right now," she said. This was mostly true. She was too dressed up to be a tourist, but her black name tag was in her purse. Along with her father's name tag, which she carried for luck and memories.

Evie crossed one leg over the other and waited. There had to be a reason Scott had decided to sit with her. She noticed him staring at her exposed ankle.

"How did you get that scar?" he asked.

Personal question.

Evie shrugged. "Growing up in an amusement park comes with all kinds of temptation."

"I would imagine."

"One summer my brother and sister and I decided to climb out to the end of the break wall even though it's officially off-limits. Our parents only found out because I sliced my ankle open when I went down between some rocks." She smiled at him. "You may have noticed the locked gate and fence where it meets the beach."

"Was it fun growing up here?"

"Every single day. We had free rein of the place."

"You still do," Scott observed.

She laughed. "Yes, but the risks we take now are far more complicated than sneaking out onto a break wall."

How true that was. Financial risks were one thing, but inviting thousands of people to Starlight Point every day and being responsible for their happiness and safety was way beyond risky. Sometimes it was downright dangerous.

"Have you heard anything more about our patient?" Scott asked.

Evie shook her head. "He was transferred, but that's all. Patient confidentiality is serious business."

"I know all about that. There are often times I wish I could find out what happened to the people I treated. We talk about that at the station quite a lot. We always review runs when they're over."

"Do you ever second-guess yourself?" Evie asked. "Wish you'd done something differently?"

"Sometimes," he admitted. "And sometimes there's nothing else you could have done."

He put an arm across the back of the bench and half turned toward her, as if he wanted to say more. Or ask her something.

She could wait. She had no plans to hurry home and sit in her lonely flat. Jack would go home with Augusta. June would go home with Mel. Her mother had become an expert at filling up lonely evenings by serving on boards and charities and making friends her age, many of them widows, too.

What did Evie have? She glanced down the midway and could barely see the carousel making a circuit at the front gates. She had Starlight Point and a basket full of big plans. Were they foolish and risky plans? What would her father say if he could see the money she was pouring into capital improvements?

He would probably love it. And that frightened her when she remembered the shock of discovering the debt he'd left behind. Ford Hamilton's habit of borrowing money for projects and piling up loans was unknown to the rest of family. It had taken them two years to dig out, and Evie hated risking their financial recovery.

"I think he'll make it," Scott continued, still on the subject of the medical emergency. "They'll probably do an angioplasty, put in a stent, stuff like that. People survive heart attacks every day."

Not always. Sometimes they die so suddenly no one even has a chance to say goodbye.

Evie ignored the pain squeezing her heart and focused on the entrance to the Sea Devil, a roller coaster partway down the midway. On a beautiful summer evening like this, the line stretched beyond the turnstile. People getting in line right now wouldn't be riding the coaster for a good hour and a half. She did the math in her head, considering the wait time and the length of the actual ride, doing the ratio of wait to fun. Calculations kept her mind busy.

And kept her thoughts off her father's sudden death over three years ago.

On a warm spring day weeks before the park opened, his heart had given out. Seeing the man having a heart attack today had made her wonder about her father's passing in a way she never had before. What had it been like for him to know he would never see his wife and children again? What would he have said if given the chance?

Evie felt heat in her cheeks and tears made her eyes heavy. She would not cry about it now. Not in front of Scott Bennett.

"Are you okay?" he asked.

"Of course. I just remembered I have to do something." She leapt to her feet and slung her purse over her shoulder.

Scott stood and stepped in front of her. "I thought we could talk about what happened today."

Evie looked down, unwilling to meet his eyes when she didn't trust her own not to betray her.

"We just did."

"There's something more," he said.

Of course. And she was certain it had to do with safety issues. He probably believed it was somehow her fault that a poor man had suffered a medical emergency in the wrong place at the wrong time.

Well, guess what, I already knew that, genius.

"I plan to meet with my fire chief tomorrow to review our procedures. I think that should make you happy."

"That's not what I meant," Scott protested.

Evie held up a hand and stepped around him. "See you later."

She stalked away, hoping her punishing pace would discourage him from following her. Instead of walking straight toward the ferry dock, she stopped by her office. Rearranged her desk. Did some file management on her computer. Sharpened every pencil she could find in her desk drawer. She pulled out her hotel plans and tried to focus on them, but she kept thinking of her father and what he would have said about the marina project, the hotel, everything.

It was time to go home, put on her purple fleece bathrobe and eat chips right out of the bag. At least two ferries should have departed for Bayside by now and, hopefully, Scott Bennett had been on one of them.

She strolled across the peninsula and exited the marina gate. The peaceful trip across the bay as the sunset colors streaked the sky was just what she needed to calm her mind after a tumultuous day. She walked down the long dock at the marina and felt satisfaction. The gas docks would open tomorrow. The restaurant would open next week at the latest. Things would be fine.

She stepped onto the ferry and headed for

her usual single seat next to the wheelhouse, but there was already someone in it.

Of course. *Him*.

She strode quickly around the boat to the other side where a similar seat was a mirror image. She sat and hoped like crazy Scott would not have the nerve to follow her. Passengers were free to change seats as long as the boat remained in dock. Only a few more minutes. She was afraid to look up for fear Scott would intrude on her solace. Again.

The boat horn signaled its departure and pulled away from the dock. She breathed. As she leaned against the engine compartment and felt its soothing vibration, she pictured Scott doing the same thing on the opposite side. That was not so soothing. She leaned forward and put her chin in her hands as she watched the waves slip past.

Next to her, a little girl played with the ribbon on her balloon. The balloon bounced around and bumped against the ceiling of the ferry, the post, other passengers. Adding balloon sellers to the midway was a new idea this year. Evie had seen the incredible revenue other theme parks earned from the souvenirs and decided to give it a try. Who didn't like balloons? So far, she estimated that almost a quarter of the children who left the gates in the evening left with a balloon with the park's logo. Not a bad return on investment.

She never thought about what happened to the balloons when the children got home. Because they were the heavy-duty Mylar kind, she assumed they lasted for weeks until children or their parents got tired of them.

The little girl's father warned her to stop annoying people, but the girl continued to hold the string and jerk the balloon back and forth like a punch ball Evie had once been given at a birthday party.

The father gave up and pulled out his cell phone. He scrolled through screens. It was a weeknight and they were probably locals if they were riding the ferry. Evie watched the girl play with the ribbon tied around her wrist and thought back to the simple joys of her childhood—not that many years ago, but sometimes it seemed a lifetime.

Suddenly the balloon caught a breeze and pulled taut. The loosely tied knot around the girl's wrist unraveled and the balloon sailed off the ferry. The father jumped up and leaned precariously over the rail, trying desperately to grab the balloon, but it was gone.

"Please remain seated," the captain said over the loudspeaker.

Evie expected tears would be next. She'd seen it before. But the little girl surprised her. She leaned over the rail and watched her balloon float away.

And she laughed.

Evie risked a glance over the engine compartment. Scott Bennett was standing, also watching the balloon float away. A small smile lit his face in the evening sunset and Evie realized how handsome he was when he let down his guard.

CHAPTER SEVEN

BABY SHOWERS, EVIE DECIDED, were not her thing. Because her college friends were too young and her siblings were just entering the wonderful world of reproduction, this was the first baby shower Evie had attended since one for her older cousin when she was eight. The magic of babies was a world she was not yet initiated into. Unpredictable, irrational, ungoverned by the laws of logic. In short, a world that was not for her. At least, not right now.

"You want to get the baby on a schedule," a woman was advising Jack's wife, Augusta, as Evie escaped for the kitchen. "Eating schedule, feeding schedule, pooping schedule."

Poor Gus, Evie thought, wondering if her sister-in-law welcomed all the advice.

Aunt Augusta, the namesake for Augusta's bakeries downtown and at the Point, was in the kitchen squeezing dollops of cream-cheese icing onto mini pastries. The shower was being held on a weekday morning to accommodate as many Starlight Point employees as possible, so the foods were breakfast-party style. A tray of scrambled eggs, artful doughnuts, fresh fruit, pitchers of milk and juice, plenty of coffee.

Aunt Augusta glanced up and looked relieved when she saw it was Evie.

"Is that woman still talking about baby poop out there?" she whispered.

Evie nodded. "It's Dorothea. She was my father's secretary and now she tries to keep track of my brother, Jack. She's been at Starlight Point longer than I've been alive."

"She isn't your secretary, too? I thought you shared an office with Jack."

Evie shook her head and grinned. "We share an office, but not Dorothea. I prefer to make up my own schedule." She sat at the counter in her former home, which Jack now inhabited with his wife. It still felt like home to Evie, and her sisterly relationship with Jack's wife, Augusta, meant she felt welcome almost any time.

"If I help out," Evie asked Aunt Augusta, "can I hide in here with you?"

"You can hide in here even if you don't do a thing. I think you're the only other woman here who hasn't had a baby or isn't pregnant right now. It's like some cult that shares way too many personal details to scare off outsiders."

"We'll stick together," Evie said. She took a pastry from the tray and ate it in one bite. "Delicious. No wonder you've made a living as a baker."

Aunt Augusta delivered the final dollop of icing and shoved the tray of confections to the end of the counter. She poured a cup of coffee and sat across from Evie. "So tell me why a beautiful young woman like you isn't out there gushing over baby booties."

"I'm only twenty-three," Evie said. "Too soon for me to think about baby anything."

"Makes sense."

Evie sipped her coffee. Aunt Augusta was one of her mother's friends, but considerably more grounded. She ran Augusta's downtown bakery all summer long while her niece Augusta ran three bakeries at Starlight Point. These days, Evie's mother ran around looking for something to do, with her old dog Betty rolling behind her in a wagon. Aunt Augusta was, perhaps, more likely to understand the heavy weight on Evie's shoulders than her own mother was. Especially since

Virginia Hamilton was worked up over the role of grandmother coming at her twice in the next six months.

"I have plenty of things other than babies to worry about," Evie said.

"What could the owner of a giant business employing thousands of workers have to worry about?" Aunt Augusta asked.

Evie blew out a breath. "Thank goodness the thousands are only here for the summer. It certainly is quieter in the off-season. Or at least it would be if I weren't trying to build marinas and hotels."

"Ambitious."

"I guess," Evie said.

"My niece told me what a lifesaver you were when it came to managing her bakeries two summers ago. Numbers and accounting are your superpower, she says."

"That's what everyone thinks."

"And you don't?"

Evie shrugged. "I love being a CPA and managing the company ledgers, but I have to contribute more than that."

"Who says?"

"I say. Unless I want to be the bean-counting baby sister all my life."

Aunt Augusta laughed. "I've been the

cake-baking spinster aunt all my life. It's not a bad gig, and it's the life I wanted. What do you want, Evie?"

The kitchen door swung silently open and Gloria, the costume mistress at the Point as long as Evie could remember, stepped in and closed the door. She leaned against it and shut her eyes.

"I hate baby showers. If one more person talks about her labor, nursing problems or stretch marks, I'm going to say something that'll get me kicked out of the party."

"I think there's some wine in the fridge," Evie suggested. "We could add it to the coffee and make up some fancy French name for it."

Gloria narrowed her eyes at the other two refugees. "Why are you two hiding in here?"

"Same reason you are," Aunt Augusta said. She poured a cup of coffee and shoved it across the counter toward Gloria. "We're not in the motherhood club."

"I have three sons," Gloria said. "But back in my day, you had the baby and you didn't talk about it. Heck, I tried to forget about all the things they're yapping up out there. Especially the parts about labor that are supposed to be between you and the delivery room wallpaper. Better kept that way, if you ask me."

Evie scooted over and made room on her seat for the new arrival. "Gloria is like a second mom to me and June. She made our ballet costumes, prom dresses, you name it."

"Made June's wedding dress for the Christmas wedding last year, too," Gloria said.

"Stunning, of course," Evie added. "Gloria's a genius."

"And it was the off-season," Gloria added. "I had time."

"Are you making baby clothes for Gus and Jack's daughter?" Aunt Augusta asked.

Gloria shook her head. "After running wardrobe for years, sewing everything from traffic vests to glitzy show costumes, the one thing I've never made is clothing for the newborn crowd. Don't think I could work on something that tiny."

Evie smiled. "I think you could do anything. But there's no need to exert yourself on baby clothes. Did you see the piles of presents out there? There are easily twenty pink baby dresses and fifteen pink sleepers."

"Dorothea's probably drawing up a schedule right now for wearing them all before the baby grows out of them," Gloria said.

The three of them sipped coffee and ate pastries while the noise level in the other room continued to escalate with each adorable baby gift Augusta opened. Evie felt a twinge of guilt because she was hiding in the kitchen instead of helping out, but she wasn't needed. June was writing down all the presents and names so Augusta could send out frilly pink thank-you notes later. And Augusta's mother was out there, also. Her parents had finally moved back to the area after Augusta's father retired from his managerial job in the auto industry. They'd bought a house in Bayside and settled down to stay close to their new grandchild.

No wonder Augusta looked so happy. Two years ago she had found a place where she belonged, fallen in love with Jack, made a successful business out of cakes and cookies, and now she would have a daughter of her own. It was a fairy tale.

Was it a fairy tale Evie wanted for herself? Right now, the happy ending she wanted had to do with construction diagrams and occupancy permits.

Virginia Hamilton came through the kitchen door and closed it behind her. "That's a lot of pink," she said.

Aunt Augusta slid over and made room for her friend next to her at the counter.

"I'll join your party for a few minutes if you don't mind," Virginia said. "I'm guessing we're not talking about strollers and diapers in here."

Evie laughed. "We're talking about getting out the wine."

"Baby talk isn't so bad, but it's just too big a group out there. You'll see someday, honey." Virginia reached across and squeezed her youngest daughter's hand.

"Right now, the marina project is my baby. And then it'll be the hotel."

"I think a real human baby might be easier," Gloria commented. She winked. "If you get the baby on a schedule."

The kitchen door opened and June popped her head in. Already beautiful with a flair for drama, she positively glowed with her pregnancy.

"There's our next new mom," Evie said. "Should I be taking notes for your shower in a few months?"

"I suggest serving plenty of food." June eyed the tray of pastries. "Are those ready? Can I take them out?"

"Did you eat through all the food I already set out?" Aunt Augusta asked.

"I had help," June said. "And now that I'm not squeezing into tiny dance costumes and I have a good excuse for gaining a little weight, I'm enjoying it."

Aunt Augusta and Gloria stood and picked up trays. "Back to the party," Gloria said. The two of them followed June through the door, and Virginia and Evie were alone in the kitchen.

"Nice to have the kitchen to ourselves again," Virginia said. "We've had a lot of talks over this counter."

"Do you like living down the street in Jack's former bungalow?" Evie asked.

Virginia shrugged. "It's just the right size for me and Betty. She has a nice run in the backyard and a sunny place in the living room where she can watch the birds."

"Maybe I should get a dog. Or a cat," Evie said. "My new apartment is a bit lonely. Lucky for me, I'm hardly there except to sleep and shower."

Virginia gave Evie a searching look. "You should make time for yourself, maybe go on a date. Otherwise, that apartment will stay lonely."

Evie laughed. "If you happen to see an eligible bachelor who doesn't mind that I'm married to Starlight Point, you just let me know."

Virginia smiled. "There's probably one right under your nose."

"I doubt it. I'd like to think I would have noticed." Evie sipped her coffee. "They're taking down the big cottonwood tree in the marina this morning," she said. "The one where we had picnics in the summer."

"Probably a good thing," Virginia said. "We're lucky that old tree hasn't come down in a storm and killed someone by now."

"Aren't you sad to see it go?" Evie asked. "I tried to keep it, even had the restaurant built so it wouldn't be harmed, but it ended up a casualty, anyway. Too close to the fire lane, according to the new fire inspector."

Virginia shrugged. "Can't be too sentimental. I love the old hotel, too, with its rolling floors and outdated everything, but I'm excited about your plans to renovate it."

Evie smiled. "You're like Dad. Always looking forward to the next big thing."

"Of course. That's why we were such a pair. If he could see you now, he'd be so proud."

"Do you think so? I thought he expected me to be an accountant."

"Honey, parents expect their kids to be whatever they want. And right now, you're thinking about the future of this place. All our futures." Virginia leaned closer and lowered her voice. "To tell the truth, I'm starting to think you're the one who's most like your father. Taking a big risk like this surprises me, coming from you, but Ford would have loved it."

Evie knew her mother meant it kindly. But why did she feel like she'd swallowed a brick when she compared her big capital improvement risk to the risks and loans her father had taken?

Her mother meant it as a compliment, but Evie wasn't sure it was.

IT WAS A shame to see the tree come down, but there was no choice. Blocking the fire lane was a safety risk, and the sheer age and size of the tree made it a hazard with the strong winds that came off the lake during storms. Scott wondered why the Hamiltons had delayed cutting down the tree this long.

He parked the ambulance at the entrance to the marina, closing off vehicle access. While that massive tree was being taken down with a bucket truck and a crane, no one was going into or out of the marina, no matter what.

"Those guys are crazier than we are," the fire chief commented. He sat in the passenger seat of the ambulance and stretched his legs. "I wouldn't want to be clear up there cutting down branches. That's higher than the ladder truck from the Bayside station."

Scott and Link Harlan watched through the windshield as the massive tree came down piece by piece. Workers in orange hard hats sawed limbs and lowered them on ropes to crew members waiting below. The tree service hired from Bayside had started at first light so they would have at least four hours until the park opened. Half that time had passed, but they were making progress. There would be plenty of clean-up work once the limbs were all on the ground, but that wouldn't pose a threat to any Starlight Point guests, aside from the noise of chainsaws, which couldn't be heard over the roller coasters anyway.

Scott rolled down both windows and turned off the diesel engine. It was a beautiful morning, the last week of June. As soon as this tree was done and the fire lane was complete, he would sign the paperwork to officially open the marina restaurant and shower house. And then Evie could check that off her list of things to worry about.

What had caused the distress in her eyes a few nights ago when they'd met on the bench in front of the train station? Was it just the sadness and chaos of the heart attack she had witnessed, or was there something else?

"I'm sure they know what they're doing," Scott said. His eyes cut to the outriggers locked in place on the crane truck. The orange cones set out. The ropes tied to the workers. Hard hats on each man. Safety procedures firmly in place.

"I hope they won't need us, but Evie insisted we bring an ambulance and sit over here, at least until the park opens."

"I'm surprised she's not here," Scott commented. She was usually right around the corner, he'd discovered in the six weeks the park had been open.

"Some big family breakfast thing this morning. I think it's a baby shower for Jack's wife," the chief said. "I remember when Jack was a baby himself."

Scott swiveled to look at Chief Harlan. "You've been here that long?"

Harlan nodded. "Lots of us year-rounders have been here that long. It's a nice place to work. Plenty of excitement in the summer, you can take it easier in the winter. We're like a family."

Scott pictured himself working at Starlight Point for the next thirty years. At twenty-seven, he still hadn't put down roots anywhere. But the fire inspector job at Bayside was a huge incentive to stay in the area. Especially if his sister decided to stick around when she finished college next year.

"Don't know if you've heard the rumors," Harlan said, "but they're true. I'm planning to retire at the end of the season."

"You are?"

Harlan nodded. "When the snow flies this winter, I'll be in Florida. My wife is a retired teacher, and we're finally going to get our schedules coordinated. For the last thirty years, she's had the summer off and that's been my busy season. When I've had time to have fun during the winter, she's been grading papers."

"Congratulations," Scott said. He tried to imagine giving up firefighting and taking up golf or playing cards. *I don't think I'll ever be able to give up the fire service.*

"No idea what they'll do for a replacement," Chief Harlan continued. "It'll have to be someone with experience and a degree. Maybe young enough he'll stick around a long time."

Scott blew out a long breath but said nothing.

"I let Evie know about my plans recently, so she'll have plenty of time to start hunting the next chief." Harlan chuckled. "I'll sure miss her and June and Jack. They used to climb on the running boards of our old fire truck—we replaced that one a long time ago—and swing their legs. I let them blow the siren in the off-season when there was no one in the hotel to annoy."

"Must be strange being here in the winter," Scott commented. "Snow instead of tourists."

"It is, but you'd be surprised how much work goes on. There's maintenance, of course, but a few winters ago we got to watch the Sea Devil being built. There were huge cranes lifting pieces of track into place and workers climbing all over it. Lots of onlookers wanting to see what was going on kept the security staff busy. There's only a few cops who winter over, the same ones who've been around as long as I have."

"Did you see the plans for the marina project over the last winter?" Scott asked. If the chief was here on-site, why had he let deficiencies slide?

"I saw them, but it wasn't my job to inspect and approve them. We're under the jurisdiction of Bayside. That means you now. I'm hearing lots of talk of the massive hotel renovation Evie's got planned for this winter, so I imagine it won't be long before you hear about that straight from her."

Interesting. Maybe that was the reason Evie was playing nice, especially now that her marina project was getting the green light. *Almost.*

"I met with her a few days ago to review our safety plans, after the heart attack run at the Space Race," the chief continued.

"And?"

"And we didn't change much. You can't predict everything. But that's when I told her I planned to retire at the end of the year and she ought to let the new guy have a say in modernizing the department, procedures and all."

Scott wondered how far Evie's interest in

modernizing the department went. He had
plenty of suggestions if she ever asked. Or
even if she didn't.

CHAPTER EIGHT

ON THE THURSDAY before the July Fourth weekend, the Starlight Point Marina finally opened officially. Although seasonal and transient dockage had been going on for almost a month, it had been low-key and spotty without the amenities Evie's plan had promised. Now, with an adequate fire lane, a clear space around the electrical panel, signage in the restaurant and all the safety valves a person could want—even someone as fussy as Scott Bennett—the whole place was open for business.

And just in time. A local boat dealer, Port Huron Yacht & Boat Sales, had rented the space for the entire weekend. Food trucks set up in the parking lot and offered everything from steak sandwiches to organic cheese. Vendors hawking boat-related clothing, shoes and supplies took up position between the parking lot and the docks. A person could eat fish tacos and browse high-priced fish-ing poles at the same time. Top-end new and used boats docked in all the slips, inviting guests to take off their shoes and step aboard.

The sales force for the boat dealership set up tents where they hoped to entice buyers to seal the deal—*only ninety-six payments larger than your house payment and you can own something you'll probably use five times a year.*

Evie shook her head, marveling at the money the boat crowd poured into their hobby. They were either unaware of the concept of return on investment or they had so much money they didn't care.

Guys in expensive polo shirts and sunglasses drank colorful drinks as they chatted with other guys dressed the same way. Evie decided the second part of her theory was correct—they had so much money they didn't care about those ninety-six payments.

Wearing her usual uniform of knee-length navy skirt, crisp white blouse, black name tag and low-heeled sandals, Evie walked the length of each of the six docks, checking out the boats for sale. Of course she wanted to make sure everything was operating smoothly, but it was no hardship cruising the docks on a sunny Thursday afternoon with a view of the sparkling bay.

And with a heart full of relief. *Finally.* The marina she'd talked her brother and sister into spending big bucks on was open. Local boaters—her target audience— would pour in this weekend, see what the marina offered and come back with their money again and again. They would eat at the restaurant, buy seasonal or temporary dockage, pay for admission to the park, eat ice cream, have a beer…it all added up to revenue eventually topping her capital expenditure. It was the return-on-investment plan she'd sold to June and Jack while crossing her fingers she wasn't wrong.

The few locals who had already paid for seasonal dockage were moved closest to the new restaurant, the prime location compensation for being uprooted for the weekend. The coupons for free dining in the restaurant also softened the blow, and Evie hadn't heard a single complaint. The Hamilton family boat, a large, white powerboat called *The Starlight*, had also been moved to the end of the long dock by the restaurant.

Evie remembered sunset cruises on the boat when her father was alive. He'd had a special hat that said Captain that he insisted on wearing. Sometimes they would take *The Starlight* through the drive-through. A family joke, since it was really a McDonald's on the other side of Bayside that happened to have a dock. Cheeseburgers and fries tasted so much better on the open deck of the family powerboat.

Jack still used the boat occasionally, but it was more or less a permanent resident of the marina. Maybe she should change that. In her new spirit of bravery and optimism and throwing caution to the wind, perhaps she should learn to run the boat and take her own sunset cruises whenever she wanted. She could take her mother's dog Betty along for company.

Like you have time.

Evie put her memories and plans aside and focused on her job. At the end of the middle dock, she paused to talk with the owner of the boat dealership that had rented her space. A man in his early fifties, Bryan Landino had *boat guy* written all over him. Expensive sunglasses, silk polo shirt with the company logo embroidered on it, dress slacks with a crisp crease. And boat shoes, of course. Not the kind available at discount stores, either.

"Hey," Bryan said as he stood on the swim platform of a huge cabin cruiser, "the only thing prettier than my boats is you."

Evie smiled. The guy was slick in a salesman sort of way, but he was attractive. And the rental fee he'd paid for the weekend was generous—it *almost* made her feel better about the lost revenue while they satisfied the fire codes. Her accountant side said, *Play nice.*

"I hope you like the weather I ordered for you," she said. "Tomorrow looks great, too."

"Perfect. Just right for taking buyers out for a cruise. Really drives home the sale."

He stepped off the boat and moved closer to Evie. She glanced at his left hand out of curiosity, a gauge to determine the nature of his attention and whether he was trying to sell her something or flirt with her. Bryan did not wear a wedding ring and there was no impression where one had been.

Caught. He saw her ring-check and sidled close enough she could smell his cologne. At least it wasn't the cheap stuff. Even in the breeze, she caught the hint of department store rather than drugstore. But she still had no intention of sailing off into the sunset with the guy. She had work to do.

"I hope you sell every one of your boats," she said. That was actually true. And reminded her she ought to ask for a partial commission on sales if they did this again next year. "And you'll want to come back next year," she continued.

"Best invitation I've had all day. Why don't you come by later when the show officially closes and I'll take you out on whichever boat you want."

Evie didn't answer right away. On one hand, yuck. On the other hand, she had to consider the man's company as a potential revenue source for next year. And it was a free boat ride on a beautiful summer evening.

While she considered his offer, Scott Bennett breezed down the dock and passed right between them. The sleeve of his firefighter uniform brushed Evie's bare arm. He didn't look at her or her companion, but went straight to a box mounted on a dock post. A reflective sign on the post announced the contents of the box: a fire extinguisher. Scott flipped it open, peered in and shut the cover. He made a mark on his clipboard, turned and brushed right between them on his way back down the dock.

Bryan rolled his eyes at Scott's retreating

figure. "What's with Mr. Safety, huh? Anyway, what do you think about you and me taking in the sunset later?"

"I think I have to pass, but thank you for the offer. This is our biggest weekend of the year, and I should probably earn my paycheck. But let's get together after the show and compare notes. I could use some feedback about my marina, and I hope you'll be celebrating many sales."

"Later," Bryan said. He added a wink and Evie turned and headed down the dock. The guy was old enough to be her father. He shouldn't be winking at her, but she also didn't need Captain Bennett muscling between them. Had he heard the offer of the boat ride? Had that prompted his fire extinguisher check?

Knowing him, he checked the fire extinguishers every other hour and had no interest in Evie's personal life.

It was obviously none of his business. Right?

So why did she find it oddly comforting to see Scott Bennett standing, arms crossed over his chest, at the end of the dock as if he was waiting for her to say no to a date with he-of-the-expensive-boat-shoes?

That theory lasted about six seconds. Because as soon as she neared the end of the dock, Scott got in his truck and drove off. Maybe he hadn't been waiting for the resolution of her encounter with the boat salesman, after all.

"I saw that," June said.

Evie swiveled and found June sitting at a temporary dockside table with Mel and their son, Ross. The six-year-old was missing two front teeth, but he had recently gained a stepmother who doted on him. The three of them had baskets of food from one of the food trucks.

"What did you see?" Evie asked. She sat in the fourth and empty chair at the table and stole a French fry from her sister's basket.

"You flirting with a slick boat salesman."

"Hi, Aunt Evie," Ross said. "Are you buying a boat?"

"Let's get refills, Ross," Mel said. He and his son picked up their empty sodas and headed for the food area.

"That was business," Evie told her sister when they were alone. "I was making sure the owner of the boat dealership was happy with the venue he paid big bucks for."

"That wasn't the interesting part," June

said. "I liked it when America's favorite fire inspector broke up your date."

Evie laughed. "Scott wasn't breaking up anything. He was checking the fire extinguishers." She sat back and looked at the boats. "He loves safety."

"Adorable," June said.

"He is not adorable," Evie said. "He's a pain in the neck."

"But?"

"But we need him on our side. So I'm being nice."

"A noble sacrifice for the company." June smirked and waggled her eyebrows.

Mel slid a chicken sandwich and an iced tea in front of Evie. "I feel guilty eating while you're working."

She smiled. "Thanks. This is going to be a wild weekend."

"Calm before the storm," Mel agreed.

On Friday evening Evie was in the office at the front gate checking the attendance figures for the holiday weekend, and the news was fantastic. The weather was perfect. And the Saturday figures should be even better because of the fireworks marking the halfway point of the season. *Halfway.* Although her marina was open, the hotel was still a dream on paper. And she had a lot work to do.

As she was leaving the glass-walled office at the front entrance, the radio she had recently acquired buzzed with the dispatcher's voice.

"Boat fire in the marina."

Heart sinking, Evie raced toward the marina on foot. She held her radio to her ear and listened to the Starlight Point Fire Department acknowledge the call. She knew half the crew had taken an ambulance run to the hospital in Bayside only a little while ago. *Hopefully it's only a small fire.*

Evie dashed through the park gate closest to the marina and saw the smoke. Clouds of smoke rolling and obscuring the overhead lights in the marina. In the darkness, orange flames leapt from one of the boats. She gasped, fear and resolution urging her onward. She knew the fire truck would take several minutes to arrive because it had to wind around the outer loop. *How bad will the fire get before then?*

A siren from the opposite direction arrested her thoughts. The Starlight Point ambulance was coming back across the Point

Bridge, and it careened into the marina lot. The firefighters on board barreled out and grabbed the hose lines specially installed on the new docks for just this purpose.

But they didn't have turnout gear or helmets. One of the firefighters was Scott. He yelled at Evie to stand back and make sure no one walked down the dock where the boat burned ominously.

It took her a moment to decide which boat was on fire. The smoke and flames came from the dock closest to the restaurant where the seasonal boats had been moved for the weekend. Her family's boat *The Starlight* was tied up on that dock, helplessly in the line of fire if Scott and his partner didn't put out the flames. It might be burning already.

If *The Starlight* were destroyed, it would be another piece of her childhood sacrificed to her oversize dreams for the marina. Maybe she had gone too far, dreamed too big.

There was nothing she could do now except wait and hope.

She blocked the dock entrance and watched as Scott and his partner battled the fire. Should they be risking their lives like that? Was saving the boat and dock worth it, or should she march down and tell them to retreat and wait for the pumper truck?

Even though my family's boat and a guest's might be destroyed.

Being the head of the safety department was a much more complicated job than she had imagined when she'd taken it on. Every day it seemed to bring a terrible choice, testing her and forcing her into tough decisions: people or property, profits or caution.

When the flames subsided and the two men emerged from the smoke, Evie breathed a sigh of relief. The pumper truck pulled up and the crew worked together to knock down the remaining fire. Scott and his partner stepped back and let the men in turnout coats and helmets handle it.

Evie kept her post at the end of the dock and watched Scott in the glow of the lights from the restaurant. He wiped his face with his shirtsleeve. *I hope he didn't breathe in any toxic fumes from burning fiberglass.* Thankfully, the night breeze carried the smoke away from them.

Evie wished it would carry all her problems out across the lake.

An hour later, she and Jack stood at the dock in the new marina while Scott wrote up the fire report. A twenty-seven-foot pleasure boat was connected to the dock only by the grace of several sturdy dock lines. Half on its side, its white hull a sickening gleam in the dark water, it was a sorry sight.

"Who knew you couldn't set off fireworks from a boat?" Jack asked. "I'm sure it sounded like a great idea about five seconds before they did it."

"You'd think the guy might have waited until tomorrow night," Scott said. "I guess he wanted to get a jump on the Fourth of July."

Evie felt the heavy weight of what could have happened, her mood grim as she surveyed her mercifully undamaged marina.

Jack nudged Evie. "You could try laughing about it," he said. "Imagine the guy who owns the boat calling his insurance agent in the morning."

Evie smiled, the weight lifting just a little.

Dear Agent. Last night I was celebrating the Fourth of July weekend when my buddies and I got the bright idea to set off fireworks from the bow of my boat. Drinking? Just a little. Honest.

"What do you think our insurance company will say?" Evie asked.

Jack shook his head. "Nothing. We have

the drunken fool liability clause that kicks in for things just like this. And there was no actual damage to the dock or *The Starlight*."

The Hamilton family boat was moored a boat and a walkway from the burned shell and had sustained no damage at all.

"Not that we can see," Evie said. "But we'll have to look at the dock again in the daylight."

Scott handed her a flashlight. "Scorched the neighboring boat before we got it out," he commented. "Not bad, but he'll want to get the fiberglass buffed out at the very least."

Evie sighed. "Happy Fourth of July weekend."

"Cheer up," Jack said. "Tomorrow could be even rowdier."

"This isn't the worst one I've had," Scott said. "At my old department, we just left the trucks running around the Fourth since we got called out so much." He shook his head. "Idiots with homemade fireworks setting their lawns and roofs on fire."

"Where was your old department?" Jack asked.

Evie wondered the same thing, but she felt awkward grilling Scott about his past. Something about him made her think there was a ready-made wall just waiting to go up if the conversation turned personal.

"About an hour away. Yorkville. It's where I grew up."

"What brought you to Bayside?" Jack asked.

Evie pretended to scrutinize the damage on both boats, using the flashlight and listening to the conversation.

"Better opportunity for a career firefighter. Yorkville was too small to offer much advancement."

Jack leaned against a dock post. "How long were you there?"

"Five years." He shrugged. "It was a good job, and there was plenty of time to do my college work while I was sitting around, but I felt like I was going backward."

"Are you talking about Dorkville?" Caroline, dressed in her all-black security uniform, appeared out of nowhere and trained a flashlight on her brother's face. "Of course it might not be so dorky anymore since you moved out."

Scott wrapped his fingers around her flashlight and lowered the beam to the ground. "Don't you have someone you're supposed to arrest right now?"

"Where's the genius who owns this boat?" she asked. "I have to take his official statement about the…uh…accident on his boat, and I better talk to him before his wife finds him and kills him."

Scott handed her the makeshift canister used to shoot off the fireworks. "You might want to add this to your report."

"Thank you, oh wise fire inspector. I don't have to salute you or anything, do I?"

"Your humility and respect will be enough," Scott said.

Caroline poked him in the gut with her flashlight. "Too bad you couldn't put it out before it sank."

"We didn't have a pumper truck at first," Scott said. "We needed a better water supply."

His sister opened her hands and gestured to the marina and the lake.

"It's not that simple. You can't just scoop water out of the lake and throw it at the fire."

"So you say."

Evie found herself smiling. She couldn't imagine teasing Scott like his sister did, but then again, people probably thought her brother was intimidating, too. Evie glanced over at Jack, who was now leaning away from the dock trying to take a picture of the boat with his cell phone, putting himself at great risk of falling in the water.

Maybe not.

"Hey, Evie," Caroline said. "I ate lunch in the new restaurant today before I had to go to work." She nodded toward the marina restaurant, which had been open only two days now.

"How was it?" Evie asked.

"Great. But really busy. We had to wait for a table."

"We?" Scott asked.

Caroline rolled her eyes at her brother. "Luckily some rich boaters shared their table with us. Good-looking older men with lots of money to spend," she added.

Scott huffed out a breath.

"Just kidding. But the food was great. Thought you could use some good news."

"Always," Evie agreed.

Caroline headed toward the men sitting on a picnic table at the end of the dock. Evie did not envy her the task of getting a truthful statement. They all appeared to be in their forties and fifties. *With age does not necessarily come wisdom.* The thought made Evie feel just a little bit better about being the youngest amusement park owner in the country. She'd stack her twenty-three years of sensible behavior against their foundered boat any day.

"Now what?" Jack asked.

"We get the salvage boat to come in and tow this wreck to one of the service marinas in Bayside," Scott said. "Chief Harlan already called it in. Luckily, this doesn't seem to be leaking anything. It'll save that moron's insurance company a hefty bill."

"Will you stand by and handle the towboat?" Jack asked Evie. "Or do you want me to do it? One of us should get back in the park and keep an eye on June."

"She'll be okay," Evie said. "Just because she's pregnant doesn't mean she can't handle a few long days and some excitement."

"That's not what I meant," Jack said. "She may stage a takeover and we'll be looking for new jobs."

Evie laughed. "You go back in there. I'll hang around here and clean up. I'm the one who thought a marina expansion was a great idea."

Jack shook his head. "We all used to think you were the smart one."

"So did I."

CHAPTER NINE

SCOTT STOOD ALONE in the dark with Evie as they waited for the towboat. Perhaps alone wasn't the right word. There were dozens of boats docked in the marina. Booths and food vendors just closing for the evening. Evie had been anxious to have the marina open for the boat show weekend. She got her wish —just in time—but probably never expected some fool would make a mess of things by setting his boat on fire.

You can never predict what people will do. That's why his job was to save them from themselves by trying to make the world idiot-proof. Fire lanes, sprinkler systems, exit signs. How much would be enough?

"Thank you for putting out the fire before it got any worse," she said. "I'm so grateful you were close by."

"You're welcome. Just doing my job."

Evie leaned against a dock post and glanced across the bay. Even in the low marina lighting, he could see she did not look happy.

Maybe he should try to cheer her up. It was a holiday weekend, after all. And he hadn't exactly made her summer easy so far.

"It's not so bad," Scott said. He meant it. The damage could easily have been a lot worse. "Only one boat was destroyed. The guy had it coming, anyway, for being a reckless jerk."

Evie shrugged. "Maybe he's not a reckless jerk. He's got vacation-brain syndrome."

Was she making an excuse for the guy?

"There's no excuse for playing with fire." He heard the hard edge in his voice but couldn't help it.

Evie crossed her arms as she continued to look across the bay. Probably waiting for the towboat so she could get out of here as soon as possible. She turned back to him. "Don't you ever play with fire?" she asked.

Scott felt her words like a punch. Felt the air grow ten degrees colder. "No," he said.

He was sorry he'd tried to be nice.

"So those stories about firefighters being closet pyromaniacs are just rumors?"

Heat crept over his neck and ears like a burn. "No one I know or have ever worked with," he said, clipping off the words with deadly deliberation, "would think it was fun to mess around with something that could kill."

He stopped himself before he said too much. Opening his heart to Evie was not on his summer to-do list. He had a job here, and getting too friendly with her would make it more difficult.

"Hey, I was just kidding. Maybe you could lighten up. The whole world isn't directly under your protection."

Was she serious? Of course it was. Overlooking hazards was dereliction of duty. Negligence. Unthinkable.

"I won't apologize for taking my job seriously," he said.

"I take my job seriously, too, but—"

"If that were true, this marina would have opened on schedule," Scott said, cutting her off.

Maybe it was a good thing he could barely see the expression on Evie's face.

"You suck," Caroline said as she passed him. She'd been close enough to hear what he'd said to Evie and was far more candid than his boss.

His boss. He should try to remember that. If he got himself canned from Starlight Point, he'd lose the opportunity to watch over his sister. But the truth was Evie needed him just as much as he needed her.

"I'm cutting off your lunch money," Scott called after his sister. She held up her hand in a rude gesture as she kept walking. *Maybe she doesn't need my protection as much as I think she does.*

He did not like that thought at all. *Of course she needs me.*

"Looks like Caroline doesn't need your lunch money," Evie said.

Why did he wish he could wipe away the hurt and anger on her face? He shouldn't want to smooth the lines of frustration and kiss away the tension in her jaw. She was his boss. And she probably only tolerated his company because she had to. He needed to change the subject before he alienated her completely or pulled her into his arms.

Wouldn't his sister love to see *that*?

Maybe he should dive into the water. He could make up some excuse like looking for hazardous materials leaking from the foundered boat. Yes. A cold bath in the interest of preparing the boat for towing would be smart.

But stupid. The water was dark. He wasn't

a certified diver. And the towboat handled this kind of navigational hazard every day. He should focus on business.

"We've got some time before the towboat gets here," he said, trying for neutrality in his tone. "Why don't you tell me about your hotel renovation plans?"

Evie's head snapped up and she drilled him with her stare. "I'm not ready to present them for your approval yet."

"I wasn't asking for an official submission," he said. "Just curious."

The owner of the boat walked over and stood looking at the burnt out shell with an expression of rue and shock. His friend joined him and they mournfully examined the listing craft.

"Your wife isn't going to believe your story," the owner's stocky friend said.

"She's not that bright. She believed it when I told her the trash truck hit her car in our driveway. If you don't go along with my story, I'll tell her you were to blame."

"Hey," the stocky man said. "It was dark. And I swear that car wasn't parked there when I showed up for the poker game."

The owner shrugged. "Accidents happen. Just like the accidental fire on the boat docked next to mine that spread to my boat before they could stop it."

"You're not going to lie to your insurance company, are you?" Evie asked. "Because when your agent talks to mine, the truth will come out. I think you should know I have no intention of lying for you. You could have burned down my entire marina. Would have if it weren't for my excellent staff of fire-fighters."

Scott was surprised by the steel in her tone. She'd been ready to sock him in the gut a moment ago and now she was endorsing him?

"You owe this man a thank-you," Evie said, pointing directly at Scott. "He raced to put out the fire without his turnout gear and helmet."

"Why didn't you have them with you?" the boat owner asked.

Scott cocked his head and stared at the reckless fool. "Left them in my other fire truck. You can read all about it in the full report the fire inspector sends to the insurance company."

"I haven't seen any inspector here."

"You're looking at him," Scott said. "You

should call it a night before you say something you'll regret."

The boat owner and his friend swiveled and moved down the dock.

Scott watched them go and tried to relax the tension in his shoulders and fists. When he hazarded a glance at Evie, she was smiling.

"Remind me not to fight with you," she said.

Her smile made his tension disappear like salt dissolving in water. It was dangerous, letting himself be drawn to Evie. For so many reasons.

"We're on the same side," he said.

"Then I'll give you a sneak preview of my hotel plans. But it's not public knowledge yet. I'm supposed to make a grand reveal this summer." She laughed. "I should probably get going on that since the summer is now officially half over. On the day of the marina ribbon cutting, I told the press that there would be an upcoming media event about the hotel."

Scott flashed to an image of that day—Evie in a soaking white dress walking along the outer loop, vulnerable and beautiful. He cleared his throat.

"What?" Evie asked.

"Nothing. I was just thinking about the… rain that day. I meant to change the windshield wiper blades on the pumper. I'll set a reminder in my phone."

He pulled the smartphone out of his pocket and pretended to swipe through screens. The electronic light from the phone cast an eerie glow over them in the darkened marina.

Scott had no idea how to make a note or set a reminder in his phone. He pushed buttons for a reasonable amount of time and then slid it back in his pocket.

"I'm trying to bring the hotel up to date without losing the old-fashioned feel," Evie said.

Scott nodded. He pictured modern fire-suppression systems. Integrated alarms. High-output sprinkler heads.

"Flat-screen televisions, state-of-the-art bathrooms, high-efficiency lighting and ventilation," Evie said.

Perhaps their interpretations of up to date *aren't the same.*

"And?" he prompted.

"It's a big project," she said. "I want to leave the central rotunda and original lobby, plus two of the century-old wings. But if I can get the project moving on time—" She lowered her voice and glanced around.

Scott felt that he was being let in on a family secret. *Great Aunt Tillie buried ten million bucks in the vegetable garden.*

"—I want to tear down the two outer wings and rebuild them from the ground up," Evie finished.

Scott let out a low whistle. "That's ambitious." *And, boy, would it require a reconfiguration of the current fire-suppression system.* He'd seen the old system lumbering away in the Lake Breeze, barely adequate and in grave danger of failing if ever taxed with an actual fire. It was truly a miracle the Hamiltons had gotten away with it for as long as they had. Probably the historic status of the hotel was the only thing keeping it legal. It was too old to force compliance with modern standards. Unless it was renovated or rebuilt.

"Ambitious." Evie cocked her head. "That's exactly what Aunt Augusta said."

"The lady who owns the bakery?"

"Her niece actually owns it. Aunt Augusta is part inspiration and part assistant."

"I love those doughnuts," Scott admitted. Maybe they should stick to safe topics like sprinkles versus powder or maple cream filling versus lemon. Had he eaten dinner today? He couldn't remember. "It's an occupational hazard having the shop right down the street from the fire station. Guys can take a radio and walk over there and still stay in range. We might need to add a fitness center to the fire station."

"That's a good idea. It could go in one of the new wings," Evie said. She brushed back her hair and looked across the bay as if he wasn't even there. *She was managing to stay on topic even if he wasn't.*

"So you'll have building plans for new wings," Scott said, back to business. "A general site plan with water mains and access considered. That comes first."

"And we'll modernize and update the rotunda and original wings," Evie added, her voice sounding miles away. "Mostly cosmetic there, but still enough glitz that guests will want to come back."

When Scott heard the word *cosmetic* in reference to a building renovation, hairs stood up on the back of his neck. Cosmetic changes were responsible for lurking hazards in buildings all over the globe. False ceilings where fire traveled silently, waiting to kill.

False walls trapping heat and endangering firefighters who were using an old schematic for the building.

Cosmetic changes covering up the old and ugly were a raging fire menace. He rolled his shoulders, trying to keep his opinion to himself but struggling. No way would he approve plans that created hidden danger. He would fight them with every single word in the fire code, even if he had to stretch the code. He had to ensure no one ever died in a hotel fire.

A searchlight swept over him and Evie. The red towboat motored silently into the marina and illuminated the upturned hull of the burned boat.

He and Evie would tangle about the hotel renovation. It was as inevitable as summer turning to fall. Just not tonight.

EVIE JUMPED ON the ferry fifteen seconds after it should have left the dock. The captain had seen her coming and stood waiting, deck line in hand. This was not the first night she'd grabbed the eleven-thirty ferry back to Bayside. With an official closing time of ten o'clock, it was often after eleven before the park was clear, the receipts under lock and key, and she could retreat to the quiet of her downtown flat.

She used to walk across the parking lot to the family home, but she was slowly getting attached to the idea of a little distance. Tomorrow night would be a different story. With fireworks and a midnight close and who knew how long until the guests all left and the accounts matched, she would crawl home so late she'd wonder why she bothered.

Maybe she should see if she could get her car started in the morning. It would give her the luxury of wheels and freedom just in case she missed the last ferry after the Fourth of July crowd finally headed home.

"Thanks, Ken," she said.

"Heard you had a little excitement here tonight. Did some guy really set off fireworks from the bow of his boat?"

Evie smiled. "News travels fast."

"I have my sources."

Evie sank into the closest seat, not wanting to stall the ferry any longer on its last run of the night. It was dark and she brushed against the other person on the bench seat.

"Sorry," she said.

There was no answer. And the guy was taking up far more than his share of the space. Maybe she should move. She took a closer look.

Scott Bennett—arms across his chest, long legs extended, head leaning against a post—was sound asleep. He hadn't bothered to change his clothes, and the white fire department insignia on his chest stood out against his dark shirt. His shift must have ended at eleven. As the head of the safety department, she knew the schedule.

But did she know why a man left work so tired he slept soundly even when the captain tooted the horn as they backed out of the dock?

She decided not to change seats. As her eyes adjusted to the shadows, she studied Scott's face. The line between his brows that made him look serious by day was gone now, relaxed away by sleep.

His square jaw was the same, just darkened by stubble. His mouth, often drawn into a tight line at work, fell open a little. His lips looked soft.

Maybe she should change seats. But the boat was in motion and she knew Ken hated it when people moved around. Especially in the dark. It seemed everyone was a safety fanatic.

Evie leaned against the seat back, resisting the temporary insanity that suggested Scott would be a lovely pillow if she just laid her head on his chest and closed her eyes. She was tired. Her eyes burned. Maybe just for a moment. To test the theory.

She smiled, imagining what Scott would think when he awakened with her sprawled over him. The employer-employee relationship would explode like an overstuffed suitcase.

She settled for watching over him as he slept soundly all across the bay. This was a side of Scott Bennett she hadn't seen before. And it occurred to her that he wouldn't like it—this exposure, this vulnerability.

Evie felt vulnerable, too, and she was afraid everyone could see it. Could see her uncertainty about the major projects she'd started, her uncertainty about where she fit in the family dynamic.

She watched Scott sleep peacefully and envied him. He had a stressful job and plenty of responsibility. She wouldn't want to face what he did every day. But she couldn't remember the last time she had slept as soundly as he did right now.

When the ferry bumped softly against the

downtown dock, Evie waited. What should she do? The other dozen passengers, mostly summer employees, got off the boat, rocking it with their movement. Scott still slumbered.

Evie laid a tentative hand on his chest. A very solid chest. She felt it rising and falling beneath her palm. "Scott," she said quietly. No reaction. The man was unconscious. She knew he worked at least three shifts a week at the Point. Probably at least that many at the downtown station. Plus his inspector duties. When did he sleep?

She repeated his name. Nothing. She moved her hand to his chcek and leaned in close. Razor stubble teased her fingers. She could probably kiss him without waking him. *The definition of insanity.*

Evie decided to say the one thing that would catapult him off the bench and out of dreamland. It was going nuclear, but necessary.

"Fire," she said.

Scott struggled up as if he'd been under water. He looked wildly around. Evie laughed. "Sorry," she said. "I wanted to get your attention. The ferry ride's over. We're in Bayside."

"Is there a fire?" he asked. He rubbed a hand over his face and sat bolt upright.

"No."

"That was mean," he said.

Evie leaned close. "Next time I'll let you sleep on the boat."

"It's more comfortable than my bed at the station."

"But there are probably over a hundred lake spiders on board. They creep out at night. You probably swallowed one in your sleep," she said, shuddering at the thought.

"Are you cold?"

"No."

"Did you sit next to me while I slept all the way across the bay?" The line between his eyebrows was back and Evie knew she was right about his reluctance to let down his guard when anyone was around.

She had the same problem.

"I'll walk you home," he said. He stood abruptly and thumped his head on the low ceiling of the ferry. He rubbed his scalp with the palm of his hand.

"Maybe I should walk you home," Evie suggested. "You could fall into the lake or walk out in front of a car."

"Good night, kids," Ken said. He waited

on the dock for his last two passengers to stumble off.

She headed up the slight grade that led to a row of buildings overlooking the marina. A warm hand enclosed her elbow. *So we're walking together. Okay.* It would be a very short walk.

Neither of them said anything until Evie paused at the street door of her building and used the overhead light to find the keys in her purse. Scott waited silently as she inserted the key and opened the door. He held it open with one hand and, for a moment, Evie felt like they were returning from a date and he would lean in and kiss her.

To her surprise, he followed her into the building. Matched her steps on the stairs leading three floors up.

"Do you have a fire extinguisher in your apartment?" he asked as she unlocked her door.

"No," she admitted. "But there's one in the hallway."

"Show me."

Rats. I have no idea which way it is. She glanced down the dark hallway and saw the outline of a box. "How about right there?" she asked.

Scott strode to the box and opened it.

"See you tomorrow," he said. He let go of the door, turned and walked away.

CHAPTER TEN

THE LOBBY OF the hotel rotunda didn't provide privacy for their meeting, but Evie doubted any of the guests passing by on their way to breakfast or getting ready to hit the roller coasters would pay any attention to three people sitting around a table with coffee and laptops. Somehow, it seemed fitting to sit in the century-old hotel for their conversation about renovating the structure.

Typical of beach hotels from the early twentieth century, the Lake Breeze Hotel had a large central lobby with wings sprouting off each side. The side wings that angled toward the beach offered guests excellent views and pleasant breezes. The windows' green shutters and awnings lent an old-fashioned appeal.

The rear wings angled toward the parking lot with a roller coaster view and a lower price. Only a few decades after the original structure was built, two detached wings were added next to it. Time had not been kind to the exteriors of the buildings, which had been exposed to harsh winter winds off Lake Huron for a century. The interiors had enjoyed a renovation and update roughly forty years ago, but the whole place had the appearance of a middle-aged woman searching through her closet for something to wear that would make her look younger.

"What about the floor?" June asked. Evie and her brother and sister glanced at the sunlight reflecting off the highly polished wood floor. The narrow planks were laid in an octagonal pattern in the rotunda. After a century of use, the wood rolled up and down. There were a few boards patched in that didn't quite match. A thick rug covered the center section, concealing a long-unused drain tile. "You're not planning to sacrifice character in your remodel, are you?"

"There are beautiful laminate floors that look like real wood and would stand up to traffic a lot better," Evie said. "Sand, shoes, strollers. They kill floors. Do you know how much money we spend every winter completely stripping and re-varnishing this floor?"

"No, but I bet you do," Jack said. He ate a

doughnut left-handed while he used his right to scroll across the screen of the laptop in the center of the table. "I like this one," he said. He pointed to a patterned floor advertised on the website Evie had bookmarked.

June leaned closer. "It's pretty. And it looks like real wood. It probably won't fool anyone, but this place still gets to feel like an old beach hotel."

"Exactly my plan," Evie said. "We spend the big bucks tearing down four of the wings and totally rebuilding them."

"Which wings?" Jack asked.

"The two off the back of the lobby and the two detached ones. They've never been as nice as the two front wings, anyway," Evie said.

"This is more major than I thought," June said.

Evie rolled her eyes. "We've been talking about it for two years."

"I was busy," June said.

"So we totally rebuild four wings and we just pretty up the rest?" Jack asked.

Ouch. The way he said it made it seem like Evie's plan was lacking. Did they have any idea how much this was going to cost?

"Don't make it sound like we're cheating," Evie said. "This plan adds rooms and makes the whole place more attractive. We fill rooms, we make money. If people like the place, they stay longer, eat more meals, buy multi-day tickets. I'm trying to get the most return on my money."

"Our money," Jack said.

"That's what I meant."

Jack smiled. "I know. I'm just trying to protect my job. With your brains—" he pointed at Evie "—and your talent—" he pointed at June "—I'm afraid you won't need me anymore."

Maybe she was too sensitive about her place in the family business.

"I have a personal relationship with the account books. Kind of how you two feel about the rides and shows," Evie said lightly.

"I'm glad you handle the money," June said. "It's much more fun to pick out sparkly costumes and soundtracks than worry about which numbers are red and which ones are black. This is fun, too," she added, pointing to the design website on the computer screen.

Evie nodded enthusiastically. "If we refurbish the central section of the Lake Breeze, update the lobby, spruce up the rotunda and beach entrance, I think guests will love it. It will still be the same place they've visited for years, but it will look new. It sets us up for the next twenty years, too, if we're careful about choosing materials that will cut our maintenance and utility costs."

"Can't argue with that," Jack said. "We're keeping this intact, aren't we?" He pointed to the skylights far above them. The floors of guest rooms circled the rotunda, but they had an open banister where guests could look up to the tenth-floor skylights or down to the wood-floored rotunda where the Hamiltons were seated.

"Yes," Evie said. "I think there would be a public outcry if we changed this dramatically. New floor, new lighting fixtures, new paint and carpet, and new furniture where we're sitting. That will bring the area up to date while still having the feel of an old beach hotel."

"Which it is," June said.

"Take a look at this." Evie opened a new tab and showed her brother and sister some of the design elements she hoped to include in the renovation. A colorful life-size carousel horse would be a focal point in the lobby. Evie had already found one in storage that could be brought back to life with paint.

Giant artwork inspired by postcards from old-time amusement parks would cover the walls—huge black-and-white photographs of people strolling the beach or riding the quaint old-fashioned roller coasters that used to undulate along the boardwalk. Plush seating in pink and green beach colors would fill the rotunda and lobby areas, inviting guests to sit and take a trip back to the days before cell towers and the internet.

"I feel like I'm on vacation just looking at it," Jack said.

"And it's not a budget-breaker."

She showed them another picture on her computer. "I found these old photographs of the Lake Breeze from about seventy years ago. Apparently it had a stamped tin ceiling, but they removed it in the last renovation before we were born. I want to bring it back."

"Is that hard?" June asked.

"There's an easy way and a hard way. The cheaper way is to install a dropped ceiling just a foot or so below the old one. They still make the stamped tin tiles, but they're a lot easier to install in a new framework."

"Do we sacrifice anything by dropping the ceiling?" Jack asked. "It's already pretty high up there, so I doubt anyone will notice."

Evie shook her head. "I was worried about the stained-glass windows because I thought they went all the way to the ceiling. Turns out, they don't. If you go in the lobby and take a good look, they actually stop about ten inches from the current ceiling."

"What's this part?" June asked. She pointed to a diagram on the table with boxes and lines.

"Redesigned beach entrance," Evie said. "What do you think of fire pits?"

"People love fire," Jack commented. "Unless it's consuming their boats. Have we heard the end of that, by the way?"

"The boat's in dry dock, being assessed by the owner's insurance company," Evie explained. "There was no damage to our docks, but I'm tempted to bill that idiot for the fire services and the cost of almost ruining my Fourth of July."

"If we're lucky," Jack said, "that's the worst thing that'll happen all summer and we'll be laughing about it by Halloween."

"So this is the entrance out front," June said. She was still looking at the diagram on the table. "I see the boardwalk area marked out, but what are all these squares?"

"I'm thinking of rows of seating with

gas-fired rocks out front. Decorative metal guards around them, of course. Maybe some flaming torches. It will encourage people to sit outside and listen to the waves. They can unwind after a day of queue lines and hot dogs."

"We could extend the bar service outside," June suggested.

"Right here." Evie pointed to the drawing. "The existing bar here in the lobby can be bumped out and we can add an outside entrance."

"Our guests will live like kings," Jack said.

"I hope so. And I hope this place will be one hundred percent booked from May until September."

June sipped her tea and sat back in the wicker chair. "All those years that I thought you were a boring accountant with an internal calculator, you were actually a visionary. Who knew?"

"Wait until you see if and how this turns out before you give me too much credit."

"Do we have building and construction permits yet?" Jack asked.

"That's the next step. Almost all the plans are drawn up—as long as I get approval from my two partners." Evie offered her untouched doughnut to both of them. "I'll bribe you if I have to."

June laughed. "You don't have to. But that doughnut does look pretty good."

Jack snatched it and took a bite.

"Next, I have to work with the fire inspector to get initial approval to go ahead with the demolition and work out any potential problems with the plans before they're real problems," Evie said.

"Do you think Scott will be cooperative?" June asked, grinning at Evie.

Evie let out a long breath. Scott was such a mixture. She couldn't decide if he was trying to help her or slow her down. Sitting next to him as he slept all the way home on the ferry a few nights ago made her feel closer to him even if they hadn't exchanged a word. Seeing him in action, treating the man with a heart attack and fighting a fire, made it clear he was dedicated, loyal, tough. All things she admired.

He was a mystery, but one thing was for sure. He wouldn't give his approval for something unless it was exactly right. All she had to do was make sure things were exactly right. *How hard can that be?* The thought made her wish she hadn't given away her doughnut.

"I hope Scott will be helpful," Evie said. "He does work for us. And I keep reminding myself that those marina plans were initially approved by someone else. This time, Scott has a chance to be a pain in the butt right from the start."

"Much better," June said. She smiled at her sister. "I'm glad you're the one dealing with construction permits. It sounds picky and miserable."

"It is," Jack agreed. "I honestly never knew much about the process until I helped Dad get the Sea Devil going a few years back. I didn't know at the time that I'd be the one finishing the job and getting the permits to open the ride." He glanced at the entrance and watched a family pass through the doors. A bright flash of morning sun off the lake lit up the table where he sat with June and Evie. "Seems like a lifetime ago."

"Did you ever imagine the three of us would be running this place?" June asked.

"Maybe," Jack said. They were all silent for a moment. "Someday. I thought Mom and Dad would hand it over to us when they were old enough to move into one of the senior citizen trailer parks in Florida."

Evie's vision of the future had been similar. She'd pictured herself working at Starlight Point as her father's accountant. Being in charge and sharing complete ownership with her siblings was not something she'd ever imagined until it suddenly happened.

"Do you think Dad would approve of how we're handling Starlight Point?" Evie asked. As the youngest, she had enjoyed the least time with her father and had been off at college in his final years. June, too, had been gone for years, off dancing on Broadway, living out her dream.

Jack was the one who'd finished his business degree as quickly as he could and dove into the daily business of Starlight Point. He knew the most about his father's method of running the place, but he discovered the hard way, after Ford Hamilton's death, that there was a chasm between what he knew and what he *thought* he knew.

"Dad would probably congratulate us for cleaning up his mess," June said. She smiled and clinked her paper cup against Evie's and Jack's. "We're smarter about spending money than he was."

"I hope you still think so after you see what this is going to cost," Evie said.

"Don't tell me," June said. She put her hands over her ears. "Let me live in my fantasy world."

Evie wrote a number on a paper napkin and shoved it at Jack. He raised both eyebrows and his mouth fell open just enough to let a piece of doughnut pop out and land on the table.

"Fantasy world sounds like a wise plan," he said.

"It's not so bad. And," Evie added, "if we can stay on budget, or even better, come in under budget, I have a plan I want to run past both of you."

"I'm starting to wish you were still our penny-pinching accountant," June said.

Evie rolled her eyes. "Did you know that sometimes you have to spend money to make money? It's called calculated risk."

"Now I do."

"What's the big idea for the buckets of leftover cash?" Jack asked.

"I'm not sure you'll like it," Evie warned, "and I'm not sure I love it myself because there's no obvious return on investment. And

I haven't thought it entirely through yet because I don't know if we'll have the money."

Jack and June stared at her, their full attention riveted on Evie. "Don't say roller coaster," Jack said. "Or campground."

"We could put a theater in the hotel," June said, her eyes lighting up. "Or a spa."

Evie laughed. "No. I'm thinking we could tear down the old employee dorm and rebuild it." She said the words as quickly as she could, fearing their reaction. "Glamorous, huh?"

"That's it?" June asked. "I thought you had some huge announcement."

"Sorry," Evie said. "But I think the investment will be worth it in the long run."

She imagined Scott applauding the decision to build safer dorms. It would be nice to earn his approval on that project, but she needed him to go along with her hotel plans first.

June laughed. "Since I'm afraid to look at the napkin with the price, I'll just have to put my faith in my little sister."

CHAPTER ELEVEN

EVIE STOOD IN the shadow of a pillar in the back of the Starlight Point ballroom, ready to watch the first night of the STRIPE classes.

Because Virginia Hamilton viewed a summer job as more than a *summer job*, she had instituted the Summer Training and Improvement Plan for Employees when Evie was just a baby. Almost anything was fair game and, over the years, Starlight Point employees had learned French, knitting, ballroom dancing, swimming, horseback riding, cake decorating and how to wire a circuit.

Evie was there for the STRIPE classes, but all she could think about were the hotel plans she'd officially submitted that morning. It was already two weeks into July and, even though Evie trembled at exposing her proposal to the fire inspector, it had to be done. If she didn't get things moving, the renovations would never be finished in time for next year. Already a costly expenditure, the project would be even more expensive if the Lake Breeze failed to open on time for the following season.

And so she'd bravely gathered her hopes and dreams into one large file and dropped it off at Scott's office in the Bayside Fire Department station before catching the ferry to the Point for a fourteen-hour day.

The architect she'd hired had done a beautiful job translating her ideas into the final scheme. Her construction superintendent had helped her work out costs and foresee potential stumbling blocks. The three of them had put their heads together the day before yesterday for a final discussion and review. The plans were solid. Evie drew a deep breath. The investment would be worth it.

All she had to do now was hope Scott Bennett's response was positive. When Evie pictured him poring over the electronic and paper documents, looking for a flaw, her stomach contracted into a fist. He didn't have to like them. He had to approve them. She had been angry when he'd nitpicked her marina plans and delayed the opening for almost a month. It had cost her financially, professionally and personally. She was convinced her brother and sister were worried about the same thing happening again. They had to be. They were just too nice to their little sister to bring it up.

This time had to be different.

Maybe she had won Scott over a little since their first meeting six weeks ago. But that wouldn't matter at all when it came to *the code*.

Watching Scott run the STRIPE class— fire safety and first responder training this year—was not making her feel better about getting his signature on her site plans so she could start construction. He was exacting, almost fanatical about following the rules. What made him so zealous? One of these days, maybe she would find out.

Evie sighed. She leaned against a post and watched summer employees, tired from a long day working, nodding off in metal folding chairs. The large ballroom above the arcade on the midway had been the classroom for the STRIPE program for years. Some of the topics had taken the classes outdoors. Water rescue, swimming and horseback riding weren't exactly suited to an art deco ballroom from the earlier part of the twentieth century. But a stage and chairs worked just fine for most topics. Including tonight's How to Stay Alive Until You're a Thousand Years Old presentation.

Maybe letting Scott Bennett run the class wasn't such a good idea. Evie had argued against it, but Jack won out. Having a willing teacher was such a novelty for the program that it was practically irresistible. Jack assumed Evie didn't want Scott teaching the session because she had tangled with him over the marina project and the employee dorms. Was that part of the reason? Yes. But wasn't it already enough he worked there, his sister worked there, and he was in the uncomfortable—for Evie—position of passing judgment on building plans? Did she want to allow Scott one more source of power at Starlight Point?

She hated to admit—even to herself—how threatened she felt when she had to cede power.

Evie watched Scott speak with passion about overloaded circuits, burning cigarettes and picnic tables blocking exits. She glanced around the room. Many of the young females present were managing to stay awake. They watched Scott's every move, followed each gesture and sweep of his muscular arms. Eyes on his face, darkened with evening beard.

Eyes on his broad chest filling out his uniform just right. Evie had felt his chest under her hand on the ferry. Had put her palm on his cheek.

If he had leaned in for a kiss at her door, what would she have done? She would have told him it wasn't a very safe move. Yes. That would have sent him packing.

Evie stood a little straighter and forced her mind back to the business at hand.

Scott had just finished a lecture about workplace hazards such as extension cords—fascinating stuff—and was moving on to how to operate a fire extinguisher. A few teenagers perked up when Scott lined up five fire extinguishers and called for volunteers. They probably imagined an advanced squirt gun fight, pelting each other with pressurized streams of water. *Boy, are they going to be disappointed.*

He chose four employees from the audience and assigned them a spot behind a fire extinguisher. There was one position left. Scott stared right at Evie and crooked a finger at her.

He saw me standing back here in the shadows? Great. She had no choice. This was the first of ten nights of classes and she had to set a good example for the sunburned and foot-sore crowd of summer workers. She'd been on her feet for twelve hours, but at least she didn't have a sunburn. She wound through the rows of folding chairs and took up position behind the first fire extinguisher on the stage.

"Step one," Scott said. His deep voice boomed throughout the ballroom without the need for a microphone. "Assess your situation. Keep the fire in front of you and an exit behind you. Never trap yourself."

A girl in the front row yawned loudly. Evie waited for Scott to deliver a safety lecture of mythical proportions with gruesome anecdotes about *the girl who yawned about safety until it was too late.* But he didn't. He moved on to the glorious types of fire extinguishers.

Who knew there was so much to think about when choosing a fire extinguisher? Evie imagined herself grabbing whichever one was handy in the event of an emergency. Scott was now explaining why that could be a disaster. *Sigh.*

Something about Scott Bennett made Evie, the rule-following accountant, want to be reckless.

However, she dutifully stood behind her

assigned fire extinguisher and read the label while Scott talked about chemical fires, electrical fires and paper fires. He revealed the wonderful mysteries of kitchen fires and vehicle fires. She should pay attention in case he quizzed her in front of the kids who worked the food stands and roller coasters.

"This one, for example," he said, stopping right in front of Evie and pointing at the tall silver fire extinguisher at her feet. He looked Evie directly in the eye. "Miss Hamilton, would you use this fire extinguisher if hot oil in the French fry stand was on fire?"

Evie wanted to drop her eyes and review what it said on the back of the silver can at her feet. But Scott held her gaze, daring her to cheat. *Rats.*

A, B, C. That's what it said, right? She didn't remember him covering a type D. So this one was good for any kind of fire…yes. She squared her shoulders and looked confident.

"Yes, I would," she said.

"That's correct," he said. He moved on to the next volunteer.

Evie let out the breath she'd been holding. A kid in the front row, a young man still wearing his parking attendant uniform complete with reflective safety vest, grinned at her and gave her a thumbs-up. She chuckled.

And this was only the first night of the STRIPE class. *Double sigh*. Although the program had become voluntary the past two summers because of a combination of mercy and manpower issues, Evie had gone along with the mandatory clause this year. She'd seen with her own eyes the minefield kids in the dorm were living in. Perhaps gutting out an hour-long lecture on fire safety would save a life. It had also gone a long way toward appeasing Scott and persuading him not to close the employee dorm.

If Evie's hotel plans went the way she hoped, there would be leftover money for a new dorm for next year. But she wasn't sharing that part of the proposal with anyone besides June and Jack. There was no sense planting a seed unless she knew she'd be able to water it.

"See this one," Scott said, holding up a red fire extinguisher. "The only safe use for this is putting out paper or wood. You don't want to put water on an electrical or chemical fire, so you don't want to reach for this one."

Do we have that kind of extinguisher in the food stands and ride locations? Evie had never thought to check. But Scott was slowly stripping away any sense of security she had about Starlight Point. If he stuck around much longer, she'd be wearing body armor, maxing out her life insurance and trading in her old car for a used army-surplus tank.

She glanced at the clock. Only fifteen more minutes and she could call it a night.

"Can I give you a ride home?" Scott asked. It was late. The class attendees could catch the last ferry if they didn't dally.

Evie was going to miss it. She and one of his partners stuck around after the summer workers had dashed out of the ballroom. Scott pictured them heading back to their dorms and testing out the fire extinguishers. He hoped they wouldn't.

He watched Evie turn out the lights and carry a fire extinguisher to his pickup. Because the park was closed for the night, he'd left the Starlight Point Fire Department truck right outside the back door.

"You have a car?" she asked.

"Truck."

Evie glanced at the red pickup.

"Not that one. My own. It's back at the

station. I have to drop Charlie off since he's on duty, but I'm headed home to Bayside."

"What color is your truck?" Evie asked.

Why would she want to know that?

"Black," he said. "Dodge. Six years old. Three-quarter ton. Just in case you're fussy about what you ride in."

Evie laughed. "Have you seen my car?"

He shook his head.

"No, you wouldn't have. It hasn't run in weeks."

Scott's partner got in the truck and slammed the door. He sat in the passenger seat, waiting. Scott leaned on the bed of the truck and looked at Evie. He wanted to give Evie a ride home, but he couldn't explain why. He'd probably be better off if she turned him down.

"What color is it?" he asked.

"Baby blue," she said. "Four-door sedan. Nine years old. One taillight out. You would hate it."

He smiled. "I hate even thinking about it. Why don't you ride in the Starlight Point limousine?"

Evie leaned next to him on the truck. "My brother got the limo and my sister got the

Starlight Point helicopter because they're older. So now I'm stuck."

"Stuck riding in my truck?"

He could see her thinking about it. He knew what his hesitation would be, but what was her reason? Was it because of their work relationship?

Did they have a relationship?

He didn't know. But he did know he had a large file of plans to review as soon as he found time. He had briefly opened it but was afraid of going too deep just yet. Reviewing building plans was like opening a bag of chips. Once he started, he wasn't coming up for air.

So he'd indulged in a tiny peek. And, holy smoke, the dollar figure had to be in the millions.

"Why don't you get a new car?" he asked. *Seriously.* Why did the owner of a resort that employed half the county, and must bring in a hefty revenue every single day of the summer, drive an old car with a missing taillight? It made no sense.

Evie cocked her head and scrunched her lips to the side as if she were considering the question. It didn't seem like a difficult one to him.

"For a long time I didn't need a car. I lived in my parents' house on the Old Road and walked to work. And then my brother took that house, my mom moved into his, and I got my own place downtown. That was right before the chaos leading up to season opening, and I haven't had time to worry about it."

"You like taking the ferry?" he asked.

"I do. But I keep having the strangest experiences." She leaned closer to him and smiled. "I wouldn't be surprised if it was boarded by pirates one of these nights."

She was too close. It was a beautiful warm night. He could hear the gentle lapping of waves on Lake Huron. Smell the aroma of flowers in a planter nearby. Starlight Point was starting to get under his skin and make him feel like he could belong there. Evie made him feel like taking chances.

And that kind of feeling was dangerous. It led to complacency. He was tempted to try to make life easier for Evie, smooth over the approval process. But was Evie being nice to him so he would approve her plans? He was treading on dangerous ground that would make it hard for him to live with himself in the end.

Giving her a ride home would be asking for trouble. *Please say no.*

"I've love a ride if you don't mind," Evie said. "Otherwise I'll have to sleep in my office. Again. People will talk."

He should have run while he'd had the chance.

"Get in," Scott said.

When his partner saw that Evie was riding along, he got out of the truck so Evie could sit in the middle. Understandable from a guys-don't-sit-right-next-to-each-other perspective. However, it meant he'd be so close to Evie their thighs would touch. Their arms would brush. Her hair might spill over onto him.

They left Charlie at the fire station and got into Scott's truck where a safe section of bench seat separated them. To avoid the long, slow drive around the peninsula, Scott took advantage of the fact that it was almost midnight and drove straight through the closed amusement park. There would be no traffic on the Point Bridge this time of night. He could unload Evie before she even thought to ask him if he'd looked at her hotel plans yet.

"I know I just dropped them off this morning..." Evie began.

Son of a biscuit. They weren't even past the midway train station yet. He was doomed.

"And I don't want to pressure you," she continued. "I just wondered if you'd taken a glance at the building and site plans for the hotel reconstruction."

Scott shook his head. "Sorry. No."

"Oh. Okay. I'm just…anxious."

Of course she was anxious. It was a huge project she was sinking millions into. And Scott was beginning to wonder where the millions were coming from if she was driving an ancient car and her family members were swapping houses. Come to think of it, he'd seen Jack driving an ugly brown SUV across the bridge one day and wondered what junkyard he'd stolen it from.

What was going on with the Hamiltons? It was none of his business. He knew what his business was. According to the Bayside city charter, he had thirty days from receipt of plans to approve, reject or return them for revision.

He glanced over at Evie as they passed under a streetlight. Head down, she toyed with her name badge, opening and closing the pin enclosure.

"I have STRIPE classes the next ten days,"

he said, trying for a mild tone. "And two jobs."

"I know," she said. "Bad timing."

"And it takes a lot of time to go through the plans and make sure everything is up to code."

"Of course."

"I can't rush the process," he said. This was true. He should have stopped there. "Even for you."

He wished he could take back those three little words that were never supposed to come out. Three little words that suggested his feelings for Evie had crossed a very hard line. *Crap*.

"What's that supposed to mean?" Evie sounded angry. Scott stopped at the red light at the end of the Point Bridge. Why on earth was the traffic light on when there wasn't a soul around? Forty-five seconds before it turned green was going to be a lifetime.

He considered running the light. Evie was making him a maniac.

"Do you think that because I'm your employer I'm going to ask for special favors?" Evie asked.

That was not what he meant, but it would

certainly be a convenient answer. Better than the truth.

"No," he said.

"Then what?"

Green light. *Yes.* Maybe he could stall on an answer until he dropped Evie off at her building. He risked a sideways glance. She was waiting.

"What?" she repeated.

"I, uh, just meant that you...that is, Starlight Point, is a big deal around here."

"And?"

"And you might think you should get special treatment from the...city because you probably pay a lot of taxes."

"Is that right?" she asked.

Scott nodded. He was doing a lousy job. A very lousy job of this.

He cruised through a residential section of town that opened onto the waterfront. He could almost see the lake at the end of the street. Soon they would turn the corner and—

"I don't appreciate your insinuation that I'm some sort of mob boss calling in favors," she said.

Scott laughed. He couldn't help it. The image of willowy blond Evie with her beautiful eyes and smile being a no-neck mob boss…it was too ridiculous.

Laughing at her was the wrong thing to do.

As soon as he came to a semi-complete stop at the entrance to her condo, she jumped out of the truck as if she were riding with the scariest kid in the driver's ed class. She didn't say a word. Just slammed his door and walked away. Scott idled in the street until he saw her enter the building and watched the door close securely behind her, all the while thinking about what a tangled mess he'd gotten into.

Fighting fires is safer than getting close to people who might burn you.

Although Evie didn't seem dangerous, letting himself get involved with her beyond a purely professional relationship tempted him in a dangerous way. He would never compromise his bone-deep belief in following the codes. His codes and the ones written into state legislation. But Evie made him wonder what he would do if he were somehow forced to choose between those codes and her.

CHAPTER TWELVE

THIS WAS THE first Saturday of the season that Scott was not on the schedule at Starlight Point. It was a nice break. Saturdays, especially hot ones like this mid-July day, were wall-to-wall emergency runs inside the amusement park. Guests passing out after standing in long lines in the sun while neglecting to eat or drink. Kids doing headers into concrete while racing for the next queue line. Bee stings. Sunburns. Alcohol. Never a dull moment, and exactly what Scott had signed up for as a paramedic firefighter.

Days like that went by quickly. But this peaceful morning at the Bayside fire station was nice, he thought.

He opened the overhead doors and let the breeze off the bay blow around a few leaves that had made their way into the station. He'd checked the oil in all the trucks. Checked the tires and lights. Opened the back doors on the ambulance and climbed in with a clipboard to inventory the supplies. One of the squads was out on a diabetic emergency. Two more of his partners were in the bunk room completing an online training unit. Another was cooking breakfast in their shared kitchen.

This was heaven. He inhaled the scent of tires, hoses and bacon. Scott scratched the burn scar on his back absentmindedly while he looked into compartments inside the ambulances. Splints, oxygen tubing, bandages, blood pressure cuffs, stethoscopes. Everything lined up exactly where it should be.

The cell phone in his pocket buzzed and he glanced at the caller identification. Smiled. His sister.

"Big Brother Advice Line," he answered.

"I'm bored," Caroline said.

"Go back to school and become a teacher or a nurse or a dolphin trainer."

"Thanks. Great advice. Glad I called."

"I'm at work. I give better advice when I'm on my own time," Scott said.

"Which is never."

"Right. Working all the time prevents me from having to think," Scott answered.

He climbed out of the back of the ambulance and shut the doors. Walked out to the bench in front of the station as he listened to his sister.

"I'm on traffic duty on the Point Bridge," Caroline said. "Do you have any idea how boring it is to sit around waiting for someone to have an emergency?"

"No idea," Scott said. He sat on the bench and leaned back. "Don't know what you're talking about."

"I'm sitting here with the flashers on while my partner moves the orange cones around. We're trying to open up an extra lane for the toll booths because everyone in the Midwest is coming here today."

"Good news for Starlight Point," Scott observed. Did they take all their revenue and pour it into projects? He was starting to think so. *Evie doesn't seem like a risk taker, but you never know what's going on in someone else's head.*

"Who's your partner?" he asked.

"Mark Stein. And he just got engaged to his high school sweetheart, so don't worry about me running off with him."

"That wasn't what I was worried about," Scott said.

"You should offer to take me out to dinner

tonight," Caroline said. "It gives me something to look forward to."

"Maybe I have a date," Scott said.

Caroline laughed.

"Fine," Scott said. "My shift ends at seven tonight. Talk to you then."

"I love you, pain-in-the-neck brother."

"Are you sure you don't want to be a tour guide or a concert pianist? You're a sitting duck in all that traffic."

Caroline huffed at him and hung up. He smiled and slid the phone in his pocket.

EVIE IMAGINED THIS was what it would feel like to stand in the middle of a giant beehive. Worker bees were everywhere. On July Saturdays, almost every seasonal employee was on duty. Cars lined up on the bridge, guests lined up at the front gate, roller coaster trains lined up on the rails.

This was the kind of day that strained the Starlight Point peninsula to the breaking point. But it also brought in ticket sales, parking fees, food sales, souvenir sales and one hundred percent occupancy in the Lake Breeze hotel. Evie pictured the black side of the account books outweighing the red side in an easy victory.

She stood near the midway train station where she felt her finger on the pulse of the whole place. Was this how the queen bee in a hive felt? Evie laughed. *Thank goodness no one expects me to lay eggs to ensure the future of the hive on top of everything else.*

Her radio, tuned to the security and safety frequency at the Point, weighed down the waistband of her skirt. *Five minutes until opening.* The opening ceremony at the front gate was the same every day. A local high school band played the national anthem, which was broadcast all over the Point. Workers way back in the Wonderful West would hear it over the park's loudspeakers and they could get ready for the crowds.

Evie picked a piece of trash out of the flowerbed in front of the train station. Walked through the nearby restrooms for a cleanliness check. They were ready. She returned to her spot where the two midways diverged in front of the train station and waited for the explosion of people through the front gates. She would have sat on the bench there, but she was too full of nervous energy.

Right on time, the "Star Spangled Banner" blasted over the speakers. Evie's heart raced. This was a moment she loved every day. And it was especially thrilling on hot summer days with the promise of huge crowds.

The radio at her hip vibrated with traffic. She pulled it off her waistband and held it to her ear, but she couldn't make out what was being said. The music continued, drowning out the dispatcher's voice. Evie strained to hear, desperately wishing the high school band had not chosen to launch into a second verse. *Does anyone know the words to the second verse anyway?*

Seriously? A third verse? That band was never getting invited back...

As soon as the music ended, Evie heard a siren.

And then she heard what the dispatcher was saying. "Multiple vehicles involved. Calling in Bayside Fire."

Where? Where was the accident? She'd missed the earlier transmissions, but it had to be either in the parking lot or on the Point Bridge. If her dispatcher was calling in Bayside Fire, it was either a bad accident or the crash had happened on the far end of the bridge. Or both.

Evie hustled to the Starlight Point police station located at the back corner of the arcade. A huge building, the arcade housed a ballroom on the second floor and games and shops on the lower floor. The police station in the back was technically in the middle of all the action but off the beaten path at the same time.

Guests raced past Evie as she speed-walked to the arcade. Teenagers and families were hurrying to be first in line for their favorite rides, but Evie's heart raced with fear instead of fun.

Maybe it wasn't as bad as it sounded. Multiple vehicles could tangle and have only minor damage. Bayside Fire may have been called in as a precaution.

She swept through the door of the usually quiet police station to find it even quieter than usual. But it was the hush of tension. The dispatcher, Louise Higgins, had her palms pressed to both sides of her face. The police chief, his back to the door, was on the phone.

Evie's radio squealed when she approached the dispatch center. She had forgotten officers were required to shut their radios off because of feedback within the station.

"Turn that damn thing off," the chief yelled as he whirled around. When he saw it was Evie, his expression softened and he told whoever he was talking to that he would call them right back.

This was not good.

"There's been a terrible accident," he said. "One of my cops is seriously injured." He lowered his voice and it trembled. "Possibly dead."

Shock replaced Evie's fear. "What? What happened?"

"Accident on the bridge. Two cars collided by the halfway hill. One of my guys was setting out cones in the lane pattern we use on Saturdays and got hit by one or both cars."

"Which guy?"

He shook his head. "I don't know. A motorist called 9-1-1 on a cell phone and reported a police officer lying in the road. Bayside 9-1-1 called us. Our police and fire are headed out. Bayside police and fire are already on their way."

"Do you know which of our officers was out on the bridge today?"

"Several. Mark Stein, one of our bonded guys who's been here a few years. And a new non-bond this summer. Caroline Bennett."

Evie sat in the chair usually reserved for teenagers caught shoplifting or fighting.

Caroline Bennett.

"There's more," the chief said. "One of the cars, according to the bystander report, is hanging off the bridge."

Evie locked eyes with Louise and took a long breath. Tried to think logically. Even though she had known the chief and the dispatcher all her life, she needed to be strong in front of them. She had to be a leader. "I have to get out there," she said. "Right now."

"We'll take my car." The chief picked up his hat and radio and told the dispatcher to call Bayside 9-1-1 and ask for updates.

They raced to the gate where the chief's patrol car was parked and got in without a word. The chief turned toward the road that would take them around the outer loop.

"No," Evie said. "Cut across the park."

"Are you sure? It just opened. There are people on the midway."

"One of our people is down. Yes, I'm sure."

"If you say so."

Evie rolled down the window. She was afraid she might be sick. The thought of any member of the Starlight Point family being injured or killed was horrible. The fact that it could be Caroline Bennett was devastating. Evie pictured Scott's face. How would he stand it? She knew he hated his sister being a police officer.

Where was he today? Her blood ran cold. What if Scott was working at the Point today? What if he was the first one on scene and found his sister in the road? The thought was too terrible. Evie braced an arm on the door as the chief cut across the midway behind the Scrambler and out a vehicle gate near the marina.

The moment he pulled onto the outer loop, he switched on the siren. Raced past the parking lot and the toll booths. As soon as they cleared the hill up ahead, they would see the accident scene.

Evie hoped she was brave enough to face whatever waited on the other side of that bridge.

Both Starlight Point ambulances blocked the road in front of them. The chief parked on the side of the bridge and Evie got out and ran. She sped around the ambulances and the first thing she saw was Caroline Bennett on the ground. She was kneeling next to a man dressed all in black. It had to be Mark Stein. Starlight Point firefighters were tending to him. They had a backboard, neck brace…

That had to be a good sign. If he were dead

they wouldn't be getting him ready to move. *Please be alive.*

Evie took a quick glance around. Cars were backed up as far as she could see. One vehicle with damage on the front end sat in the middle of the bridge. Another car had its rear wheels hanging off the bridge, but the guardrail had stopped it from falling over. Onlookers clustered in groups.

The chief stalked straight to where Mark lay on the road, unmoving. He got down on the ground and talked to the firefighters treating the victim. Evie watched him pull the radio off his belt and speak to the Starlight Point dispatcher.

When she didn't hear the transmission, she realized her radio was still switched off. It didn't matter. She wouldn't have known what to say, anyway. The chief knew. The firefighters knew. She watched them work on Mark for a moment, impressed by their calm professionalism even though he was a colleague, possibly a friend.

Scott was not on scene. Thank goodness. Maybe he had the day off, or he could be working his other job.

Evie put a hand on Caroline's shoulder and leaned down.

"Caroline, are you okay? What happened?"

Caroline scrambled awkwardly to her feet when she saw Evie, who grabbed her, afraid she would fall over. The girl was covered in blood. Evie pulled her aside to see if she was truly uninjured.

"I was in the car with the flashers running, driving alongside Mark while he put out the last few cones." She spoke so quickly Evie was afraid she wasn't breathing.

"Slow down," Evie said. "Are you hurt?"

Caroline shook her head. "But…Mark." She put her hands over her face, leaving streaks of blood. Mark's blood. "A car came over the hill. It was in the outbound lane that we were switching to an inbound. It hit an inbound car and Mark was right between them. He went up in the air…"

Her words trailed off and Evie pulled her close, hugging her and hoping Mark would make it.

She glanced over at the injured man. His eyes were open and he seemed to be talking to the firefighters who were strapping him onto a backboard.

"I did a lousy job calling it in," she said. Tears started to run down her face, mixing with the blood. "My radio was in the car and

Mark's was gone. I didn't want to leave him, so I had a bystander call it in."

"You did the right thing. You got help on the way. No one could have done better."

Evie handed Caroline over to one of the year-round Starlight Point police officers who'd just arrived. An older man she had known all her life, he would treat Caroline like a daughter. "Take down the details for a report," Evie said. "Take care of her," she added quietly.

She walked over to the police chief, trying to control her breathing and her heart rate. In her peripheral vision she could see them loading Mark into the ambulance. "Was anyone else hurt? What about the people in the cars?"

"No. As bad as it looks, it was a pretty low-speed head-on. Air bags are made for that kind of thing. I've checked with the occupants of both cars. Nothing serious."

Evie let out a long breath. "Good."

She was so relieved she thought her knees would give out.

"Still got Bayside coming in. I didn't have time to call them off, and we may still need them. Some of those folks might need transport to the hospital, just out of precaution.

It's never a bad idea to document even minor injuries."

Evie nodded. She heard sirens approaching. A lot of them. She and the chief had probably been on the scene for two minutes. Cutting across the park had saved them so much time they'd beaten the Bayside Fire Department. She realized the Starlight Point ambulances must have cut across the park, too, with just minutes before it opened. *Life or death only.*

She looked at the end of the Point Bridge that connected with the city streets of Bayside. A huge red pumper rounded the corner at such a high speed Evie thought it would roll over. She could hear the engine laboring, the air horn hammering as if the truck were outrunning an avalanche.

The driver of that fire truck was handling it like an absolute maniac. And Evie knew who it was.

CHAPTER THIRTEEN

THE RED PUMPER from Bayside careened to a stop on the opposite side of the wrecked vehicles. The man driving it wore full turnout gear, minus the helmet. He jumped out of the truck and ran like an Olympian. Evie walked swiftly, anxious to intercept Scott and relieve his mind. The sooner he realized his sister was not injured, the safer everyone would be.

"Where is she?" he growled. He took Evie by the shoulders. He was crazy-eyed. Almost terrifying in his intensity. His eyes dropped to Evie's neck and white blouse. "There's blood on you."

"It's not mine. It's from Caroline —"

Scott's grip on Evie's shoulders tightened. "Caroline. Is she…?"

Evie had never seen another human being look so haunted. She hardly recognized Scott's face. She knew he loved his sister deeply, but his reaction was so extreme she wondered if there was something else.

"She's fine. Completely unhurt," Evie said, enunciating the words clearly.

To her amazement, Scott hauled her against him and hugged her so tight she could feel his heart racing, even through his heavy coat. Of course she knew his arms would be strong. He was a firefighter. But she'd never imagined how good it would feel to be held by those strong arms.

It should not feel this good. Especially after the way they had parted several nights ago.

Scott released her suddenly and gently set her away from him. He held her at arm's length. "Sorry," he mumbled.

"Come see your sister," Evie said. She grabbed his sleeve. "Caroline is right over here in the cruiser with one of our best guys."

Before they reached the Starlight Point cruiser, Caroline saw her brother and jumped out of the car. Scott crushed her with a hug. Evie smiled, glad for at least one happy ending on this disastrous morning. She started to walk away and leave the siblings alone, but she was still close enough to hear Scott's voice. "The report on the radio said officer down on the Point Bridge," he said. His voice sounded like he'd just struggled up out of a deep canyon. "And I knew you were out here."

"My partner, Mark, got hit by a car," Caroline said.

Evic didn't hear Scott's immediate reply but then she heard him say, "I couldn't lose you, too."

Caroline answered quietly, but her words were muffled against her brother's turnout coat. Evie walked away, fearing she had already heard too much.

"Somebody move that truck," the Starlight Point chief yelled. The fire engine Scott had driven was blocking the exit lane and the ambulance was trying to leave. One of the firefighters from Bayside who'd arrived in a different ambulance stalked over to the truck and backed it out of the way.

Evie thought about Scott's reckless driving and parking. For a man so devoted to safety, he'd thrown it out the window when he feared for someone he loved. *Interesting.* There was something Scott was afraid of more than failing to follow the rules.

"Hey, Evie."

She turned, recognizing her brother's voice. Jack's suit coat flapped in the breeze as he walked up. He glanced at her face and shirt. "Are you okay?"

"Fine," she said. "It's not my blood. I got it thirdhand."

"How bad are things?"

Evie loved her brother. And she was completely certain he loved her, too. But his reaction was entirely different from the one she'd just witnessed from Scott. How would Jack behave if he thought she or June was injured or dead?

I couldn't lose you, too. What did that mean?

"Things are bad," Evie said. "One of our police officers, Mark Stein, is headed for the hospital. Badly injured but alive. Occupants of these cars—" she pointed to the damaged one in the middle of the bridge and the one straddling the guardrail "—are probably okay but may go to the hospital as a precaution. Traffic will be snarled until tomorrow, and this accident has taken ten years off my life."

Jack nodded. "That could be a good thing. You don't want to get old. Especially since you're going to be a spinster and all."

"Not funny."

"Sorry." Jack buttoned his coat. "I'll go

start with the two families and see what we can do to help them out."

"Thanks," Evie said. For some reason she wished her brother would give her the kind of hug she needed right now. The kind Scott had given his sister. But she was a grown-up in a job with a lot of responsibility. She could tough this out.

Jack started to walk away and stopped. Turned. He came back and embraced his sister, pressing her cheek against his suit coat. "I sure am glad you're in charge here. This kind of stuff makes me want to hide in my office."

It turned out to be exactly what Evie needed to hear.

She stood by, helping direct the safety forces while the accident site was cleared. The Bayside Fire Department took the driver of one of the cars to the hospital as a precaution, but the second driver and the passengers signed off. Evie sent one of the Starlight Point ambulances back to the amusement park, where thousands of people were filling the midway. She approached Scott, who leaned against his pumper, listening to his radio and awaiting orders.

"I understand it's protocol to keep a fire truck on scene while the wreckers load the cars," she said. "In case of fire or hazardous fluids leaking."

He nodded. "It is."

"I'd like to get my firefighters back in service as soon as possible," she said.

"I can see why."

"So I'm hoping you can stay a little while longer. Just until the cars are cleared."

"The Point Bridge is technically the city's jurisdiction," Scott said. "So I'm not going anywhere."

The rules. Of course.

"Will you give Caroline the rest of the day off?" Scott asked.

"Yes. She's headed back to her dorm to clean up. I'll see if someone can check with her later and maybe give her a ride to the hospital to see Mark."

"I appreciate it," Scott said.

Evie wondered if they should talk about what had happened, but Scott's posture and tone told her they weren't. Fine. She had plenty of work to do.

"I'm going to go direct traffic," Evie said. "No matter how hopeless it seems right now."

She started to walk away, but Scott put a hand on her arm. "Wait," he said.

He walked to the side of the pumper and

dug through a compartment, pulling out a reflective vest.

"Put this on if you're going to be out here. It's dangerous."

IT HAD BEEN a very long day, Scott thought. The run to the Point Bridge this morning had nearly ended his life. He shouldn't have driven the truck as hard and fast as he had, but a call for a Starlight Point cop down, possibly dead, on the bridge… He didn't think he'd ever recover from the panic he'd felt. Losing Caroline was not something he could think about.

Lucky for him, there was a long string of minor fire calls and squad runs to take his mind off the accident for the rest of the day. Grease fire at a downtown eatery. Fender bender with a car leaking gas over by the mall. Suspicious smoke smell at the auto factory across town. Nothing serious, but it passed the hours until he could see his sister for dinner and put some closure to the events of the day.

On one of the return trips to the station, he'd noticed a baby blue sedan in the lot outside Evie's building. Since she didn't seem in a hurry to fix her car, he should avoid riding the ferry after the last four STRIPE classes. Bumping into Evie was making it harder for him to stay focused on his job.

Caroline had texted him earlier to say that Mark was out of surgery and stable. He faced a long recovery, but the doctors were hopeful. Lucky Mark, he thought.

He glanced at his watch. Almost five o'clock. Scott rolled a fifty-foot stretch of dirty hose out on the concrete apron of the station. He wet down the white hose and began scrubbing it with a stiff broom, washing off the dirt and oils it might have picked up when they'd used it at the fender bender earlier.

The sun was lower in the sky, but it was still a hot July day. Too nice to sit inside and wait for a call. Too nice to sit in his office and review the hotel plans. Plans he was stalling on. He hadn't even opened them since his first cursory glance several days ago.

What was he waiting for? With only thirty days by law, he was cutting into his time to review them. This was the largest project he'd seen in his short time as a fire inspector. And it was the first set of plans for new construction and renovation. Checking pre-existing structures, walking through them with a list to note violations and hazards—that was easy. Looking at something on paper and imagining it in three dimensions…that was different.

What if he screwed up? Overlooked a construction flaw that would result in the deaths of occupants or firefighters down the road? At fire school, he'd heard those stories. A design flaw that caused a structure to weaken catastrophically when exposed to flame and water. Seven occupants dead at a hotel in Missouri. Nine firefighters killed in a hotel in Boston.

Maybe he didn't want the heavy weight that came with a building inspector's job.

He scrubbed the hose harder, making his way down the length of it.

A shadow fell across his feet. A long, thin shadow. Scott wiped a bead of sweat from his forehead and looked up.

Evie held the reflective vest he'd given her earlier in the day. "I wanted to make sure you got this back on your truck," she said. "In case you need it."

"Thank you."

"Things got crazy after you left with the fire truck. Do you have any idea how hard it is to get cars to spread out evenly over three lanes and stay put?"

"Never tried it."

"I have a newfound respect for our traffic workers. It was a war zone out there. And I appreciated the vest. It gave me confidence if nothing else." She stepped closer and handed it to him.

He laid his scrubber down and headed inside the station. Evie followed him, watching as he carefully folded the vest and put it back in the side compartment of the truck. He would never use it again without thinking of Evie. He rolled his shoulders and turned to face her.

"Have things settled down at the Point?" he asked. He didn't know why she'd followed him into the station, but he hoped talking about something other than the hotel plans would prevent her from asking about his progress.

Evie shook her head. "It's nuts over there. Long lines for rides and food. Given the weather, I think people are planning to stay until the midnight close."

"Can't blame them," Scott said. "Any fire or ambulance runs?"

"One trash can fire in the Wonderful West.

Cigarette, I think. And a diabetic teenager forgot to eat because she preferred to wait in line for the Silver Streak. Those were the most serious things."

"So far."

Evie sighed. "Yes. So far. I took the ferry home so I could change for the evening. I plan to stay late."

"I'm having dinner with my sister tonight," he said. Not that there was any reason to share his personal business with his boss.

"I know. I checked on Caroline this afternoon when I had a minute. She was in her dorm room enjoying some peace and quiet."

"Was she okay?" Scott asked. Maybe she shouldn't be alone.

"I think so. She said she'd had a shower and some ice cream."

Scott smiled. Caroline loved ice cream.

"I think she puts up a tough front," Evie continued. "But seeing someone get hit like that has to be terrible."

Scott swallowed. Seeing someone badly injured or die was terrible. He rubbed the back of his neck where a scar rippled just under the edge of his shirt.

"I should get going. On a busy day like this, anything can happen over there."

Scott walked outside with Evie and picked up his brush. If he finished washing this hose, it would have just enough time to dry before his shift ended.

Evie watched him work for a moment. He glanced up.

"I just want to say I'm glad your sister wasn't involved in that accident today."

"She was involved," he said.

"I mean not hurt."

Evie fidgeted with the set of keys in her hands. She seemed to be stalling, as if there was something more she wanted to say. Perhaps she wanted to mention that incredibly impulsive and stupid hug he'd given her earlier. He couldn't help it at the time but he'd been kicking himself all day for being reckless and losing his tight grip on his emotions.

Had Evie heard what he'd said to his sister about not losing her, too? He hoped not. It was not her business and he didn't want to explain himself.

"Is there any additional information you need as you review my application for a building permit?" she asked.

And there it was.

"Not that I know of right now," Scott said.

"I'll get back to you within the thirty days allotted. Careful reviews take time."

She didn't move. He knew she wanted to ask if he'd even looked at them. He would if he were in her shoes. But he didn't feel like answering that question today.

He got out the water hose and started rinsing off the soap from the length of fire hose. The wind picked up the overspray, dampening Evie's skirt and legs. She jumped back, turned and walked quickly away.

Mission accomplished.

Scott took his sister to a chain restaurant she loved in Bayside. She put away enough pancakes to assure him she would survive at least for the night. He drove her back to her dorm and saw her safely back to her room. Checked that the fire exits in the dorm were clear and the fire extinguisher in her hallway was in its box.

It was almost nine o'clock and the lights chased furiously on all the roller coasters. The parking lot at Starlight Point was still full of cars. Evie had been right. Guests were staying until closing.

Scott walked back to his truck parked in the marina lot. Drove with the windows down across the Point Bridge. He should call it a night.

But his brain was on overtime. He drove to the Bayside fire station and let himself into his office. Shutting the door, he booted up the ancient computer and laid the blueprints for the Lake Breeze Hotel project out on his desk.

It was time to review the plans.

CHAPTER FOURTEEN

SCOTT SAT AT the kitchen table in the Starlight Point fire station. The early morning light streamed in the solitary window and illuminated the fact that everything in the kitchen was a shade of brown. The countertops, cabinets, floors and laminate-topped table were all at least forty years old. Chief Harlan poured them both a cup of coffee and pulled out the chair across from Scott.

"I heard you have the plans for the hotel project locked up in your office," he said. "Still."

"It's only been twelve days," Scott said.

"Not that anyone's counting."

"I'm sure Evie is counting."

"So why the delay?" Link asked.

Scott drank his coffee and weighed his words. "Have you ever had to review a site plan for a new construction project? Calculate the size of the water mains necessary for the fire-suppression systems? Measure the width of access and fire lanes?"

"I've seen quite a few things in my career," Link said.

Scott stared at his coffee and waited the chief out. Link Harlan was his elder by thirty years and Scott respected the man. *What if I ask his advice about the project?*

"But I never had to do a review like this, exactly," the chief admitted. "It's a big responsibility. But it's your job. A job I heard you jumped at when Marty retired."

"It's a job I don't take lightly," Scott said.

"Didn't say you were."

"And a mistake on my part could cost someone's life one day."

The fire and police band radio buzzed with talk about a gate left unlocked overnight and a guest with a dead battery in the hotel parking lot. Scott and the chief sat silently, listening.

"So you've looked at the plans?" Harlan said.

Scott nodded.

"What do you think so far?"

"Evie has a good construction super. Plans follow the code right down to the inch."

Harlan sat back in his chair and smiled. "Good."

How much do I say?

"I think the plans for the tear-downs and totally new construction won't be a problem," Scott said. "The rules for new builds are cut and dried."

"But?"

"Did you know Evie plans to renovate the old part of the hotel? The rotunda and two of the original wings?"

"I'd heard about it," the chief said. "Probably saves a lot of money and keeps the historic status of that part of the building."

"So you did know about this."

"Know about what? It's no secret. Everybody knows the hotel's on the national register of historic places. There's a big bronze plaque on the beach in front of it. Of course she wants to respect the history of the place."

"Not what I mean," Scott grumbled.

"So what do you mean?"

"You knew she meant to use the historic status of that old fire hazard to avoid bringing it up to code."

"Maybe she has another reason for renovating the old part," Chief Harlan protested.

"Like nostalgia. Or not throwing out the baby with the bathwater."

"I didn't see nostalgia evident in her marina project. And she doesn't seem to mind tearing down at least two of the wings."

"Not following where you're going."

"State fire code," Scott said. "Old hotels are not required to have sprinklers in every room. If you do a substantial renovation, you have to follow the law for newer buildings. I'm saying Evie is staying just on the edge of that line."

"So what if she is? It probably saves a lot of money and effort. Maybe she wants to spend that money and time somewhere else."

"So guests in the new wings will be safer than guests in the old wings," Scott said. "Maybe they should add that to the brochure for the hotel. Lakeview wings in the front come with an added thrill—potential death by fire."

The chief stood. "If you're accusing Evie of doing something shady, you might want to keep your opinions to yourself. As long as you're working here."

The dispatcher's voice came over the radio on the table. "Dispatch to SP Fire. Back injury, Last Chance Bakery."

Scott glanced at the wall clock. "Must be an employee this early."

"Let's drive the ambulance," Chief Harlan suggested. "If it's a back injury, I don't think whoever it is will want to ride in the scooter. Park doesn't open for two hours yet."

Only the two of them were on duty until then. Scott was sorry he'd started a quarrel with the chief about the hotel plans. He should have kept his opinions to himself until he was ready to approve or reject the proposal.

They drove the ambulance through the gate nearest the Wonderful West, past the Gold Mine roller coaster and across the train tracks. As they approached the Last Chance Bakery, the first thing Scott noticed was a baby blue sedan parked in front of it. His chest tightened. *What is Evie doing here this early? Is she the injured person?*

He shot out of the ambulance as soon as the chief parked it and crossed the front porch of the western-themed bakery. There was no one in the front of the shop, even though it already smelled like cookies and doughnuts.

"Back here," someone called from the work area in the rear. Scott recognized Evie's voice, but it sounded strained. It only took him three long steps to get to the swinging door separating the two areas. Augusta Hamilton, hugely pregnant, sat on a chair with one hand supporting her back. Evie knelt next to her, lines of worry wrinkling her forehead. There was something different about Evie this morning... What was it?

"What happened?" Scott asked, relieved Evie wasn't the one injured, but a glance at Augusta's face told him this was serious. He leaned down, picked up Augusta's wrist and felt her racing pulse. Chief Harlan swung through the doors behind him.

"I came in early as usual to get the ovens going," Augusta said. She stopped and seemed to hold her breath for a moment as if she were in great pain. She clutched her apron with her free hand and wrinkled the fabric mercilessly. Scott glanced back at the chief, whose expression was somewhere between "uh-oh" and "holy smoke." This was Jack Hamilton's wife. They treated every employee and guest injury with great care, but this was kid-gloves territory.

Augusta drew breath. "Slipped on something. Fell to my knees."

"Did you hit your head?" Scott asked. "Lose consciousness?"

"No. I just…jolted myself."

Evie moved behind Augusta and put her hands on her shoulders, rubbing them gently. Augusta relaxed for a moment, leaning back into the chair. She let go of her apron and smoothed the fabric. "I think I'm okay."

"I'm not," Evie said. "You scared me to death when you called me so early."

Scott looked up at Evie and realized what was different. She wore a Starlight Point T-shirt. Shorts. Sneakers with no socks. No makeup, hair wild. She'd just gotten out of bed. *Who fixed her car for her? When?*

"I couldn't call Jack. He'd panic. He's probably still in bed." Augusta grimaced. "Only one of us keeps baker's hours."

"That'll change when your baby arrives," Chief Harlan said. "When are you due?"

"Two weeks," Augusta said.

Scott moved behind Augusta. Evie stepped aside for him but she was still close enough for his arm to brush against hers. "Can you point to where it hurts?"

Augusta shook her head. "Sort of everywhere. It's a strange feeling."

Scott and the chief locked eyes over Augusta's head. The chief raised an eyebrow and Scott guessed what he was thinking. They had both seen this before.

"What time did you fall?" Scott asked.

"About six," Augusta said.

"An hour before you called me?" Evie said.

"So," Chief Harlan said, "you've been feeling like this for almost two hours now?"

Augusta nodded. "It wasn't so bad at first."

Scott leaned closer to Evie, his lips brushing her ear. "You need to call your brother."

Evie frowned and her mouth parted with a question.

Augusta gasped and gripped her apron again, clenching both hands into fists. Her shoulders hunched against the pain.

"Not even five minutes apart," the chief said.

Scott turned to Evie. "Call your brother and tell him his wife is in labor."

Augusta shook her head. "No, it's just… I fell and…"

The chief leaned down and put a hand on Augusta's shoulder. "I think your fall got things started. The ambulance is right out front. When this contraction passes, we're going to walk you out there."

Evie got out her phone and Scott overheard

her arrange for Jack to meet the ambulance at the marina gate.

"Was he panicked?" Augusta asked.

"My brother?" Evie asked. "Cool as a cucumber, of course."

"I don't need an ambulance," Augusta protested.

"But Jack probably will," Evie said.

When Augusta gave the word, Scott and the chief each took an arm and walked her slowly to the ambulance. Scott had transported women in labor before, but he'd never delivered a baby. He wondered if the chief ever had and if they'd have to deliver one today. *No. First baby. These things take time.* He hoped.

Evie held the shop door for them and then opened the back doors of the ambulance. Scott gave her a reassuring smile as he helped Augusta step up into the vehicle. The chief got in with her and Scott had almost shut the door when he heard Augusta call Evie's name. He held it open so Evie could climb in.

"My shop," Augusta said.

"I'll run it until reinforcements arrive," Evie said. "I got pretty good at that two summers ago."

"Thank you," Augusta murmured. Her face was as white as the sheets on the gurney.

"Time to go," Harlan said.

Scott shut the doors and headed for the driver's seat. Evie walked alongside him. "Take good care of her," she said.

"Of course." He noticed Evie's pale face and the way she clutched her shaking hands in front of her. He put his own large hand over both of hers. "You take care of yourself. Augusta will be fine. Babies are born every day."

He got in the driver's seat and drove down the trail, trying to miss the tree roots and bumpy spots. As soon as they picked up Jack and got on smooth pavement, he planned to hit the siren and test out the horsepower under the hood.

EVIE PULLED HER hair back and put on a Starlight Point baseball cap she found in the workroom. Dug lip gloss out of her purse and applied it. She lowered doughnuts into the fryers and called Aunt Augusta to let her know what was going on. She would have called Augusta's parents but she didn't have their number.

Aunt Augusta was thrilled to hear the

news, and also told her which summer employees would be the most helpful in an emergency. Evie found their cell numbers on a list hanging over the desk in the workroom.

She called her mother and June next to assure them both she would hold down the fort if they wanted to go to the hospital.

Now all she had to do was make doughnuts and bake cookies until help arrived. After that, she just had to run an amusement park. By herself. *I can do this.*

Only thirty minutes went by. Evie knew this because she'd been watching the clock wondering how Augusta was doing. They would be at the hospital by now. The ambulance was probably already back at the park. She wished she had grabbed her radio before she'd left home. If she had, she could hear the customary announcement from the firefighters when they were back on the grounds of Starlight Point.

The swinging doors of the Last Chance Bakery squeaked, but Evie didn't see who came in. She was in the workroom, gloves on her hands as she boxed cookies in half-dozen sets. *Augusta must have gotten here very early.* The icing was already dry. The cutout cookies in the shape of landmarks at Starlight Point had been Augusta's brainstorm two summers ago, and Evie had plenty of experience helping her with them. Although she had mostly done the accounts and ordering for Augusta's three bakeries at the point, she had pitched in with the baking and decorating as needed.

She put a carousel horse, Ferris wheel and four other cookies in a box while she waited for whoever had come in to find her in the workroom. *Please be a bakery employee reporting early for work.*

Scott Bennett strode in and leaned on the counter next to Evie. He wouldn't be helpful with the pastries, but he had something she wanted. News.

"I thought you'd like to hear the report," he said.

She was glad her hands were busy and no longer shaking.

"I do. Thanks for coming to tell me." She glanced up but immediately refocused on her work. Scott had a way of unnerving her. She didn't know if he would hug her or turn a fire hose on her. *Why is he staring at me?*

"Well?" she asked.

"We got her there," he said. "In time. They

wheeled her into the maternity ward and we left."

"Did Jack pass out or anything?"

Scott chuckled. "Not that I know of."

"There's still time. Jack can be squeamish."

"But not you," Scott said. "Is that why you're in charge of safety?"

"Part of the reason. Hold out your hand."

Scott slanted his eyebrows but complied and opened his right hand.

Evie chose a sugar cookie shaped and iced to resemble the Lake Breeze Hotel and laid it in Scott's palm. "Thank you for your help this morning."

Scott looked at the cookie in his hand and then met Evie's eyes. "Just doing my job."

Although Evie wore an apron, her long legs were bare. She felt exposed in front of Scott without her usual professional attire. She didn't even have her name tag on.

"When did you get your car fixed?" Scott asked.

"Two nights ago. Mel came over and put a new battery in."

"Did he also fix the broken taillight?"

Of course that would bother Mr. Safety. *He*

*probably wishes he had the power to write
me a ticket for the infraction.*

"Yes," she said, even though it would have
been more fun to make him wonder. Just as
she wondered if her hotel plans were anywhere close to approval.

Scott bit the cookie in half and ate a whole
wing of the hotel.

"How long do you think it will be?" Evie
asked.

Scott leaned on the counter and ate the rest
of the cookie. He crossed his arms over his
chest. "Never know with first babies."

"I can't imagine," Evie said.

She continued to arrange cookies in pink
boxes, wanting to stay busy. She tied string
around each box and stacked them. Sur-
rounded by food, she was too nervous to eat
any of it.

"Have you had anything to eat today,
Evie?"

She shook her head.

"You've had a stressful day and nothing
to eat," Scott said. "Bad combination. It's
supposed to be humid and over ninety degrees today. I don't want to have to scoop
you off the midway when you faint in this
afternoon's heat."

Scott turned toward her and tapped his fingers on the countertop. She wanted to ignore him but she had just boxed the last cookie on the counter and she had no choice but to look at him. *Why is he concerned about me?*

"Especially since you're going to be pulling double duty," he added. "For at least several days."

"I'll try to keep my cool." *If you really want to show you care about me, you'll approve my hotel plans so I can stay on track with the project.*

She faced him and met his eyes for a moment. *What makes you tick, Captain Scott Bennett?*

"I'm sure you will," Scott said. He walked out and she heard the squeaking door at the front of the shop open and close.

CHAPTER FIFTEEN

SINCE THE BIRTH of Jack's daughter on Thursday morning, Evie and June had shared the daily responsibility of running Starlight Point. Friday was busy but tolerable. Very warm but not dangerously hot. June had battled morning sickness the first part of the day, but she'd stayed by Evie's side until past sunset, doing her part.

Saturday was a different story. Crowded and hot, the peninsula was like a hill of ants. If someone dropped a spoonful of peanut butter into the mix, it would be pandemonium.

"Go home," Evie told June late Saturday afternoon. "Or I'm calling Mel and having him pick you up."

They were sitting on Evie's favorite bench in front of the train station where the midway parted. Although they never talked directly about their father and how he loved that bench, Evie, June and Jack often used the spot for a break. Walking through the park, they would find each other sitting there having a soda and watching crowds. Sometimes they talked about business and sometimes they just sat together and enjoyed a moment's peace. Evie had discovered June resting there as she'd walked from the Wonderful West toward the front of the midway.

"I hate leaving you alone," June said.

"I'm not alone. We have almost three thousand employees. I can't believe I managed to look busy all day."

The first-aid scooter drove past them with Curt at the wheel and Scott on the bench seat next to him. Evie had heard the call for a twisted ankle near the Midway Carousel. Because it was not an emergency, she was glad to see Curt driving slowly as he navigated the shoulder-to-shoulder crowd. When the scooter passed Evie and June, Scott lifted his hand in greeting. Not an enthusiastic wave. More of an I-see-you gesture. He made eye contact with Evie but he didn't smile.

"That is one intense man," June said. "Hot, but intense."

Evie huffed out a sigh. "Everyone's hot. It's still ninety degrees at this time of day."

"Not exactly what I meant."

"I'm too tired to think about what you meant."

June took a long drink from the bottle of ice-cold water her sister handed her. "I doubt most people have any idea how hard it is to run an amusement park."

"That's why we're a team," Evie said. "But I can be a team of one for the rest of the night because you—" she pointed at June "—are going home."

Evie watched June from the marina gate to be sure she got in her car and left. The live shows would run themselves the rest of the day, especially at this point in the summer where the performers knew their routines like their middle names. June's other responsibility was human resources, but there was no hiring or firing happening on a Saturday night. She hoped.

Handling Jack's areas of responsibility—rides and foods—was a challenge, but Evie had wisely chosen pants and comfortable shoes she could walk in all night long if she had to. Her own departments—resorts and safety—were familiar territory, and she hoped for a quiet night even though she found every day brought its challenges. Issues with a reservation or a guest complaint at the hotel. Fires and medical emergencies. There was a reason she went to bed tired every night.

With at least thirty thousand guests in the park, Evie wanted to be ready for anything. Her siblings were depending on her more and more as they began families of their own. Last summer she'd spent more time in the office watching the money than she had on the midway watching people. This year was different. She just hoped she was doing the right thing.

She felt for the radio at her hip and made sure the volume was up, even though there was not much chance of hearing it over the crowds and coasters.

She checked in at her office and smiled at the framed baby picture Jack had already put on his desk when he'd stopped in that morning. Baby Nora had her first ride in the car yesterday on the way home from the hospital. Jack was probably hanging over the crib marveling at her perfect little ears and fingers right now.

Evie took a lap around the entire peninsula. Past the Sea Devil, through the Wonderful West, up the Western Trail and a loop around the carousel at the front of the park.

There was a line at every ride and food stand. Balloon sellers made change and handed over fun on a string. Lights in the games area whirled and flashed as people exchanged money for chances.

Evie stopped and watched a dad try unsuccessfully to win a stuffed monkey for his toddler. He'd be better off buying one at the toy store. What was it about amusement parks that made people do things they wouldn't do elsewhere?

She stopped by Bernie's Boardwalk Fries for dinner. If she didn't take advantage of the lull right now, she might not eat until tomorrow.

"Are you in charge tonight?" Bernie asked. Evie smiled at the man she'd known her entire life. As far as she could tell, he'd always been the same age. Somewhere between middle-aged and the great beyond. This evening she noticed the lines around his eyes. More gray hairs than black. A fixture from her childhood, Bernie probably would retire one of these years. And it wouldn't be the same without him.

The past seemed to be slipping away a little at a time, but she had to let it go. The future was her job.

"Can you believe my brother and sister left me in charge?" Evie said.

Bernie shook his head. "Would never have imagined it, even just a few years ago. But things have changed fast lately."

"For the better?"

"Some of it. I miss your dad. And I miss seeing you with pigtails skipping down the midway."

"Maybe I'll do that later and surprise you," Evie said.

She picked up her food—greasy fries in a cardboard box with a soda on the side— and headed for the bench near the fry stand where she could watch people twirl away on the Scrambler.

The lines were long and the sun dipped lower. Midnight was still another five hours away. Evie finished her dinner and took a walk through the restroom building to wash her hands. Made a phone call to housekeeping to have them come by and do an extra cleaning. *Too many people in one place.* The trash cans overflowed and the paper towel dispensers were empty.

Evie headed down the midway toward the front ticket booths with the intention of checking on sales receipts for the day. With so many guests in the park, the money rolling into the Point bolstered her confidence. *Imagine if there were twice the number of hotel rooms so guests could stay another day.*

Her radio crackled and she lifted it off the waistband of her navy linen pants.

"Fight. Officers needed in the Silver Streak ticket lines," the dispatcher said. Evie heard the excitement in the dispatcher's voice. Fights were unusual and serious, and she hoped there were officers nearby.

Evie was only two rides away from the Silver Streak. She dashed past the antique cars and the dodgem cars as she tried to think of the last major fight at the Point. Two summers ago when the Sea Devil was new and the queue lines weren't nearly long enough, a few punches had been thrown on hot, crowded days. Those were fairly minor scuffles and quickly quelled by the in-house police department.

The Silver Streak, just past forty years old and one of the tamer wooden coasters, didn't seem like the scene for a rumble. But… *Oh, man.* A crowd had already formed. Cops in black uniforms dashed past Evie and entered the fray. She ran, too. *What would Jack do?* Would he dive in and start swinging? Announce his presence and his credentials as owner? Should she call Bayside police for backup?

Evie worked her way through the crowd at the entrance to the turnstiles. One cop passed her, hand clutched over a profusely bleeding nose. She paused and called dispatch on her radio to request medical help. Beeping of the first-aid scooter was audible over the melee and Evie knew she wasn't the first to realize medical help was needed.

She pushed on, working her way through the silver bars and trying to reach the knot of shouting people bunched around the steps leading to the ride platform. Maybe she should let the trained police officers handle this. Did her one hour of self-defense training qualify her to step into a fight? *Battling the accounts on the computer seems like a vacation right now.* Was she in over her head?

The situation was completely out of hand and the fight stormed quickly her way. A woman wrestled another to the ground and pulled a chunk of hair loose. One man body-slammed another. Evie watched in horror as the target hit the concrete.

It was a mob scene. Adrenaline raced

through her. She had to do something. This was her park, her responsibility.

"Stop!" she yelled. "Stop fighting! Separate or you'll be arrested."

A huge man swung around and pulled back his fist. He was taller than Evie and twice as heavy. And he had a full head of angry steam behind his punch. Evie had no time to react. The massive fisted hand was heading straight toward her face. She froze, expecting the worst.

Suddenly an imposing figure stepped between them and shoved the assailant, blocking the shot with an upraised arm and knocking him backward. Evie saw a flash of navy blue uniform and mile-wide shoulders. Scott Bennett.

Scott swung around and made eye contact with Evie, raking her with an assessing look. It only took a second, but his attention was diverted from the fight. The man staggered to his feet, fist drawn back again, face twisted with rage.

"Look out!" Evie yelled. She pushed Scott to the side so he wouldn't take a blow to the back of the head. But the punch was already thrown and it caught Evie right in the face.

The world went white and Evie fell back

onto the silver rails of the queue line. She grabbed the rail and tried to find her balance. Everything seemed to be moving, even the concrete under her feet and the cold steel under her hand.

A face she recognized swirled before her. Scott's lips were moving, but he spoke too fast. She couldn't understand him. She tried to shake her head to tell him she couldn't hear him. The sunset slanting across the rows of queue lines blinded her. Nothing made sense.

Scott put an arm under hers and her feet left the ground. *No. I'll fall.* She tried to fight him for a moment until she realized he was carrying her away from the fight, dodging through people and heading for the exit to the ride.

She closed her eyes against the shouting, the fear and the pain in her head. Completely trusting Scott, she surrendered and relaxed in his arms. He would keep her safe.

"It could have been a lot worse," Scott said. "The guy was aiming for me so his trajectory was off when he hit Evie."

"No offense," Jack answered, "but I wish he'd hit you instead."

"Agreed," Scott said. *I would have taken that punch for Evie any day.*

Evie sat on a vinyl bench in the first-aid station, ice pack held to her eye. Jack stood over her like an angry giant whose village had been defiled by raiders. Scott had never seen Jack in anything but a white shirt and a suit, but tonight he wore cargo shorts, a faded gray T-shirt and loafers with no socks. And an expression full of adrenaline and hostility.

"I can't believe I was stuck clear back in the Wonderful West when it all went down," Caroline said. "It would have been my first fight."

"Cheer up," Evie said. "I may take a swing at the guy who did this and you can jump in that fight if you want to."

Scott sat next to Evie and felt the pulse in her wrist. He counted her heartbeats for a full sixty seconds and then did it again. It was reassuring.

"Bayside Police hauled off the three biggest offenders," Caroline told Jack. "Dispatch sent me over to tell you that because they didn't want it going over the radio. Those guys will face criminal charges, including assault."

"They certainly will," Jack said. "Especially the one who clocked my sister."

"I'll happily testify," Scott offered. "I saw it all."

"Thanks. Now, what's next with Evie here? Does she go to the hospital? What do you think?"

"I'm right here," Evie said. "Don't talk about me like I'm a little girl."

Jack leaned closer to Evie. "You'll always be my little sister," he said in a quiet voice.

Scott was still sitting next to Evie on the vinyl bench, his hand over her wrist. *I have a little sister, too.*

"Aside from a bruise, I'll be fine," Evie said. She lowered the ice pack and Caroline gasped.

"Holy shiner. You don't want to look in a mirror for the next two weeks."

"It can't be that bad," Evie said. She turned toward Scott. Sitting on her right, he hadn't noticed the color spreading around her left eye. But when she removed the ice pack… yikes!

He tried to keep a neutral expression on his face, but he was torn between shock at the massive purple bruise and bone-rattling fury. He would have knocked that ham-fisted guy into next week when he'd hit Evie, but his main concern had been getting her out of danger.

As he'd carried her through the sea of Starlight Point cops and guests, two thoughts competed in his mind. He'd thought of his sister and hoped she wasn't one of the cops rushing into the fight. And he'd thought of the beautiful woman in his arms and realized something he was afraid to say out loud. Ever.

"I think an X-ray would be a good idea," Scott said, refocusing on a practical matter. Patient care. *I'm a professional. I can set my feelings aside.*

Evie carefully felt her cheekbone and the area around her eye. "It seems to be intact," she said. "You're just trying to scare me."

"No, we're not," Jack said. "I'm calling Mom. I'll have her meet you at the marina gate with her car. Even if you think nothing's broken, I want your injury documented."

"Scott can document it," she said. She turned to him for verification. The sight of her colorful eye made anger rush from his heart straight out to his fingers and toes.

"Conflict of interest," Jack said. "Scott works for us. The emergency room is a neutral party. And I'm not taking no for an answer."

Conflict of interest. He knew what Jack meant. In a police investigation, his testimony could be considered slanted because his employment put him squarely on the side of the Hamiltons. Was his consideration of the hotel plans a conflict of interest, too?

"Fine," Evie said. "But I can drive myself. I've got one good eye."

"I'll take you," Scott said.

"You're on duty," Evie protested.

"No, I'm not. My shift ended fifteen minutes ago."

"Good idea," Jack said. "And you'll call me and let me know what you find out."

Scott nodded. Jack's tone was hard. Demanding. But Scott didn't begrudge him his attitude. If Caroline had just gotten slugged in the face, he'd act the same way. Maybe worse.

"I will," Scott said. "And then I'll take her home."

Jack reached out a hand. "Thanks, Bennett. I hate handing my sister over, but I need to stay here and clean up."

"Hey," Evie said, "you're talking about me like I'm a piece of luggage."

Scott stood and pulled Evie up. He held her by her upper arms for a moment just in case she was dizzy. "Your car or my truck?" Scott asked.

"Believe me," Evie said. "You don't want to drive my car."

"Why not?"

"The taillight is still out. I guess the new bulb Mel put in wasn't the fix."

"So you've been driving around like that for days?"

Scott pictured cars rear-ending Evie's car because they didn't see it. *Why do people take risks like that?*

"I've been busy, Mr. Safety," Evie said. "In case you hadn't noticed."

Scott wanted to either fix her car or take it to the impound lot so she couldn't drive it. But he didn't have any authority over her and now was not the time.

"My truck is right outside," he said.

On the drive around the outer loop, Scott tried to keep his eyes on the road, but he kept glancing at his passenger. He was glad it was too dark to see her black-and-purple eye. The vision of that huge man's fist smashing into her face kept replaying in his brain, driving him nuts. *Why didn't I react faster?*

"What ever happened with the sprained ankle call at the carousel?" Evie asked.

"Nothing really. A man twisted his foot when he stepped off the ride, but it was already better by the time we got there. He walked it off."

"Good."

"It's always nice when something turns out not to be an emergency," Scott said.

"You're not disappointed about wasting your adrenaline?"

"Never."

They were silent a moment and Scott decided to ask something he'd been wondering about for weeks.

"What is it about that bench?"

He heard Evie let out a long breath.

"The one in front of the train station," he prompted. "I swear you're so busy you never seem to sit down, but I've noticed you sitting on that bench at least three times this summer."

In his peripheral vision, he saw her head swing toward him.

"You didn't notice me the one time," he said. "You were lost in thought."

They passed the employee dorms and marina, and Scott was afraid Evie was going to ignore his question.

"Three years ago," Evie finally said, "a few weeks before the park opened for the season, my father had a fatal heart attack. He was only fifty-four." Her voice wavered and Scott wanted to kick himself. *Wasn't it bad enough she got punched in the face tonight?* And now he'd opened a wound.

"He loved sitting on that bench and watching the crowds," Evie said. "It's in the center of the park and almost every single guest has to pass by it. Once when I was younger, I saw him kissing my mom on that bench."

"I'm so sorry," Scott said. He wanted to reach over and take her hand, but he was afraid to. He felt her grief and knew from experience he might make her emotions spill over completely by touching her.

"My family never got to say goodbye, so sometimes we sit there just to feel his presence."

Scott thought of the heart attack victim at the Space Race. Remembered him making what he believed were final farewells to his family. No wonder Evie's expression had been troubled. It had brought her own memories and sadness to the surface, but she had handled it. Had done what was necessary. Not many people were that strong.

"It's hard to lose someone you love," he said.

He heard Evie sniff. He reached for the tissue box on the floor and handed her one. He was sorry he'd asked the question, but the story about her father somehow made him feel even closer to her. It hadn't been hard to figure out who the other name tag in her purse belonged to, but now he understood why she carried it with her.

He carried a family burden with him, too.

They passed the toll booths and Scott was afraid it was going to be a long, silent ride to the hospital.

But he was wrong.

"So," Evie said, her voice sounding stronger, "is this a bad time to ask when a certain building inspector we both know will have an opinion on my hotel renovation plans?"

Scott tensed at the thought of the reservations he had regarding her plans, but at least if Evie felt well enough to ask him about them, she must be okay. And if talking about business helped ease her painful memories, then he would take the hit. The fact that he cared more about her well-being than the safety issues he found in the plans left him feeling chilled.

Conflict of interest.

He was too close. To Starlight Point. To Evie.

Tomorrow he would talk to the Bayside fire chief and ask him to reassign the Lake Breeze plans to an independent inspector— perhaps one from nearby Port Huron. More than anything, Scott wanted to have a say in those plans, especially because they involved a hotel. A shiver ran over the burn scars on his back. This was his life's passion, but getting too close to Evie meant he had to withdraw.

Right now, he needed to buy time while he processed the thought of backing away. He didn't feel like explaining it to anyone, especially Evie.

"You can't be in a hurry to have a press conference," he said. He was careful to keep his tone neutral and not look at Evie. He couldn't do neutrality when he looked at her. "You don't want anyone taking a picture of you for about two weeks."

"So you'll have my plans returned in two weeks?" she asked.

Scott huffed out a long breath. "That would be within the thirty-day window."

"Of course." Evie sighed. "That's the regulation. You love playing by the rules."

A metaphorical knife sliced his chest and twisted in his heart. He did love the rules. They kept people safe. But he was beginning to realize he wasn't following them. *I can't approve building plans for a place where I work. No matter how much I want to.*

"Rules are important. They're there for a good reason."

"So you never take a risk and deviate from them?"

"No."

"I could blackmail you," Evie said with a lighter tone. "When we get to the hospital, I could tell them you punched me in the eye because I refused to make you a sandwich."

"Not funny," he said. "Not even a little bit."

"I know. Sorry. It's been a tough night." Her voice wavered and he wanted to reach across the seat and put his arm around her.

But he couldn't.

Tonight he'd already discovered two things that shook him right down to his boots. He was falling in love with Evie Hamilton. And his feelings for her meant he could not do his job—a job he thought meant more to him than anything else. The chance to make hotels safer and to right a terrible wrong from his past was one of the reasons he'd pursued his fire inspector's certification.

And now he had the chance, but he had to give it up. Someone else would approve Evie's plans, no matter how dangerous his gut told him they were. It couldn't, and wouldn't, be him.

CHAPTER SIXTEEN

ON MONDAY MORNING, Scott sat across from the fire chief at the Bayside station. Chief Portman had awarded Scott the job of building and fire inspector less than two months earlier based on Scott's experience, education and passion for the position. Instead of proving himself, though, Scott was letting himself and the chief down. Evaluating the construction plans for the hotel project at Starlight Point was his first major job, and he was removing himself from it.

Scott laid the construction diagram and blueprints open on the chief's desk. "I've done all the legwork on the new construction. It's solid. Meets code."

Portman nodded. "Good to hear. And the renovation of the old part?"

Scott shrugged. "It's trickier."

"Does it follow the law or not?"

"Depends on how you look at it," Scott said.

Chief Portman huffed out a breath and held

his hands in the air, palms up. "I appointed you to do this pain-in-the-neck paperwork so I wouldn't have to look at it."

"I know. And I want to do it, but I can't," Scott said. He paused. "I have a conflict of interest."

The Bayside chief leaned back in his chair and tapped a pencil on the desk. "You didn't have a conflict of interest earlier in the season when you made the Hamiltons dance over the marina plans."

That was before I thought about Evie's feelings with every decision I made.

Scott cleared his throat. "That was a clear-cut case."

Portman put down the pencil and leaned forward. "If it was so clear-cut, why did you overrule the plans Marty had already approved before he retired?"

Scott's heart accelerated. Was his boss disagreeing with his ruling on the safety issues at the marina? Why hadn't he said so at the time?

"I have nothing but respect for Marty," Scott said.

"But?"

"But he let a few things go that…on a

closer inspection of the updated codes, maybe it wasn't the best review of the plans."

"You're dancing around it," Portman declared. "Marty was ready to retire. He was friendly with Starlight Point and other places around town. Didn't want to make trouble for people by enforcing some pickier parts of the fire code."

"I think all the parts should be enforced," Scott said.

"Officially, yes. But we both know some of the code is bendable."

"I don't like bending it."

"So why are you really backing out of doing your job now?" the chief asked. "What's going on over there at Starlight Point?"

"I'm not backing out of my job. I just don't want to be the one to sign off on this particular set of plans."

"I still don't see what's changed since the marina issues two months ago," Portman said.

Scott had no desire to explain his feelings to his boss. He didn't even want to admit them to himself. He shrugged. *I feel like a kid trying to explain to his dad that he didn't mow a patch of the front yard because there was a scary dog walking by.*

Chief Portman blew out a long, noisy breath. "So you've worked there all summer and gotten friendly with somebody there. And now you don't think you can be objective."

Scott stared at the wood grain on the ancient desk. "I'm happy to work with whoever you appoint. But it's a conflict of interest for me to make the final judgment."

"Fine. I'll review the plans myself," Portman said. "I used to do it all the time before we instituted the inspector job twenty years ago."

Scott got up. "Thanks."

"Not so fast. First, tell me what it is you don't like about the plans to remodel the old section. Whatever it is, I think you're afraid to come out and say it."

Scott stood with his hands gripping the back of his chair. How much was he willing to tell the chief?

"You know how it is with old buildings. Dropped ceilings, false walls, chases cut through fire walls for modern plumbing and electrical. Fixing up old buildings creates fire hazards."

"Old buildings are a nightmare," Chief Portman agreed. "And we've got them all over downtown. It gives me heartburn."

Scott's hope lifted. Maybe the chief would see it his way, even if it took a stricter line than the code technically required. The chief would be the one to say no to plans he thought might endanger firefighters and hotel guests in the future.

"But the Lake Breeze is a historic building," Portman said. "It's on the register. Got a big bronze plaque. It was built long before there were fire codes and it's exempt from most of them."

"Look at those plans," Scott said. "They're renovating most of the building. More than fifty percent. Probably endangering their historic status."

"They can give it up if they want to."

"But if they lose the protection of that status and make substantial changes, they could be forced to modernize safety systems," Scott insisted. "Like sprinklers in every room."

Portman put his elbows on the plans and stared at the newest member of his department. "You're a hell of a firefighter, Bennett. And I like your ambition. But sometimes I wonder what force is driving you. I swear you've got the devil at your back sometimes and you're trying to outrun him."

"The same force drives me as everyone else here," Scott said. "I don't want to see anyone die, not on my watch, not now or on some distant day in the future when a fire breaks out in a building whose plans I approved."

The chief raised his eyebrows. "I'll look at the hotel application this week. If I have questions, I'll consult with the inspector from Port Huron. You're off the case since you want to be, but you have to agree to stay out of it and abide by my decision. No matter what this conflict of interest is that you think you have, you're giving up your right to say anything."

Scott left the chief's office and went into his own tiny one. He shut the door and sat behind his desk. Evie had sat across from him just weeks ago, but he didn't want to think about her right now. He didn't want to think about her smile, her eyes or the way she laughed. Because all those things added up to his failure to do the job he'd sworn to do. Falling for her was a huge mistake.

For the next three days Scott avoided Evie. He worked one shift at Starlight Point and he was lucky to have a quiet night and keep a low profile. If he had to interact with Evie and she asked him about the plans, he didn't want to lie about the status of the application. But he sure didn't want to explain why he'd felt compelled to hand them over to a neutral party.

He was no longer neutral, and the feeling burned him. He considered quitting his job at Starlight Point so it wouldn't jeopardize his work in Bayside, but as long as his sister Caroline insisted on doing dangerous work at the point, he would be there. Watching over her as best he could.

FOUR DAYS AFTER the fight in the Silver Streak queue lines, on a hot evening after the park closed, hundreds of summer employees were still on the premises. Instead of working, however, they were lined up for rides on the Sea Devil, Silver Streak, Space Race, Mine Ride and even the carousel. The lights of the midway were on, loud music blasted from the speakers, and the food vendors were open late to serve up food courtesy of the owners of Starlight Point.

Employee appreciation night at the end of July was a longstanding tradition meant as both thanks and inspiration to carry the summer workers through the rest of the season. When August came around, staff would peel off like layers of an onion as college campuses and local schools reconvened.

Because it was tradition, the entire Hamilton family worked the event. They spread out over a small section of the front midway. Evie put her mother, Virginia, to work handing out prefilled cups of soda at a table in front of the carousel. She heard June over the microphone on the loading platform of the Sea Devil reeling off safety instructions. She laughed at Jack as he ran around and checked seat belts and door latches on the Scrambler.

Every year, the siblings chose jobs for each other. Evie had assigned June to the Sea Devil where she could use her stage voice but not wear herself out. June had chosen the Scrambler ride for Jack because she thought it would keep him awake. *New baby at home.* Jack had selected a job on the midway for Evie because of her notorious dislike of games and gambling.

Evie considered her assignment to be a three-hour sentence. Running the age and weight guessing game. At least people weren't throwing away their money tonight, she thought as she looked at the long line and groaned. Usually, chances to win an inflatable banana or a plush gorilla cost guests three bucks each. Tonight, the game was free.

Evie's job was to guess either age or weight—player's choice. Players stepped up and wrote their age on a slip of folded paper or agreed to get on the scale after Evie stated her guess over the speaker for all to hear. If she was within three years or five pounds, the player went away empty-handed. If her guesses were farther from the mark, she gave them their choice of souvenir.

She sighed. *Thanks a lot, Jack. I'll get you back next year by making you clean the restrooms.*

A burly teen who still wore a green uniform designating him as one of the trash collectors stepped up.

"Bet you can't guess my weight," he said.

You're probably right, Evie thought.

She gauged his height and tried to guess accurately based upon some algorithms she had looked up online to prepare for her job. *About five foot ten, lots of muscle.*

"Two hundred," she said.

The teen laughed and got on the scale, an old-fashioned ornate model with an array of numbers at the top. There was a moment of drama while the assembled crowd waited for the needle to stop. The gold arrow pointed to two hundred and twenty.

"Fooled me," Evie said over the microphone. "Pick your prize."

She gave away ten more prizes to the next ten contestants, and her line started to grow. *I'm an easy target. If I don't improve my success rate, I'll run out of inflatable bananas.*

A petite girl with a baby face was next. "Age," she said. She wrote a number on a piece of paper, folded it and held it behind her. Evie studied the girl. *She will probably still be getting carded when she's forty*, Evie thought. *But I'm getting wiser.*

"Twenty-three," Evie declared.

The girl's smile faded and she handed over the paper. "Twenty," Evie read aloud. *Finally got one right.* "Sorry," she told the girl. "Get back in line and I'll guess your weight next time. I'm terrible at that."

The next person, a rail-thin retiree who took tickets at the front gate, moved forward.

"Don't make me guess your age," Evie said. "I'd have to say you don't look a day over forty. Give me a fighting chance."

The man laughed. "Fine," he said. "Guess

my weight. I want to win a gorilla for my grandson. Not that I'm old enough to have grandchildren, mind you."

Evie laughed. "One hundred and fifty pounds," she said.

"Let's see." The man stepped on the scale and the needle stopped at one hundred and sixty-five. "My wife's meatloaf," he said. "Does it every time."

This was going to be a long night. Evie was glad she wore comfortable shorts, a T-shirt and sneakers. Because of her bruising, she wore her hair long and parted on the side so it would sweep over her face. Even with stage makeup— thanks to her sister June's expertise—she still looked like she'd been in a fight. Evie didn't want to answer any more questions. There'd been more than enough for the police report and at the hospital.

To her great surprise, Scott and Caroline were her next two contestants. She hadn't recognized them in the dim light beyond her game booth. Caroline smiled and looked closely at Evie's eye.

"Would never know," she whispered.

Evie laughed. "Sure. That explains all the comments I've had."

"You're beautiful, anyway," Caroline said.

Scott stood behind his sister. He was dressed casually, like most of the other employees. She hadn't seen him since four nights ago when he'd dropped her off at her door after the trip to the emergency room. He'd lingered, making her wonder if she should invite him in. She hadn't.

Evie was surprised to see him at the employee appreciation night since fun wasn't exactly something she equated him with. *He's probably here to spend time with his sister.*

"It wouldn't be fair for me to guess your age," Evie said to Caroline, "because I already know you're one year away from being old enough to be a bonded officer. How about weight?"

"Sure," Caroline said.

Evie made a big show of looking Caroline over. She cocked her head and closed one eye. Because Caroline was very similar in size and build to Evie, Evie gave her own weight.

"One hundred and thirty-two."

Caroline grimaced and got on the scale.

The needle hovered for a moment and settled on one hundred and twenty-six.

"Is that all you weigh?" Scott asked his sister. "You need to bulk up."

"Every woman's dream," Caroline said. She rolled her eyes at her brother.

"Winner!" Evie announced into the microphone. She rang the bell and told Caroline to choose a prize.

Scott stood in front of her and Evie's pulse raced. All summer long she had tried to view him as a professional. An employee. A potential friend or adversary in the matter of the hotel plans. He held the fulfillment of her dream and future plans in his hands.

He'd held her in his arms a few nights ago. Despite the pain and shock of the punch to the face, she remembered clearly what his arms felt like. His scent, the warm skin of his neck as her forehead had pressed against it.

She held his eyes and drew a long breath. "Age or weight?"

"Whatever you want."

She handed him a slip of paper and a marker. "Age," she said.

He wrote down a number and handed it to Caroline. She opened the paper and looked at it. "Just checking," she said. "Keeping my brother honest."

Evie smiled at Scott. The warm lights

around the booth played over his face. His dark eyes looked soft, sweet.

"Forty-two," she said.

Scott laughed. A deep, rich sound. Had she ever heard him laugh before?

"Exactly right," he said. "If we fast-forward fifteen years."

Evie rang the bell. "Winner!" she announced over the microphone.

Scott didn't move to grab a prize. *Was he going to say something?*

Evie's security radio sat on the table next to her. She could barely hear it and had not paid much attention to it this evening as the park was closed anyway. But now it came alive with noise.

Scott turned his head and zeroed in on the radio. Stepped closer. He appeared to be listening intently.

Evie made out two words: Bayside Fire.

She picked it up and handed it to Scott. "Do you need to go?"

He turned up the volume and held the radio in the air between him and Evie so she could hear, too.

"Boat accident, Starlight Point break wall. Request fireboat and dive team."

"That's my dispatcher's voice," Evie said.

"Security here must have called it in, but it's Bayside's territory. They cover the break wall."

"Are you on the dive team?" Evie asked. She hoped the answer was no. Sliding under the dark waters of Lake Huron...it was a scary thought.

"No. But I'm going, anyway."

"I'll come with you," she said. Evie glanced down the line of people. *Should I close the booth and disappoint them? No choice.* Scott was already running toward the beach exit.

"Sorry," she said to the waiting staff. She shut off the lights in her booth. "There's another guessing game over by the dodgem cars. Good luck."

She clutched her radio and ran after Scott. He was way ahead of her and she couldn't see him in the darkness. *He wouldn't be crazy enough to go out on the rocky break wall in the dark. Would he?*

Caroline ran up beside her, matching her stride. Good. Maybe she would convince her brother not to take a terrible risk.

CHAPTER SEVENTEEN

SCOTT HAD HEARD the stories about boats wrecking on the long break wall that jutted into Lake Huron. During the daytime, the half mile of jagged rocks was picturesque and formed a divide between the lake and the sheltered opening of the bay. Local boaters knew the wall had only a small, utilitarian lighthouse at the very end, but at least one out-of-towner hugging the shoreline crashed into it each summer.

He'd heard the stories this summer and wondered why no one had installed lights along the wall. *Why would Starlight Point know of a hazard and do nothing to change it?*

There was no moon tonight. A glow from the Lake Breeze Hotel down the beach barely illuminated the break wall. Scott had no flashlight. The only thing he could see was the shiny-white upturned hull of a boat glowing eerily far out on the rocks.

A Starlight Point police officer stood on the beach near the fence that enclosed the entrance and a sign prohibiting pedestrians and climbers. The jagged rocks were no place for recreation.

"Any idea about injuries? Survivors?" Scott asked the officer. He was winded from his run and took a minute to catch his breath.

"No idea. Also don't know how long the boat's been there. No distress call that I know of, which isn't a good sign."

"Got a flashlight?" Scott asked.

The officer nodded. "But you're not going out there. Not in the dark."

Evie and Caroline raced up.

"Unless the boss says it's okay," the police officer continued. "Standard orders are to never unlock this gate."

Scott turned to Evie. In the darkness he couldn't read her expression.

"You're an idiot if you think you can climb over those rocks," Caroline said. "Just wait for the fireboat. It can't be that long."

"It would be a whole lot easier for them if I get there first and signal with a flashlight," Scott protested.

"You don't know what you're walking

into," Evie said. "It's been a while, but boaters have been killed on this wall."

"All the more reason for me to get out there," Scott said. *And for you to install more lights.*

"The rocks are jagged and spaced unevenly," Evie said. "It's too dangerous, especially in the dark." A sound carried to them on the night breeze from the direction of the wall. It could have been someone crying. It could have been the boat grating on the rocks.

He heard Evie sigh. "Unlock the gate, Sam, and give Scott your flashlight. Please."

Sam nodded. "Your decision."

"I'll come with you," Caroline said.

Scott turned on her fiercely. "You will not." He directed the flashlight beam at Evie. "I expect you to make sure she doesn't."

Evie's face in the circle of light was grim. Lips in a tight line, eyebrows drawn together.

"Be careful," she said. "Take my radio. Stay in communication with us."

Scott took the radio and clipped it on the waistband of his shorts. It felt warm in the cool night air. Wearing a T-shirt and sneakers, he was not dressed for a rescue, but he couldn't just wait on the beach while someone out there was clinging to the rocks. Possibly clinging to life.

Sam unlocked the gate and Scott held the beam of light just ahead of his feet. He leaped from one flat rock to another and got on to the break wall itself. It was going to be a long trek out to the end. He navigated a dark cavern that loomed between footholds. Good thing he had the flashlight.

He balanced on the sharp edge of an upturned boulder and decided Evie was right. This wall would be barely navigable in the daytime. He wondered if she could see his small circle of light. He had no doubt she would be watching. He risked a glance back to shore and noticed a vehicle on the beach. Probably a patrol car. The headlights illuminated the first thirty feet of the break wall, but he was beyond that now. The firefighters on duty at the Point should bring the pickup with the big search lights on the back. Those lights would stretch hundreds of feet. He hoped Evie or someone would think of it.

He would radio but he needed both hands for balance.

As he tried to move faster, his foot slipped and he raked his shin on a rock. It stung like crazy, but there was no turning back, not when he could hear the unmistakable sound of a person crying. He toggled his flashlight, searching ahead of him. The white hull was now more visible. With the light focused ahead of him instead of at his feet, he misjudged a rock and fell. He broke his fall with his left hand, but his shirt caught on a sharp rock and he heard the fabric tear as he got up.

As he neared the boat, the damage became all too clear. *How fast had they been going?* The powerboat was sliced nearly in two. It was fairly large, maybe a thirty-foot cabin cruiser. The kind of boat that could easily have ten people aboard. The part he could see was on its side on the rocks. *But where are the people?*

"Hello?" he called. He knew there had to be at least one person alive. He shivered in the night air as he waited for a response. His lower leg felt wet. *Probably blood from the slip on the rocks.*

"Over here." The voice was anguished, high-pitched.

Scott swung his flashlight toward the sound. A man and a woman were on a flat rock. The woman was sitting, but the man lay unmoving. Scott held his flashlight between his teeth so he could use his hands to scramble faster across the rocks. He felt his torn shirt flapping in the breeze.

The woman held her arm at an unnatural angle, but at least she was conscious. The man had an ugly gash on his head, but he didn't move.

Scott took the flashlight from his teeth and raked it over the man. Found a pulse. *He's alive, but in bad shape.* "I'm Captain Bennett from the Bayside Fire Department," he said to the woman. "Help is on the way. Are you the only two victims?"

"Yes. It was just us on the boat," she said. *At least no one is in the water.*

"What happened?" Scott asked as he continued to examine the man. He already knew, but keeping the woman talking helped him assess her condition and keep her calm.

"We dropped our friends off in Bayside and were headed home. We never saw the rocks." She choked on a sob. "We crawled out of the boat and then Aaron passed out and I've been calling for help."

"How long has it been?"

"I don't know," she said, sobbing. "It seems like forever, but maybe an hour? We left Bayside about nine."

Scott did a mental calculation. The employee party hadn't started until at least ten-thirty when the last guests had left. It was a short boat ride from downtown Bayside, which meant these poor people had been stranded and suffering here for hours.

And this accident could have been pre-vented if someone had added lights along the break wall as they should have done years ago. It was inexcusable.

"Can you help me by holding my flash-light?" Scott asked. He handed her the light, hoping to free his hands and give her some-thing to do to take her mind off her compan-ion's injuries. She had one good arm that he could see and he needed her to remain alert.

He realized his mistake too late. She shone the flashlight on the man, getting a good look at his bloodied face. With a cry, she dropped the light.

Scott heard it rattle down between the rocks and splash into the lake. *Great.*

He took the radio off his waistband. "Cap-tain Bennett to Bayside Fireboat. Boat ac-cident location south side of the break wall, fifty feet from the end. Two victims. One possibly critical. Both out of the water at this time."

He heard the roar of the fireboat's engine

as he clipped his radio back on his shorts. *Thank goodness*. There was nothing he could do for the victims in the dark.

He stood. Waited for the searchlight on the bow of the fireboat to find him. Signaled where to bring the boat alongside the wall.

Scott helped his fellow firefighters immobilize the man on a backboard and transfer him across the rocks to the bow of the fireboat. He put an arm around the woman and assisted her down to the boat. When it surged upward in the current, the woman panicked and clutched Scott's arm. She made it safely onto the boat, but he wasn't so lucky. He lost his balance and fell in the lake.

Scott felt himself slip under the dark water. He surfaced quickly, hoping not to misjudge and hit his head on the bottom of the boat.

"Man overboard," someone yelled. A beam of light hit Scott in the face and a gleaming white life ring sailed his direction. He grabbed the ring and towed himself in on the attached rope, then swam around to the back of the fireboat. Chief Portman was waiting. He pulled Scott over the low stern and flipped on an overhead light.

"Want a ride back to town with us?" he

asked. "We could put you in a first-class cabin since you helped us out even while you were off duty."

Scott grinned. "Do I look like I need a ride?"

His leg was bleeding, most of his shirt was missing, and he was soaking wet.

"Nah, you look like you're in great shape. We gotta get moving. Riding with us or going back across the rocks?"

"My truck is at the Point. And my sister's waiting on the beach," Scott said. He saw big floodlights set up there now. They would light his way back. "If I don't get back soon…well, you know."

The chief handed him a flashlight. "Hop off the front of the boat and take your time getting back. And thanks for coming out here. You went above and beyond."

Scott put the flashlight between his teeth and used both hands as he eased off the bow of the boat and found his footing on the rocks. The lights from shore illuminated the entire section of wall he had to cross, but they also created deep shadows in the rocks. It would still be a treacherous crossing. The radio weighed down his wet shorts as he moved as quickly as he could toward shore.

His sister was waiting. *And so was Evie*. He had some hard questions for her.

"YOU GAVE HIM your radio," Caroline complained. "I wish he'd use it."

"The Bayside fireboat said Scott's coming back," Evie said. "At least he has light now, if he's crazy enough to cross those rocks a second time."

A crowd had gathered on the beach. Members from both the Starlight Point fire and police departments set up lights and waited, but when the fireboat left, Evie sent most of the safety forces back to their duties. She kept only two police officers, two firefighters and the truck with the lights.

The waiting was torture. Caroline put on a brave front as she talked with her fellow police officers, but Evie knew she was concerned for her brother's safety. Evie stood alone, arms crossed, watching the rocks for a sign of Scott.

Finally.

He moved slowly, picking his way across the wall, but he was headed her way. Evie waited for him at the gate. The fireboat had provided no specifics over the radio, and she was anxious to hear what he'd found at the end of the break wall. And anxious about him. Was he all right?

The lights were bright enough for her to see he was soaking wet, his leg was bloody and half his shirt was torn away. The expression on his face matched the rest of his grim appearance.

Evie laid a hand on his arm. "Are you all right?"

"Fine," he said. He shoved past her without even making eye contact.

"Scott, wait," she said, struggling to keep up with him as her feet sank in the sand.

He paused and turned toward her. "I'm going to make a report with the officer on duty tonight. Or do you want my report?"

"I'm in charge of safety," she said.

"Really? Then maybe you're the one who can tell me why a known hazard like that damned wall has no lights on it. Huh? Why, Evie? Would it kill the Starlight Point budget to make that wall safer?"

Evie stepped back. His rage vibrated from him in waves. She felt as if her lungs were empty and she couldn't breathe.

"Well, safety boss?" he asked. "You wouldn't be hesitating with your answer right now if you'd seen those two victims. There's no excuse for this. No excuse."

Scott swiveled and walked away from her, his shirt hanging off him. She followed right on his heels. In the merciless lights from the fire truck, she saw something that stopped her in her tracks. Scars. Mottled scars dimpling and puckering his flesh from his neck to his waist.

She gasped aloud, and Scott stopped.

"What?" he thundered.

She wanted to ask what had caused such major scarring. An accident?

Suddenly everything she had ever wondered about Scott came into brutal focus. Burns. His back was covered in burn scars.

But she couldn't ask about that. Not tonight.

"The wall," she said. Her voice sounded thin and unnatural. "It doesn't belong to Starlight Point."

"So?"

"It belongs to the Army Corps of Engineers. They built lighthouses and break walls all along the lakes years ago."

Scott crossed his arms and made eye contact. That, at least, was a good sign. He was listening.

"We've requested lights. Reported the accidents. But they say the light at the end meets the minimum requirement. Case closed, according to them, and they won't budge."

Scott opened his mouth but didn't get to say whatever he was going to say. Caroline had noticed he was back and she raced over and hugged him.

"You big dummy," she said. "I hope you're happy now that you're a big hero."

"I'm not a hero," he said. "The fireboat got there two minutes after I did."

"Why are you wet?" she asked, recoiling and looking down at her soaked shirt.

"Fell in the lake."

He took the radio off his belt and handed it to Evie. "Sorry," he said. "It's probably ruined."

Evie took the radio, her fingers brushing his for a moment. "I may be better off without it, anyway."

"You go back to your dorm," Scott said to his sister. "Or the party, whatever you want."

"Dorm. I'm changing my wet shirt before I go anywhere."

"I'm going to write up the report on this and go home. I don't think they'll let me back into the party looking like this."

Caroline hugged her brother one more time, kissed him on the cheek and said goodnight.

"We'll take down the lights and meet you back at the station in a few," one of the other firefighters said to Evie. "You can get a ride with us if you want."

"We'll walk," Evie said. She glanced at Scott's leg and second-guessed herself. "Is your leg okay? Would you rather ride?"

"I'm fine," he said, his voice hardly more civilized than a growl.

Scott started walking across the sand toward the Starlight Point fire station. Located near the back of the park, it was only a short distance from the hotel and the beach.

Evie caught up with him. "You have to talk to me," she said. "Tell me what happened to those boaters."

"They hit the wall," Scott said. "A wall they couldn't see in the dark because somebody thinks the bare minimum lighting is good enough. The woman probably has a broken arm, and her companion has at least a head injury and possible internal injuries and broken bones."

"But they'll live," Evie said. "Right?"

"Probably."

"I'm sorry they were hurt."

"Are you sorry enough to fix the problem?"

"I told you, it's not my wall. And we have tried. The Army Corps of Engineers says it fulfills the safety code, so it's good enough."

"Good enough?" Scott said. "Just like your renovation plans for the old part of the hotel. The fire safety precautions meet the code. Barely. But they're good enough."

Evie felt as if she had been slapped. Was this the holdup on approving her plans? They did meet the code. Her construction supervisor and architect had assured her of it. But there was something Scott Bennett didn't like.

"What do you mean?" she asked. Her voice was a strangled whisper.

"You're skirting along the edge. You don't have to bring that old barn up to code, so you're cutting corners. Ask Harlan about it if you want."

Scott stalked across the beach boardwalk and cut through the hotel grounds. With her long legs, Evie kept up with him. When they passed the hotel and were again in darkness along the outer loop, she grabbed his arm and forced him to a stop.

He waited, breathing heavily, but at least he stood still. They were alone in the shadows. His muscled upper arm was hard under her hand. She put her other hand on his bare chest and felt it rise and fall. Scott didn't back away. Evie stepped closer. He still didn't move.

She had never wanted to kiss a person more in her entire life. Scott made her, the rational accountant and number-cruncher, feel irrational. Dangerous. She had been resisting the feeling all summer, but tonight her nerves were stretched thin.

She shifted her hand to his shoulder and dug her fingers in, but when she did she felt the knotted scars under her fingers.

Scott flinched.

"Tell me what happened," she whispered.

"I already did," he said. His voice was low and husky. He ran a hand through her loose hair from her temple around to the back of her neck. His touch was sensuous, intoxicating. He had to feel the same thing she did.

"I don't mean what happened tonight," she said.

Scott dipped his head toward hers and their lips nearly brushed. His eyes were so dark she couldn't tell what he was thinking.

Without adding up the risk and reward factors, Evie touched her lips to his. She closed her eyes. A contrast to the cool night air, his lips were soft and warm. Even better than she'd imagined.

And Scott was kissing her back. One of his hands was on the back of her neck and the other gently cradled her cheek. It was easy to forget they had ever argued as their lips forged a bond between them.

Evie had kissed men before, a few brief flirtations during her college years. But her complicated relationship with Scott made this kiss more dangerous and wonderful than all her previous ones combined.

She touched his cheek with one hand while the other moved over the bare flesh on his back. Without thinking, she traced one of the burn scars with her finger.

Suddenly, Scott took a hard step back and broke their contact. "This is a mistake," he said.

"Why?" Although Evie could come up with several reasons herself—and probably would tomorrow when she reviewed this incident in the light of day—she wanted to hear from Scott's own lips why kissing her was a mistake.

He crossed both arms over his chest as if he were guarding a relic. "If you want to know about the scars on my back, I'll tell you just one thing about them. They're the reason I do my job."

He stormed off, but Evie stood still.

What had caused those terrible scars?

She watched him recede into the night before she turned around and faced her hotel. The massive ancient wing scheduled for demolition loomed before her.

She stumbled toward a bench on the hotel grounds and sat among the gray shadows. They reminded her of the decisions she had faced all summer long. But there was no hiding in that gray area any longer, no matter how much she wished she could.

CHAPTER EIGHTEEN

WHEN EVIE LISTENED to her voice mail from Chief Portman of the Bayside Fire Department, nervous excitement raced through her. He wanted to meet with her about the plans for her hotel project. Said he wanted to explain something. But why was the message coming from the chief and not from Scott?

She was already at work at the Point, but her car was in the marina lot. The chief's message said he was on duty all day and would be happy to make time for her whenever she came in. Evie started the engine on her old car and headed across the bridge. No way could she wait. It was already July 31, and her target date for the press conference was only a week away.

If I have good news to tell the media. She didn't want to think about what would happen if there was bad news. A delay would cost her.

When she parked in the small lot next

to the fire station, she saw a familiar black pickup. Great. Scott was on duty. Was that why Chief Portman wanted her to come today? Would they both be at the meeting?

Evie walked through the open bay doors of the station. One fire truck was missing. Her heels clicked on the concrete, echoing in the silence. There were three doors to her right. Bunk room. Inspector's office. Chief's office. *The chief is the one who called me.*

Evie knocked on the door of the third office and waited. When the chief opened the door, Scott came out and passed Evie without even a glance. His face was flushed, mouth tight.

"Come in," Portman said. "Go ahead and shut the door if you don't mind."

Evie tried to keep her hands from shaking as she closed the door and approached the chair the chief was pointing to. His office was public-servant style, but considerably nicer than Scott's. It had a window. And the chair he offered her didn't tip her out. She flushed, remembering her encounter with Scott in his office. She wondered why he'd looked so angry just now.

"I appreciate you coming over here," Portman said. "I like to keep a good relationship with Starlight Point."

Evie smiled. *This was sounding promising.* "I appreciate that."

"Used to work there in the summers when I was young," Portman continued. "Great experience. Except for that crazy STRIPE program."

Evie laughed. "Dare I ask what you had to do?"

"Watercolor painting," he said, grimacing. "Can you believe that?"

"I can believe anything when it comes to that program. Did you make a successful painting?"

Chief Portman pointed behind Evie and she turned. A framed watercolor of a red fire truck hung on the wall. Despite the fuzzy lines and abstract nature of the work, at least it was recognizable.

"I like the Star Spiral in the background," Evie said.

"It was the easiest ride to paint. Just a tall straight line. Think it looks like a fire truck?"

"Absolutely. But you didn't give up firefighting to pursue a career as an artist?"

He shook his head. "I wish the STRIPE topic that summer was like the one you had this summer. Safety procedures and fire extinguishers would have been a lot more useful for me than doing that painting."

"Scott did a great job running the classes for us," Evie said. It was a nice opportunity to bring up his name and gauge Chief Portman's response. And she still wasn't sure why Scott wasn't part of this meeting.

"Not surprised. Bennett's a professional. A real detail person." The chief leaned back in his chair and rested his hands on his stomach. "I wonder if he volunteered or got drafted for that job."

"A little of both," Evie said.

"Sets him up nicely, in case he puts his hat in the ring for the chief's job over there."

Evie's nervousness about her plans switched immediately to surprise. The man who found fault with everything at the Point and probably only worked there to keep an eye on his sister might want a year-round job there? Would become part of the Starlight Point family? The thought had never crossed her mind. "Scott wants the chief's job when he retires?"

Portman raised both eyebrows. "You didn't know that?"

"No," she said. She looked at her hands.

"There's been no formal announcement or posting at all, so I guess it hasn't come up." She met the chief's eyes. She did not want to appear as if she didn't know what was going on at her own business.

"You probably want to hear about your hotel plans," Portman said. "Long story short, you've got the green light."

Evie sighed with relief. "I'm glad to hear it."

"Sorry the process took up most of the thirty days allotted. Almost took longer when Bennett walked away from the job."

If Chief Portman doesn't stop dropping bombshells on me, I'm going to need one of those ambulances parked in the bay.

"You didn't know he refused to sign off on these, did you?"

"No," Evie said. "Did he give a reason?"

"Conflict of interest. That's all I got out of him."

"I see," Evie said. Five minutes ago she would have thought the conflict involved his feelings toward her. But now that she knew he wanted the job of her retiring fire chief, she realized her assessment of him had been all wrong. The shreds of kindness, emotion,

even vulnerability she'd seen from him—
they were never about her. *Ouch*.

She was a fool to think they ever were.

The chief pulled papers out of his desk
drawer and laid them in front of her. "As I
told you in my message, I just wanted to explain a few things before you get your project started."

Evie swallowed her disappointment and
focused on the future. Her plans. Her hotel.
Her role as an equal and important partner at
Starlight Point. Whatever she thought might
have passed between her and Scott was obviously her imagination, and she would do
well to remember her goals, personal and
professional.

*I made fun of Jack two years ago and June
last year for letting a summer romance go to
their heads. And look at me.*

She squared her shoulders and put her
hands on the desk, palms down in a power
gesture. *I'm going to have more to show for
this summer than a foolish infatuation.*

"The plan for the grounds with the utilities
and water lines looks fine. Your construction manager and architect did their jobs.
These—" he pointed to the drawing of the
hotel "—also look good. With new construc-

tion, there's not a lot of gray area. Fire codes and building plans for new occupied structures are straightforward."

"That's great news. Thank you," Evie said. She felt the *but* coming. "What can you tell me about my renovation plans? Can I order the new ceiling tiles and wallpaper yet?" She smiled, trying to keep the meeting light and prevent her coffee from burning an acid hole in her stomach.

"Trickier," he said. "Technically the hotel's old enough it doesn't have to adhere to modern codes. You run into trouble when you do a substantial renovation. Go over a certain percentage of changes and you fall under the new rules."

"Have I gone over that percentage?" she asked.

He shook his head. "No, your changes look to be pretty cosmetic. Not everyone likes the extra chases you added through walls to accommodate updated plumbing and wiring."

By not everyone, did he mean Scott?

"And not everyone likes the dropped ceiling you're adding in the lobby. And the false wall by the elevator shaft."

"And what do you think of those?"

Chief Portman shrugged. "Doesn't matter what I think. They meet code. I'm here to determine that and that only."

Evie leaned close to the drawing and saw red marks slashed across the items the chief just mentioned. "Did someone else make these marks?" she asked.

He nodded.

It was obvious who that person was. Evie wanted to be mad at Scott. He had nearly stood in the way of her professional plans. As it was, he'd delayed the approval for days, possibly weeks, with his stubbornness. And he could have ruined her chances for starting the project on time by forcing delays or revisions. But he hadn't. Instead he'd turned the plans over to someone else.

Why?

"Thank you for stepping in and approving my plans," Evie told Chief Portman. "I appreciate it and I'm happy to be able to set the project in motion."

"You've got a lot going on over there at the Point," he commented.

Oh, no, not the "for someone so young" lecture again.

"And I wish you the best," he concluded. "What's good for Starlight Point is good for the whole area."

Evie was tempted to ask him if that's why he'd approved the plans, but she didn't want to open that door. Besides, her drawings met code. As he said himself, his only job was to determine that.

Apparently, Scott saw things differently.

WHY DIDN'T I go out on that smoke alarm call an hour ago?

Watching Evie arrive to meet with the chief and get her approved set of plans was one of the most painful things he'd endured in his life.

Scott sat in his tiny office next to the chief's. He could hear nothing through the wall, but he left his door open just a crack so he'd hear Evie leave. Then it would be safe to vacate his office.

After only twenty minutes he heard Evie say thank-you and listened to her heels clicking as she walked out of the fire station. He counted to ten to be sure she was gone, and only then did he go out and start the project the chief had assigned him. Because one of their rescue trucks was scheduled for service, they needed to move some of the equipment into a different truck. Just in case.

Scott picked up a heavy set of hydraulic

cutters used for extricating car accident victims. He carried them toward one of the ambulances with the intention of stowing them in an outside compartment. But he didn't get there.

Clicking heels echoed in the station. *She was back? Why? Hadn't she already got what she wanted?*

She was standing right behind him. But he took his time settling the equipment into its temporary home before he turned around.

Instead of looking triumphant, she resembled a wayward child who'd gone home to ask for money.

"My car won't start," she said.

"I thought Mel fixed it for you."

Evie's shoulders slumped. "I thought so, too. He put in a new battery a few weeks ago, but now it won't start."

Scott leaned against the ambulance and crossed his arms. Evie was his boss. Evie was the reason he'd put his job on the line with the chief, who was also his boss. Evie was the woman who'd been driving him crazy all summer long and making him dig deep for reasons to push her away when all he wanted to do was pull her into his arms.

Loving her was not an option. It left him

vulnerable, made him put his feelings for her ahead of his passion for his work. Without the single-minded goal that had driven him and soothed his emotional scars for years, what did he have left?

And now she needed him.

When did my life get this complicated?

"Just a minute," he said. He walked over to his chief's office and leaned in.

"Evie's car won't start. If you need me, I'll be in the parking lot trying to help her out."

Chief Portman glanced up and grinned. "You're a hell of a guy, Bennett."

Scott felt bottled-up emotion closing his throat. What did his boss mean by that? Without replying, he turned and headed for the parking lot. He heard Evie's steps clicking behind him.

He made his way straight to the baby blue car, opened the door and popped the hood latch. The key was still in the ignition and he reached in and turned it, just in case.

"I told you that didn't work," Evie said. She looked irritated. Tapped her foot.

Good.

"I thought it might like me better," he said.

She cocked her head to the side and almost smiled.

Scott raised the hood and propped it open. Checked the battery cable connections. Fished his own truck keys from his pocket and clicked it unlocked.

"Are you leaving?" Evie asked.

"Bringing my truck over so I can use it to jump your car. Unless you have a better idea."

He didn't wait for an answer. Scott nosed his truck up to her car, hooked up the jumper cables and got her car started. He let it run while he put away the cables and backed his truck into its space again.

He closed her hood and kept both hands on it. It was a safe thing to do when he was tempted to touch her.

"Thank you. I don't know what drained the battery," she said. "I didn't leave the lights on, and it seemed okay when I drove here this morning."

Scott walked past Evie and leaned in the open driver's window. He switched on the headlights and took a lap around the car.

"I thought you had your taillight fixed."

"I did."

He used his large hands to shade the light and look at it closely. "It's out again. Which explains a lot. I think you have a short somewhere, which took out your light and drained your battery. You need someone to go through the electrical system or this will probably keep happening."

"Great," Evie said miserably.

Again Scott wondered why she drove such a junker, but he wasn't likely to ever unlock the mysteries of the Hamilton family.

"It's the little things you don't see just below the surface that cause you the most trouble," Scott said.

Like covering up the decrepit parts in your old hotel instead of rebuilding it the right way.

"I know what you're talking about," she said. She gestured to the hotel plans lying on the passenger seat of her car. "I'm sure you disapprove of my car, my hotel and everything else I do. But I'm too tired and busy right now to fight for your approval."

"You don't have to fight for my approval," he said. *If you only knew what I feel for you.* He cleared his throat. "But you should get your car fixed right or this will happen again."

Evie opened the door and got in. "I think I'll go back to taking the ferry to work. It runs every day and the only thing I have to think about is where to sit."

Scott leaned in her window. "I thought you liked planning things. Making decisions."

Evie put both hands on the wheel as if it were a life ring thrown to a drowning swimmer. "It's a lot more complicated than I ever would have thought."

CHAPTER NINETEEN

June and Evie greeted guests at the door of the Lake Breeze Hotel. A hot mid-August day, members of the press and media looked relieved to enter the air-conditioned lobby where a reception announcing the renovation of the old hotel awaited them.

"Good call on the red dress," June commented to her sister. "Power color."

Evie laughed. "Clearly I have acquired immense clout this summer."

"You have. You opened the marina and got the hotel project started after we'd just talked about it for years. Plus, you're the only one of us three who isn't in crazy baby land."

"Behold the magnitude of rational thought," Evie said.

"You're always the most rational one. Although I did think you might have been distracted by a certain firefighter for a while."

Evie smiled and shook hands with a local reporter, glad for the interruption. The certain firefighter mentioned by her sister hadn't crossed Evie's path in a week. Clearly, she wasn't a conflict of interest for him anymore. He had not been on the late-night ferry. When she'd responded to two ambulance calls in the park—both minor health issues—he had not been on duty at either one. His truck had not been parked in the fire station lot at Starlight Point when she'd zoomed by on a park scooter. Every day.

"Minor distraction," she admitted to her sister. "More of a complication. And now that I have my plans approved, I don't even have to be nice to him anymore."

June gave Evie a raised-eyebrow look and crossed her arms over her chest.

"I mean it," Evie said.

"But I thought you said he wasn't the one who approved the plans in the end."

Evie shook her head. "He wasn't. The fire chief at Bayside did it himself because Captain Bennett believed he had a conflict of interest."

"Humph," June said.

"What?"

"What was the conflict of interest?"

Good question. "Because he worked here, I suppose."

"But he's worked here all year. Including when he tore up our marina plans. And when he nearly closed the employee dorms."

"He didn't tear up the marina plans," Evie said.

"Fine." June huffed. "He loved the marina plans. Either way, why the conflict now?"

Evie and June left their post by the door and walked into the hotel lobby. The rotunda area had been converted for the day into a pressroom. The wicker couches and settees had been shoved back against the walls. Tables covered with white cloths held crystal glasses and trays of tempting finger foods. Local newspapers, media influencers and even the television station from Detroit were on hand to see the drawings and hear details about the hotel renovation.

Evie took a small white plate from a stack on a table and began filling it with fruit and desserts.

"You're not even going to eat that," June said. "You look calm, but I know you're too nervous. And you won't want food on your teeth for your big speech."

Evie held out the plate. "I was filling this for you. I thought you might want to eat instead of talking about Scott."

June grabbed the plate. "One more thing. If Scott was going to back out, anyway, because of some recently discovered conflict of interest—" she pointed at Evie with her spare hand "—it wasn't very nice of him to hold up the process for so long. You're dancing pretty close to your deadline at this point in the season."

Evie shrugged. "It doesn't matter now. Full steam ahead." She checked the time on her phone. "Only a few more minutes until the big reveal."

"You'll be great," June said. "I'm going to check on our big brother and make sure he's staying awake over there."

June, still dancer-slim with hardly a bump alluding to her January baby, delivered a glass of champagne to Jack and the editor of the local paper. The three of them stood by the table where framed diagrams were draped with cloths.

Speech time, Evie thought, moving to the podium. This was the moment she'd been dreaming of all summer long. At the end of her speech, she would reveal the diagrams and hand out press releases with complete details.

"Thank you for coming," Evie said. She

raised her voice to get the attention of the people in the room, but she wouldn't need a microphone because of the acoustics in the rotunda. The reporters and invited guests standing around with drinks formed a semicircle and silenced their conversations.

"For the second time this summer, we're pleased to host you as we continue our capital improvement projects here at Starlight Point."

Evie had a folded program in her hand. She'd memorized her speech, but she was glad to have something to hold on to. Her hands were damp with nerves. The butterflies in her chest were like the feeling she got whenever she stood too close to Scott. Or thought about him.

What would he think of her grand unveiling of the renovation plans? Sadly, she already knew. The red marks on the original plans were painfully clear. But he'd been overruled by his boss.

"I'm pleased to tell you the marina is practically overflowing. Docks are filled, the restaurant is booked solid, and we'd like to thank you, the media, for spreading the word about it." The reporters clapped. Smiles all around. *This is going very well so far.* "Your press kit includes a coupon for a dinner for two at the marina restaurant to show our appreciation. But you might want to call ahead and reserve a table."

Evie took a moment to glance around the rotunda. Her siblings were impressed with her planning and execution. The marina project was such a success, her mother had begun hanging out on the family boat with her dog, just to be close to the action. *I should be happy.* But there was a long way to go before her visions were realized. That's why they were here today.

"As you may know, the Lake Breeze Hotel has graced the shoreline here for over a century. It's had a few changes over the years, but my plans are the most substantial since President Eisenhower was in office."

A few members of the press chuckled. Evie reminded herself to smile. This was the grand occasion she had been anticipating for over a year, ever since she had convinced her partners to let her explore ideas and funding.

"Our hotel refurbishing is a two-part project. Part one," she said, pausing for effect as she placed one hand on the white cloth covering a large, framed picture. "The wings behind the hotel are showing their age. They were not part of the original structure and never reflected the quality and grace of the rest of the hotel. Starting next week, we're tearing them down."

A murmur went through the crowd. Evie had been thinking about the demolition for so long, she was surprised by the reaction of people who were hearing the dramatic news for the first time.

"But don't worry," she said. "We're going to rebuild them throughout the winter."

She pulled the covering off the framed drawing and the crowd moved closer. The artist's rendering depicted the new buildings and their beach-hotel design. Because they were separate from the main hotel, the drawing featured gardens, pathways and a courtyard uniting the structures.

"Instead of two stories, they'll now have three stories so we can increase our overall room count. And building a new structure allows us to include completely new amenities. The buildings have the look of an old-fashioned seaside resort, but you'll find modern comfort inside. New furnishings, world-class technology and the kind of luxurious comfort our guests and their families expect."

A reporter raised his hand and Evie acknowledged him with a nod.

"Are you tearing down the attached wings and rebuilding them, too?"

Evie looked around the room, almost expecting Scott to show up and protest.

"Not exactly. The attached wings will be renovated extensively, along with the rest of the original hotel, including the part we're standing in right now."

A reporter directly in front of Evie frowned.

"I know what you may be thinking," she said, raising a hand and smiling reassuringly. "Don't worry. We are still keeping our place on the historic register because the changes are cosmetic and functional. Not architectural."

The reporter smiled and nodded. Evie breathed. Despite Scott's bullying about the fire code, she was gratified that someone else recognized the value of cosmetic renovation. Even if he was a reporter from a tiny paper an hour away.

"All the elegance we love about this historic building will remain, it'll just be improved," Evie said. She uncovered the next framed picture and the crowd moved a few steps closer. Cameras flashed.

Judging from their expressions, they liked it. What a relief. Although she'd been bolstered by the success of the marina project, Evie still awoke in the night worrying that her grand plans for putting her stamp on Starlight Point would fall flat and cost her family their livelihood and their legacy.

"Your press kit contains details," Evie said after the reporters had perused the drawing and taken pictures of her standing by it. "But I'm happy to take any questions you have right now."

"How many total rooms will you have on property next year?" one reporter asked.

"Three hundred rooms in the hotel," Evie said. "That's eighty more than we have now, and some of them are suites and family rooms."

"Do you think you'll have the project done when the park opens in May?" another reporter asked.

"That's the plan. And that's why we're starting the tear-down of the back wings next week. We need to work on the site itself and outdoor construction before winter. We can move indoors when the bad weather comes."

Evie removed another covering. "Here's an artist's rendering of the lobby and rotunda." The new stamped-tin ceiling and carousel décor added to the old-fashioned summer resort theme. Guests would feel like they'd stepped back in time, but they would still enjoy wireless internet wherever they went.

With her official speaking role finished, Evie wandered among the reporters and bloggers, answering their questions. Some hotel guests wandered through and stopped to look at the drawings. Evie overheard them talking about returning next year to stay in the renovated hotel. *Exactly my plan.*

She and her siblings stayed until the last reporter left and then they split up to get back to work.

In her capacity as safety manager, Evie decided to walk by the fire station since she was in the vicinity. As she approached, she saw that the two scooters and all the fire trucks were lined up. Although the afternoon was hot and sunny, her radio—a new one after the boat accident on the break wall—had been quiet since she'd switched it back on after the press conference.

Chief Harlan had the hood up on the pumper truck.

"I hope the truck's not broken," Evie said as she came up behind him.

He turned and smiled at her. "Just checking the oil, boss."

Evie laughed. "You can't call me boss, not when you've worked here longer than I have."

Harlan wiped the oil off a dipstick with a paper towel and slid it into the engine. He pulled it out one more time and checked the fluid level.

"Won't be long and you'll be breaking in a new chief here," he said.

Evie sat on the bumper. "Any suggestions?"

Chief Harlan closed the hood and sat next to her. "I did have one good candidate, but I guess he decided working here is not for him."

Evie felt her chest hollow out. "Who?"

"Scott Bennett."

"Are you saying he doesn't like working here?"

The chief shrugged. "Guess not. He took himself off the schedule last week, and processed out at human resources a few days ago. His name tag's on my desk."

How did I not know this?

"I thought you knew," the chief said.

"I'm not in charge of human resources. Just safety and resorts."

"Just," he said, grinning.

"And I've been preoccupied with the hotel renovation. Apparently, I didn't notice we're down one firefighter." Evie tried to think and sound practical. "Do I need to see about replacing him, or can we limp by the rest of the season?"

"We'll get by. Some of the younger guys who need the paycheck have stepped up and picked up an extra shift. And the park's only open a few more weeks."

Evie ran her fingers over the rough, expanded metal of the bumper. Why had Scott quit? Especially if he had any interest in the job of fire chief. Had he ever mentioned the chief's job to her? No. She'd heard about it from Chief Portman. Had she just assumed that was the conflict of interest? *What if that wasn't the conflict?*

"When does the hotel demo start?" the chief asked.

Evie snapped her mind back to the present. "Soon. A couple of days. We've moved guests into the main building for the remainder of the season. My construction boss has the demo crew lined up to start Friday."

"Want me to keep a fire truck and crew with them as they tear down?"

Evie cocked her head to the side and looked at the chief. "Is that customary?"

"It's not a bad idea. Demolition involves cutting torches, sparks and usually a few surprises."

"I didn't think of that. You're pretty close here as it is."

"True," he agreed. "We're only a minute away."

"And since you're down one guy, maybe it would be hard to cover the park and the demolition project," Evie said.

"You're probably right. I'll keep an eye out over there, but keep my men and equipment here for now. Unless I see something that changes my mind."

"I'll leave it up to your judgment." Evie put a hand on his shoulder. "Thank you. And thank you for everything you've done over the years. You've been the chief here all my life."

"You're welcome. But don't start getting sentimental. You have to save some of that for my retirement party."

CHAPTER TWENTY

EVIE AND HER mother walked along the waterfront in Bayside with Jack and Augusta's new baby in the stroller. Nora was almost a month old, and Virginia had decided the new parents could use a night out. Evie decided new-baby smell was better than lonely-office smell, so she'd taken the evening off to join her mother and niece for dinner downtown.

"Augusta packed us enough stuff in this diaper bag to survive five days instead of five hours," Virginia said.

Evie laughed. "Maybe they need a five-day vacation."

"Wouldn't have any fun," Virginia declared. "Jack would probably sleep the whole time."

"He's managing better than I thought he would," Evie said. "There's been almost no complaining about night feedings and diaper changes. I think he's happy being a dad."

"That's probably because Augusta is doing all the work."

The evening light was layered with colors from the sun slowly sinking across the bay. Boats bobbed in the harbor and the Starlight Point ferry was just leaving on one of its many scheduled trips.

Evie's car was in the shop and the mechanics were taking their time chasing down the electrical problem. Not that she was in a hurry to get the old beast back in her parking space. Even when and if the car worked again, she planned to keep taking the ferry on days with good weather. The ride was relaxing, and it gave her perspective as she approached Starlight Point in the morning and sailed away at night.

They walked the length of the harbor, pausing a few times so Evie could take pictures of her niece with her cell phone. She sent a picture to Augusta with a reassuring note. The image of Nora peacefully sleeping in the stroller would, Evie hoped, help Augusta and Jack enjoy their evening out without worrying.

"Only a few weeks left in the season," Virginia commented. "It's always bittersweet to see Labor Day come."

Evie nodded. "I know what you mean. I used to think the end of summer was sad because it meant I had to go back to school or college, but now I see it differently."

"I was always sorry when you kids had to go back to homework and peer pressure and all that stuff. Not that any of you had any problems." She smiled at Evie and touched her hair. "All my kids are smart and know their own minds. Especially you."

Evie laughed. "Do I? I think you already know that's been my big struggle all summer. Should I keep track of our money and be an accountant, or be a visionary and see how fast I can spend it?"

"You've spent it wisely," her mother said. "The marina and now the hotel."

"We'll have to wait until next May to see if the hotel is a wise investment."

"It will be."

They stopped walking and Evie leaned on a railing along the water. Starlight Point sparkled just across the water. The lights on the Ferris wheel swirled, and those on the tracks of the roller coasters flashed. When the sun went down, they would be even brighter.

"I hope I haven't made a mistake at the hotel," Evie said.

Virginia set the hand brake on the stroller and leaned next to Evie on the railing.

"There were tough choices," Evie continued, glad to air her concerns. "How much of the old character to save, how much to tear down, how many rooms to build, how much can we afford in hopes it'll pay off."

Her mother shrugged. "I think you did a great job. I've seen the plans and drawings. No one could find fault."

"Even with the renovations in the old part? You don't think I'm just prettying it up instead of making more substantial changes that might be necessary in the long run?"

"That hotel has been fine for years. If you want to give it a new coat of lipstick, you can't go wrong."

"One of the fire inspectors didn't like my changes. He wanted to see the walls opened up and a whole new sprinkler system installed."

"That sounds expensive," Virginia said. "And time-consuming. I think I'd be afraid to see inside those old walls."

Evie laughed. "Me, too. So I went with the bare minimum on the fire system, basically sticking with what we already have there. It meets code."

"So?"

"It could be better," Evie admitted. "I know that. But the money I save by going a less expensive route—we're talking over a million here—I was thinking of using that to improve or replace the employee dorms."

"I see," Virginia said.

"I think those dorms are important. I'm just trying to decide what brings us the most return."

"I know you'll do the right thing. With you and your brother and sister running the place, I don't have to worry. And I'm very glad to hand over all my cares and spend my time being a grandmother now."

Once they reached the end of the boardwalk, Evie and Virginia turned back toward downtown and the harborfront. In addition to the docks and a few restaurants, the downtown area had a mix of buildings facing the water. The tall building where Evie lived on the third floor and the bakery took up the bottom floor. A newer lawyer's office across the street with an all-glass façade that suggested the lawyers were doing pretty well. A police station on one side of the city park and the fire station on the other.

As they approached the fire station, the

baby started fussing. Virginia stopped and picked her up, but quickly made a face.

"Do you smell that?" she asked. "Somebody needs a fresh diaper."

"Let's go up to my apartment," Evie suggested. "It'll be a lot easier to change her there."

Virginia laid the fussing baby back in the stroller and they started walking a little faster. As they passed the fire station, Evie noticed the big doors were open to the fresh evening breeze. Two firefighters were sitting on the bench. One of them was reading the newspaper and the other was looking directly at her.

She hadn't seen Scott Bennett in almost two weeks, not since the day he'd started her car and lectured her about doing things right. The same day she had received approval for her plans. Against his wishes.

If he read the newspaper like his friend was doing, he'd know she'd had her big press conference and unveiling. Might even have seen the pictures of her and the artist's renderings of the new construction and renovations.

That probably explains his frown.

"There's our STRIPE sergeant," Virginia said, waving cheerfully at Scott.

His face softened and he got off the bench. *He's walking toward us.*

Now that he didn't work for her anymore, Evie thought, there was nothing stopping him from unleashing a righteous defense of the fire code according to God.

"You did such a wonderful job," Virginia said as Scott came up. "We were lucky to have you."

"Thank you," he said. He frowned. "I guess you heard I quit."

Virginia tilted her head and looked puzzled. "What did you quit?"

"My job at the Point."

"You did? I was talking about the STRIPE program."

Scott put his hands behind his back and shifted his feet. He glanced up and made eye contact with Evie.

If he thinks I'm going to explain his decision to my mother, he's out of his mind. Especially since I don't know what's going on in his mind.

"Why did you quit working at the Point?" Virginia asked. Evie had known she would. Her mother was not the type to let things go.

The baby started sputtering and waving her arms, working herself up to a full-blown crying fit. "I better get Nora up to your apartment and change her," Virginia said.

"I'll do it," Evie volunteered. "You can stay here and talk with Scott about why he quit, and I'll be right back."

Virginia shook her head and started pushing the stroller. "I'm no longer in charge at the Point," she said to Evie. "But you are."

She walked away, moving quickly as the baby's screaming gained momentum. Scott's partner folded his newspaper and disappeared inside the station.

"Why do you care why I quit my job at the Point?" Scott asked bluntly.

"I don't," Evie said. "My mother was the one asking questions."

Scott stared at his feet. Crossed his arms. Turned and looked behind him as if backup were available.

"She's like that," Evie continued. "One time, a girl dumped my brother with the standard 'it's not you, it's me' line and my mother called her out on it. Wanted to know what was wrong with the girl."

Scott's lips twitched and his shoulders relaxed. "So what was wrong with her?"

"Nothing. Except that she wanted to date the captain of the basketball team."

"Not your brother?"

"Even though Jack is six foot four, he can't play basketball to save his life," Evie said. "I guess you can't make assumptions about people."

"Do people make assumptions about you, Evie?" Scott asked. His voice was gentle, barely carrying to her as she stood four feet away.

Evie had had no plans to force a showdown with the man who had been driving her crazy all summer long. But since he had quit his job, and his connection to the Point through his sister would be ending soon, maybe it was now or never.

"They do make assumptions," she said. "Recently a man assumed that since I want to keep a historic hotel mostly the way it is, I must not care about fire safety."

The gentle expression disappeared and Scott's face set into hard lines.

"This same man never gave me a chance to explain my position," Evie said. "Never asked me if I had a reason."

"Did you have a reason?" he asked.

"Since you backed out of your duty to review the plans, and then you quit your job at the Point without saying a word to me, I don't think I owe you an explanation now."

Scott swallowed hard. His ears reddened. One eye twitched. Evie had struck a major nerve.

"I don't have to explain why I quit that job," he muttered.

"You're right. You probably don't need to tell me, anyway. I can guess."

"What?"

"This shouldn't be too hard," she said. She crossed her arms and paced as if she were an attorney cross-examining a witness in court. "You think my family's business is lackadaisical when it comes to your precious fire codes."

"They are not my codes."

"Ah, but you think they are. I bet you sleep with a copy under your pillow," Evie said.

Scott said nothing.

"You hated my hotel plans, and you wanted to reject them even though there was technically nothing wrong with them. Rather than reject them and risk getting fired when I realized you were bullying me, you bowed out, citing a conflict of interest." Evie's voice rose but she tried to temper it. They were outdoors on a beautiful evening. People were walking by. Scott was on the clock, a public servant.

A muscle worked in Scott's jaw and a red flush spread over his neck. *Struck another nerve with the conflict of interest thing.*

"What do you know about that?"

"I only know what your chief said. He thought the conflict of interest might be because you wanted the chief's job at Starlight Point when he retires."

"I don't."

"I figured that out since you quit and killed your chances. But I do wonder why you had to hand over your inspector's job to someone else and then hand in your name tag at the Point if getting the chief's job was not your motivation. Not your supposed conflict of interest."

Scott shoved his hands in his pockets and said nothing.

"If staying on my good side as your boss wasn't the source of your conflict," Evie asked, her voice softened to a low tone, "what was it?"

She knew what she hoped it was.

Scott stepped closer and spoke in a gruff tone. "I don't work for you anymore. You've got your plans approved. You got what you wanted. But I won't be called a bully."

Something in his expression made Evie feel like she had just kicked a puppy. He cast his eyes downward. The color in his ears and neck faded.

"I'm not a bully," he said. "I never intended to make your life difficult with the marina plans or the hotel plans. In fact, I wanted to make your job easier every step of the way. But I couldn't."

What is he saying?

"Everything I have worked for, insisted on, and been difficult about, was for a reason," he said.

His voice was so quiet he was practically whispering.

"You once asked me how I got the scars on my back. I'm giving you a chance to back out now if you don't want to hear this."

She had to hear this. Had to know what drove Scott. Wanted to understand him, the man who made her feel things she'd never felt before. The man who wouldn't budge on following the fire code to the end of the earth, but treated his sister and victims of medical emergencies with almost painful kindness.

"Tell me."

Scott turned and faced the water, looking off in the distance. "My father was a businessman. Sales, consulting…things like that. He traveled a lot when I was a kid. Sometimes, for a treat, my family would go with him. My mom, my two sisters and me." He emphasized the word *two*.

I couldn't lose you, too. Evie vividly remembered his words to Caroline on the bridge the day of the accident. What had happened to the other sister?

"We were in Nashville for one of my dad's sales conventions. My older sister, Catherine, was twelve. She used to do a lot of babysitting for other families and my mom trusted her to watch me and Caroline. I was seven, but Caroline was only a baby."

He paused. Swallowed. Continued to focus on the water instead of looking at Evie. She was glad. She wanted to cry just imagining what he was going to tell her. If she looked him in the eye right now, she would cry.

"It was a cheap hotel. Old, with flimsy walls, but it was still like a vacation in my mind. My parents were invited to a dinner with my dad's company and they would be gone for hours. It was a boring awards dinner or something like that. My sister and I were happy to stay in the room where we could watch television and feel like grown-ups."

Scott raked his fingers through his short, dark hair. Rubbed the back of his neck.

"The people in the room next door left a cigarette burning when they went to dinner. Same dinner my parents were going to because the guy was a business partner of my dad's. I think everyone in that wing of the hotel must have been going to the same place, because there was no one around later when we needed them."

"Oh, Scott. I'm so sorry," Evie murmured.

"Caroline was asleep in a playpen and Catherine went into the bathroom to take a shower. I was watching cartoons and not paying attention to anything else. We'd been playing in the hotel pool all afternoon and I was so tired I must have fallen asleep. I never noticed the burning smell."

Scott's chest heaved, his breathing quickened. Evie wanted to go to him and put her arms around him. Protect him from what had happened, from what he was about to tell her.

She moved closer to him and put a hand on his arm. She, too, faced the water, afraid to see his face right now.

"There were no working smoke detectors in that lousy hotel. No sprinklers in the rooms or hallways because it had been built before they were required."

Evie's knees weakened. Her stomach was in her throat. *Too old.* Like the Lake Breeze Hotel.

"Catherine was in the bathroom forever, taking her time because she was twelve and we were on vacation. I remember seeing her wearing my mom's lipstick when she came out. She was singing and woke me up. Of course, she was older than I was and as soon as she got out of the bathroom she realized something was wrong. She ran over and felt the wall, saw the smoke seeping through the crack under the adjoining door. The room next door was on fire. We grabbed Caroline and opened our room door, but the hallway was already filled with smoke."

Tears stung Evie's eyes. "What did you do?" she asked, her voice barely a whisper.

"Panicked. We were afraid to go into the smoky hallway. Catherine put me and Caroline in the bathtub because she thought we would be safe there." He paused and shook his head. "The fire spread so fast. Caroline was under me in the bathtub, and Catherine got on top. The tub was cold and damp. I remember how cold it was. We huddled like that, scared to death. Three little kids. I remember my sister's voice in my ear telling me to be brave and then the shower curtain catching fire and falling on us."

Scott turned and faced Evie. As long as she lived, she believed she would never forget the look in his eyes. Regret, misery, sorrow.

"The plastic shower curtain caused most of my burns. Catherine had it worse. Between the burns and the smoke, she didn't make it."

Scott took a long, shuddering breath.

"When the firefighters knocked down the flames and found us, they said it was a miracle Caroline and I survived."

Evie could hardly breathe. She didn't know what to say. It *was* a miracle that Scott and Caroline were alive, but what a terrible price their sister had paid.

An alarm sounded in the station and Scott snapped his attention to the dispatcher's voice audible through the open door.

He turned his attention back to Evie. "I told you my reason for the way I am, the way I do my job. But you haven't told me yours. I haven't heard your reason for those hotel plans I supposedly bullied you about."

She felt as if he had pulled a rug from underneath her and left her flat on the ground. She stood on the concrete, her hands and knees trembling.

Scott loped into the station and stepped into his boots. Pulled up the bunker pants. Slipped on the turnout coat. Grabbed his helmet and climbed in a fire truck. He got in the driver's seat and pulled out of the bay. His partner hit the siren and the truck flew past Evie, the rush of wind and noise nearly knocking her off balance.

How does he do it? Race off to fight the same demons that had cost him a sister and left him scarred for life?

He cared about saving people and protecting his sister more than anything else in the world, yet he had given up the chance to reject her plans and he had given up his job at the point.

Why?

CHAPTER TWENTY-ONE

ALTHOUGH THERE WAS no one she trusted more than her brother and sister, Evie dreaded revealing her change of plans. Adding a sprinkler system to an old building meant knocking down walls. Was she opening herself up to more trouble than she could handle?

"Do we have an extra million and a half bucks?" Jack asked after she'd informed them of her revised proposal.

"No," Evie said. "Not exactly."

"How much do we have exactly?"

Evie shoved her rolling chair back from her desk. "How much can we borrow is a better question."

June yawned. "Before I take my morning nap, can someone please tell me when we're going to stop bleeding money and start making some? Babies are expensive. I'm beginning to worry."

Jack opened the lid on the white bakery box and peered inside.

"Any answers in there?" Evie asked.

"Everything's round like all the zeroes in the millions you're spending."

Evie turned her computer monitor so her siblings could see it. "There's good debt and bad debt."

"Which kind do we have?" June asked.

"Both. We have the bad kind left over from dad's overly optimistic borrowing. When we refinanced last year, we started to look better on paper. We have a plan in place for managing the old debt."

Evie pointed out the pie chart on her screen. "The red represents bad debt. The blue slice is yearly expenditures. The green slice is yearly revenue. If you look at the side-by-side from last year, you see the green is up and the red is down. We've managed to keep the blue slice—expenditures—steady."

"What's the yellow slice?" Jack said. He squinted to see Evie's computer from his desk across the room.

"Good debt like the hotel renovation and the marina project. We'll have something to show for it. A capital improvement."

"We're not doubting you," June said. She

sat on the edge of Evie's desk and folded her hands.

"Yes, you are," Evie replied. "And you should. I'm spending money like we're printing it in the back room."

"If you think it's going to pay off before the next generation of Hamiltons takes over, I'm not against borrowing money and hedging our bets," June said. "I just don't want to fall into the same trap our father did."

Evie reminded herself to breathe. She had done her homework, met with the construction superintendent and architect again. Knew the estimated costs. And was prepared for overruns in case the hotel walls had secrets. The architect had cautioned her that the dollars could double if they ran into unexpected problems. New construction was predictable, but a grand old building like the Lake Breeze Hotel might not take kindly to having its insides exposed.

"We already agreed to the giant price tag for the hotel earlier this summer," Jack said. "So tell me how the additional expense is going to pay off."

"It's technically only a half million extra," Evie explained. "Some of the money is already budgeted because I was hoping to have a million left over from the original construction loan. I told you about the plan for the leftover money already—improving or rebuilding the employee dorms."

Evie walked over to Jack's desk and took a doughnut. Maybe sugar and fat would help. The multimillion-dollar baking industry couldn't be all wrong.

"We're sacrificing that now, right?" June asked. "The employee dorm?"

Evie sighed and licked the chocolate icing off the top of her doughnut. "I hate it, but, yes. Our summer help will have to live in the drafty old dorms another year. Or maybe two."

Jack shrugged. "We never officially announced that part of the plan, so no one will be disappointed."

"No," Evie said. "I guess not. And no matter how yucky those dorms are, at least they do have a sprinkler system." She almost smiled, remembering the day she had walked through the halls with Scott as he removed coat hangers from sprinkler heads and shoved away chairs blocking fire exits. She pictured his broad shoulders and square-set jaw. That was the first day she'd seen him as a man, not an obstacle.

And how does he feel about me? Is there a spark for him or does he see me as an irresponsible safety manager?

"Do you think it's weird that all these years our summer workers have lived in a safer building than our hotel guests?" June asked.

Evie nodded. "Sprinklers were added in the 1970s after a small fire in the dorms. They didn't do a beautiful job cosmetically. They did it the cheapest way possible by leaving the pipes exposed. But it's better than nothing."

"I'm assuming we're not going with the industrial exposed-pipe look in the hotel," June said. "It would look like a factory."

Evie shook her head. "No. If we're going to this much trouble to make it cosmetically beautiful, it would be stupid to do that."

"You haven't said how this will pay off financially," Jack said.

"Insurance savings, for one. We get a substantial discount for having sprinklers in all the rooms and hallways. And we get that savings every year from now on."

"That sounds good," June said encouragingly.

"Will that add up to a million and a half during my lifetime?" Jack asked.

Evie grinned. "That depends on how long you live. If you keep eating those doughnuts, probably not."

Jack wadded up a napkin and tossed it at Evie.

"One more question. Why are you changing the plan now?" Jack asked. "Earlier this summer, you had no intention of knocking down old walls in the old part of the hotel."

"I thought about it some more," Evie said.

"You've thought about it for the past year," Jack reminded her. "What changed?"

"I studied the issue."

June laughed. "Who was your study partner? Or can I guess?"

Evie felt her face heat. She opened the top drawer of her desk and dug around in it so she wouldn't have to look at her brother and sister. She pulled out a box of staples and refilled her desk stapler, snapping the jaws back together loudly.

Jack frowned. "I have no idea what is going on here. Is Evie going to fire safety school? Was it the STRIPE program that inspired you?"

"Poor Jack," June said. "Does the name Scott Bennett ring a bell?"

"Of course it does."

June smirked at her brother. "Did Bennett talk you into these changes?"

"No," Evie said quickly. "This was my decision."

"Good," Jack grumbled. "Or the guy owes me a million and a half bucks."

"You're a grouch," June said. "And you should be happy. You've survived six weeks of parenthood already."

"Barely. You're smart to have a baby during the winter. Augusta went in to work downtown for a few hours this morning to make some flowers for a wedding cake this weekend. But I'm picking her up and we're taking Nora to get a family portrait taken. Even though I'll look half dead in the picture."

June laughed. "Tough it out, big brother."

"If you two approve of my plans, and since you're going downtown anyway, would you drop off these documents to the fire station? I need the inspector's signature on our amended drawings."

June glanced at her sister questioningly but she didn't say anything.

Evie could deliver the plans on her way

home, but she thought it was better if she steered clear of the Bayside Fire Department for now.

ON THE SECOND day of demolition, there wasn't as much drama and action as Evie had hoped. Before the heavy equipment could tear off the roof or knock down walls, interior work had to be completed.

"Wear this," the site boss told her as he handed her a hard hat.

Evie snapped it on and followed him into the building.

"We've shut off the power. The gas lines are getting disconnected and capped off next. Water is already turned off and the system is draining. Takes time."

"How long will this phase take?" Evie asked. She mentally reviewed the construction calendar, which didn't allow for many delays. Bad winter weather loomed in the back of her mind and made her wish she could grab these hot summer days and make them last.

"A few more days. We want to pull out and recycle all the old copper wire. It's worth something. And some pipes and gutters can be recycled, too. We have to inspect and document any hazardous materials we find such as asbestos."

"Do you think you'll find that?"

He nodded. "Older buildings like this one are often full of it behind the walls and in the crawl spaces. I can't even imagine what we'll find when we tear into the original part of the hotel. That's a lot older yet."

Because the park was still two weeks from closing, the historic section of the Lake Breeze Hotel remained open and full.

"I hope the updated plans will be approved by the time we're ready to tear into the old part," Evie said. It had only been two days since Jack had dropped off the new drawings and Evie had not heard a word from Scott. Would he approve them himself now that he no longer had the conflict of interest as an employee of Starlight Point?

Because it was one of the last Saturdays of the operating season, and the park would be open until midnight, she planned to be on her feet all day. Luckily, her car was back in operation and she had driven it today knowing she was likely to miss the last ferry.

She left the hotel project and entered Starlight Point through a gate concealed behind a French fry stand. As she strolled up the midway, conserving her energy, the summer heat from the concrete rolled over her feet and legs. Roller coaster riders screamed happily. Elephant ears tempted her with their smell.

Evie was very glad to be busy running the park, winding down the season and ramping up the hotel demolition. In theory, it left her no time to think about Scott Bennett. She tried not to think of him every time she passed a handsome, dark-haired guest. She put him out of her mind when she found herself noting the location of fire extinguishers in each building she entered. She wished she could forget the haunted look in his eyes when he'd told her about the tragedy in his youth.

Her childhood had been cotton candy compared to that, no matter how much work Starlight Point was.

Nothing was more important to her than securing the future of her family's park. It was also their past. Taking a risk on projects this summer was a long stride out of her comfort zone. Adding to the cost in the past week was a leap out of safety. *Did I do it because it was the right thing for our guests and our company? Or did I do it because I wanted to please Scott?*

Either way, adding sprinklers to the old hotel wouldn't erase the scars Scott carried from his childhood. What, then, was she hoping for?

Now that Scott no longer worked for Starlight Point, and Evie had changed her plans—the right thing to do—what was keeping them apart?

Fear. Had she only imagined there was something between them aside from just the tug of war of having to work together while on opposing sides? Without that conflict, did they have a relationship? She was afraid to ask herself that question and even more afraid to ask Scott.

Evie got a basket of chicken strips and fries and headed for her favorite bench in front of the train station. Her thinking bench. The place where she used to meet her father for an afternoon break on hot summer days, and the place where she felt closest to him now.

But the bench was taken. Scott and Caroline were drinking sodas on her bench. Caroline wore her work uniform. Scott was dressed like a tourist.

Evie stopped short but it was too late. They had seen her approaching.

"Hi, Evie," Caroline said. "Sit down and

eat with us. You're much better company than my brother."

Scott stood but said nothing. His face was serious, a deep line between his brows.

He's not happy to see me. Did he regret telling her about the hotel tragedy? Did he think she had only changed her plans out of pity or guilt? He had certainly seen the new proposal by now.

Why doesn't he say something?

If she had believed he had feelings for her that amounted to a conflict of interest, she had been wrong.

"I can't," Evie said. "I was on my way... somewhere."

"Scott told me this was your favorite place to sit," Caroline said. "I can see why. You can watch all the action from here."

Evie laughed, even though a heavy weight in her chest took any humor out of it. "I'm hoping for a quiet night with no action."

"No fun in that," Caroline said.

"Yes, actually there is. And I'm in charge tonight, so I better eat on the run." She couldn't stay there awkwardly with her food getting cold and Caroline trying to make up for the rudeness of her brother—*who was still silent.*

Evie started to walk away. The one place that had always brought her solace was no help tonight. She wished her father was there so she could pour out her heart and ask him what he thought of her plans for the park and her complicated relationship with Scott. She squared her shoulders. She had to face her problems without her father. She had to let him go.

"Evie, wait," Scott said, coming up behind her. "I'm on duty in Bayside starting in about an hour, but I wonder if you might...if we might meet up tomorrow."

She stopped. Turned. "Why?" Evie asked. His tone implied that it was business.

He swallowed. "I wanted to talk with you about...what happens next." Scott glanced at his sister, who pretended to be very interested in her drink. "I bought a two-day ticket," he continued. "Will you meet me here tomorrow night?"

Evie's heart hammered in her chest. She looked away from Scott's earnest but serious face. The train was just leaving the station behind him. Steam bellowed from the old-fashioned engine and the loud whistle perforated the air. How many times had that train made the same circuit? Dozens of times each day it left the station, changed passengers at the Wonderful West station, and returned—always the same but always different.

The weight on her lungs lifted. Maybe she and Scott could start over, too. He'd said *what happens next*. What did that mean?

"Eight o'clock. Tomorrow night," she said.

IT WAS ALMOST MIDNIGHT. The back part of the park had begun to clear as guests gathered at the front of the midway for their final rides on the big coasters. The food stands were slowly shutting down in the Wonderful West as Evie passed them on her way up the section of the midway closest to the hotel.

Ducking out a side gate, Evie took a stroll past the rear of the Lake Breeze Hotel. The lights in the main structure were on, welcoming guests home from a long day of hot dogs and sore feet. The detached wings toward the back were empty, silent, dark. She breathed in the cool night air, imagining what this scene would look like next year with new wings, a courtyard, a reimagined car entrance.

Her baby. Her project. She was so close to making a substantial contribution to Starlight Point. More than running accounts and securing loans to repair the damage her father had done, she was ready to take one of her visions and make it reality.

Night cloaked the construction project in darkness now.

Except for a glimmer in one of the windows. Had a construction worker left a light on when he'd finished for the day hours ago? The crew planned to work six days a week while good weather lasted, but Evie knew they would take the next day, Sunday, off.

So why the faint glow? Evie slipped around the barricade, ignoring the sign forbidding entrance. The orange light in the upper window wouldn't be visible from the main hotel. It could only be seen from the side nearest the little-used employee gate she had just come through. No wonder no one had noticed it.

Evie used her master key to unlock the main entrance door. There was no light in the building because the power had been shut off for two days. It was eerily silent.

She used the flashlight app on her cell phone to find the stairs to the second floor. Having been in this building hundreds of times throughout her life, she knew exactly where the stairs were. Could count the doors until she got there. But the building was different now. Construction equipment lay everywhere. Pipes, tools, bundles of wire. She had to step carefully to avoid falling over something.

And what was that strange smell? Opening up old walls had filled the place with dust and the smells from decades of hotel occupants. Years ago, smoking was commonplace in the rooms, and stale cigarette smoke emanated from the exposed walls.

But this was a different smoke smell. Fear seized Evie's heart. She flashed her cell phone's light ahead of her and raced up the stairs, trying to avoid tools left on the steps. On the second floor, she glanced down the long hallway.

The flashlight app on her phone died, but it didn't matter. There was no mistaking the orange glow she saw under the door at the far end of the hall. The radio at her waist broke the silence with the Starlight Point dispatcher announcing a fire.

A car fire in the parking lot. *Great*. And now she had two on her hands.

She paused at the top of the steps and watched smoke curl from under the door at the end of the hallway. It was almost mesmerizing. But it was terrifying.

She heard the fire department acknowl-edge the parking lot call and radio that they were on their way. She didn't want to call them back, not for a fire in an unoccupied building. Car fires could be dangerous. Ex-plosive. And there were sure to be many people in the parking lot at this moment be-cause the midway had just closed. Human lives could be in danger.

Maybe she could handle this herself. She'd already taken on things this summer she would never have imagined doing even a year ago. It was her place, her hotel. She had to take action. Fast.

There was a fire extinguisher box next to her. Could she try to put out the fire? It hadn't burned through the door. How bad could it be? Evie grabbed two fire extinguishers, mentally reviewing Scott's instructions for using them as she stalked down the hall. She thought of her mother and how excited she would be that someone had learned some-thing useful in the STRIPE classes.

Her mother would probably tell her to turn around and run right now, but Evie had learned to face down her problems. Since her father died, she had found the strength to confront the things that frightened her.

She felt for the pin and pulled it. Readying the fire extinguisher in one hand, her heart pounding out of her chest, Evie shoved open the door. She knew it wouldn't be locked because all the electronic locks had been disabled.

As soon as the door swung open, flames and smoke leaped out at her. The heat singed her and smoke choked her. She dropped the fire extinguisher, realizing immediately that she was overpowered.

Evie grabbed her radio and called the Starlight Point dispatcher as she ran down the hall toward the central staircase.

"Evie Hamilton to Dispatch," she huffed out as she ran.

"Go ahead."

"Fire in the hotel. Call Bayside Fire."

Evie reached the staircase and started racing down in the pitch darkness. "It's in the—"

Her words ended on a scream when her foot caught in a hose and she fell over a piece of equipment left in the stairwell. Her radio went flying and she heard it smash as she fell down step after step in the darkness, her foot still tangled and agonizing pain taking away her breath and her ability to think.

CHAPTER TWENTY-TWO

LONG, SLOW NIGHTS like this were Scott's least favorite thing about his job. Too much time to sit around and think. Since his talk with Evie about the hotel fire that had taken his sister's life, Scott had replayed his words a hundred times.

He needed to let go. He knew that. But every time he thought of the words *hotel* and *fire* in the same sentence, searing pain blinded him. He hated coming across as a hard-hearted jerk to Evie, and he didn't want her pity.

That was definitely not what he wanted from her. He had less than twenty-four hours to figure out how to tell her he had fallen in love with her. What would he say to her when they met on the midway tomorrow night? Did she feel the same way he did?

Scott had seen Jack Hamilton go into the chief's office with an armload of paperwork a few days ago, but since he wasn't on the chief's good side right now he hadn't asked what was in the paperwork. Since he'd taken himself off the roster at Starlight Point and removed himself from inspecting anything there, he had no right to ask.

Whatever happened with the hotel, he had begun to realize his feelings for Evie were separate from it.

Scott grabbed a newspaper and a bag of chips. Set the radio to scan the local departments' radio traffic, and parked himself at the dinner table in the bunk room. It was going to be a long night at this rate.

He was halfway through the chips and the paper when he heard a familiar voice over the radio. His heart contracted when Evie announced a hotel fire. Nearly stopped beating when he heard her scream and then silence.

He didn't wait for Dispatch. He raced through the bunk room and woke his shift partners.

"Hotel fire at Starlight Point," he yelled, racing for his turnout gear and the main pumper truck.

He waited for his partner to hit the seat next to him and floored the truck out of the station. The other fire truck was right behind him.

As they neared the Point Bridge, all the traffic was heading the other way, leaving the park after a midnight closing. Good. The inbound lanes were a ghost town.

His partner ran the siren and air horn while Scott negotiated the bridge and the outer loop road at a dangerous speed. He'd noticed the Starlight Point fire trucks in the parking lot, smoke rolling off a car fire as he raced by. No wonder Evie had called Bayside right away.

The Starlight Point dispatcher came over the radio while they were still on the outer loop.

"Update on hotel fire. Security reports it's in the unoccupied section that is being demolished. Repeat unoccupied wings in the back."

"That's a relief," his partner said. "We could slow down and live to get there."

Scott didn't let off the accelerator.

"It's unoccupied, Captain. You heard the dispatcher."

"I heard the original call over the scanner. The person who called it in sounded like she was in the building."

"She?" his partner asked.

"Uh-huh," Scott grumbled.

"What the heck is somebody doing in that place this late?"

He rounded the tight curves on the road around the peninsula. He thought of the time earlier in the summer when Evie had ridden next to him in the Point's fire truck. He'd been carefully pushing her away all season long, but all he wanted right now was to hold her close. He would give up anything—his job, his badge—to see her safe.

As soon as he parked the truck next to a hydrant behind the hotel, Scott flew from the cab and confronted two Starlight Point cops standing by the building. Flames were already visible coming out of the windows on the far end.

"Where's Evie Hamilton?" he asked.

"That's what we'd like to know. Can't find her. Dispatcher didn't want to say it over the radio, but she's worried."

"Did anyone go in the building yet?" Scott demanded.

"One quick pass through the downstairs, but we didn't go upstairs. The smoke was starting to get thick in there."

Scott's partner jogged over.

"I'm going in," Scott said.

"Sure," his partner said. "I hooked the hydrant and the other guys are pulling hoses. We'll put on the air packs. Ready in a minute."

Scott didn't wait for his partner to stop talking. He ran for the open door, completely ignoring department protocol. He had no fire hose. He had no air pack. He was only thinking of one thing.

He raced down the first-floor hallway, flashlight in hand, pushing in doors as he went.

"Evie! Where are you?" he yelled.

He entered one room when he thought he heard something, did a quick search, looked in the bathtub even though nausea and fear nearly took him to his knees.

The room was empty.

He dashed back to the hallway, looking wildly around like a madman. Paused. Listened.

Someone was saying his name.

Smoke came through the ceiling at the far end of the hallway. The fire was beginning to advance and burn through the floor upstairs. Scott ran toward the middle of the hallway and found the staircase. Someone had opened a hole at the top of the staircase, perhaps left a vent open during the demolition project, and the stairway was acting as a giant chimney. The very bottom was clear of smoke.

Which was why Scott's flashlight beam could pierce the darkness and smoke and find Evie, crumpled at the bottom of the steps.

Her eyes were open as she lay on the last step. Her leg was elevated, tangled in something and held at an unnatural angle.

He was by her side in a heartbeat, running his hands over her head, her face.

"Evie," he breathed. "You're alive."

She blinked, never taking her eyes from his face.

"I knew you'd find me," she whispered.

He almost smiled as the weight in his chest lifted.

"You're all I care about," he said. "I have to get you out of here."

She shook her head, a tiny back-and-forth movement. "I can't move. My leg got tangled in something and twisted. Whenever I try to move it, it hurts so much… I can't."

Scott took both her hands and squeezed. "Squeeze back," he said.

He was relieved when she did. No spinal injury, he hoped. But he didn't like the confused look in her eyes. She'd been stuck here, waiting in agony and fear for possibly ten minutes.

"Did you hit your head when you fell?"

"I hit everything."

"What's the date?"

"Last midnight close of the season," she said.

"Tell me your sister's name," he said.

"June," she said. "And yours are Caroline. And Catherine."

Scott's throat was so thick he couldn't speak.

"I've been lying here thinking about her. And you," Evie said.

Scott kissed her forehead and his chest expanded. "This is going to have a happy ending," he said.

He palpated Evie's leg. Probable fracture of the tibia. Likely a spiral fracture, but only an X-ray would tell. Good thing it had been elevated all this time. It kept the swelling and the pain down somewhat. He gently unwound her foot from the air hose attached to a compressor nearby. She flinched and gasped when her leg moved.

"I'm sorry," he said. "I have to get you out of here. Fast."

He heard voices behind him and turned.

His partners in full face masks and gear were waiting with flashlights and a fire hose. He nodded at them, bent and picked up Evie as carefully as he could. The smoke was getting thicker. One of his partners went in front and one behind him and their group made it down the hall and out the exit.

Outside, Scott laid Evie on the grass away from the burning building, the trucks, the hoses and the noise and fury of a working fire scene. A member of his crew dumped off a medical kit and a splint, told him an ambulance was already on the way, and headed back to the fire.

Scott splinted Evie's lower leg first, trying to minimize the damage and the pain. She wore the same navy blue skirt he'd seen her wear a dozen times. She'd been wearing it just hours ago when he'd seen her on the midway. Her exposed skin was cold and clammy. *Shock*.

He finished the splint, palpated her other leg and ran his hands over her torso and down her arms. She was cold all over and her eyes were closed.

"Evie," he said, rubbing the pads of his fingers over her cheeks. "Stay with me, honey.

You're safe now, you'll be all right. I'll make sure of it."

He put a blood pressure cuff on her arm, trying to think rationally and complete a patient assessment as he would with anyone.

But this was not anyone.

"I love you," he whispered to Evie.

She opened her eyes and the corners of her mouth slid upward just enough to let him know she'd heard him.

As he tried to take her blood pressure, listening to the reassuring sound of her heart through the stethoscope, Jack ran up and dropped next to Evie on the ground. He stopped, hands in midair as if he wanted to hug her but was afraid to touch her.

"Broken leg. Shock. Bruised up from a fall down a staircase," Scott said.

"Will she be okay?"

"I think so."

"What happened?"

Scott took the stethoscope from his ears. He heard the wailing siren of the approaching ambulance. "She was in the building, reported the fire, got tangled up in construction stuff and fell down the stairs. When we got here, I went in and found her."

Jack sat back on his heels, his face a mask of fear mixed with relief.

"You saved my sister's life," he said. Jack leaned over Evie and brushed her hair from her face. He turned back to Scott and held out his hand. "Thank you for my sister."

Scott felt his heart stop. And then, miraculously, start again. In that moment, he believed he heard his older sister Catherine's voice. She was asking for him, saying his name, asking if he was okay.

He turned. It wasn't Catherine. Of course it wasn't. She'd been gone for twenty years. It was Caroline, in her uniform, asking one of her colleagues where he was.

He glanced back at Evie, whose eyes were open as she answered her brother's questions. Memories of Catherine and him flooded his mind. He remembered his older sister as she had looked when she was alive. Swinging in the backyard. Eating spaghetti at the dinner table. Throwing him out of her bedroom when her friends were over.

He hadn't thought of her like that in a long time.

The ambulance backed onto the grass and the Starlight Point fire chief opened the back doors. He unloaded a gurney and placed it next to Evie. Together, they lifted her onto it and loaded her into the ambulance. Scott was about to climb in the back when someone punched him in the ribs.

"Did you run into a burning building with no air pack and no hose?" his sister demanded.

"It's my job," he said.

"You drive me nuts."

"Likewise."

Caroline kissed him on the cheek. "There's something different about you," she said, cocking her head to the side.

"There is," he agreed. He climbed in the ambulance and shut the doors.

He flipped on the overhead lights and got out the supplies to start an IV on Evie. She needed fluids to combat the shock.

As he taped down the needle and the tubing, he held her hand just a little longer than necessary.

"Thank you," she said. "I'd kiss you right now if I could move."

He smiled.

"You could kiss me," she said.

Scott leaned over her and touched his lips to hers. The ambulance hit a bump on the

Point Bridge and he braced an arm on the gurney.

"I'm not supposed to kiss my patients," he said. "It could be dangerous."

"Love involves risk and breaking the rules," Evie murmured.

Scott's heart was already racing from the kiss, and now it was sprint level.

Did she love him? How long had they both known?

Her face changed with each bump in the road and he felt her tense. He wanted to kiss her again, but instead he pulled two pillows from a cabinet and packed them next to Evie's broken leg.

"There's so much I want to tell you," Evie said.

He laid a hand on her forehead. Still clammy, but not as bad. "Later," he said. "We'll have plenty of time to talk."

CHAPTER TWENTY-THREE

"Bennett," the Bayside chief said, "you've been a big pain in the butt all summer."

Scott sat across from his boss on the Monday morning after the fire. He felt as if he hadn't slept in years.

After he'd gotten Evie to the hospital on Saturday night, he'd stayed there for hours, waiting with her mother and her sister as the orthopedic doctor treated her fracture. Scott had been much relieved that it was not the spiral fracture he had suspected and did not require surgery. The doctor's plan was to keep her overnight and release her the next day with a cast on her left leg and orders to go home and rest.

He'd returned to the fire scene to help with cleanup at dawn. Jack was there, disheveled and soot-streaked, but happy there had been no loss of life. The building was being demolished, anyway, but the project had taken a messy turn. Seeing the burned building and thinking about what could have happened took away Scott's desire to go home and sleep.

Now he focused on keeping his eyes open as he waited for his boss to finish berating him. He knew what was coming. And he deserved it.

Chief Portman paced behind his desk, arms crossed over his chest. The morning sun streaked through the window, but the chief's face was dark as night.

"You were the officer in charge and you blatantly disregarded our protocol." He huffed out a long breath. "Running into a building without a charged line. Without your air pack. Without your partner." The chief's voice rose until it thundered. "What the devil were you thinking?"

"I was thinking about the credible report of a trapped victim inside," Scott said neutrally.

"And so you wanted to add one more victim to the count? I don't think you learned anything when you got your fire science degree," he fumed. "Maybe you need a refresher at officer's training school."

Chief Portman thumped down into his chair.

"It was damned foolish, Bennett, and I ought to fire you."

A wave of panic rushed up Scott's throat. He was about to lose a job he loved. All his life he'd believed he must fight fires to atone for the early death of his sister. And to pay for the fact that someone else had died for him. It was a heavy burden he'd lived with, a dark shadow that never left.

But then he thought of carrying Evie out of that burning building and realized he didn't *have* to fight fires and save people anymore. He *wanted* to.

"Are you telling me to turn in my badge?" he asked quietly. *Please say no.*

"No."

Scott looked up. His chief's face had lost some of its anger.

"You think I can fire a guy who just risked his life to rescue someone? And not just someone, one of the owners of Starlight Point? Heck, I'd probably get fired."

So, I'm not losing my job?

"Jack Hamilton already called me and said he wanted a parade for you." The chief shook his head. "A parade. I sure can't can you now for tearing our rules to shreds and going rogue."

"Thank you," Scott said, meeting his chief's eyes.

"Don't thank me yet. I've got conditions. You have to take back the inspector's job. I have plenty of paperwork of my own to do, and I'm in no humor to look at those hotel plans again."

"Again?"

The chief drained his coffee cup and parked it in a worn ring on the edge of his desk. "They made changes at the end of last week on the Lake Breeze Hotel renovation over at Starlight Point. Jack brought in the drawings. I figured I'd face it on Monday, so I haven't looked at it yet." He sighed. "I hate paperwork."

Changes? Was that what Jack had dropped off on Friday?

"I know you had some supposed conflict of interest at the Point," the chief said. "But since you don't work there anymore, I don't see why you can't take those plans off my hands."

Scott didn't answer. He was still thinking about what the changes could be and whether his conflict of interest was better or immeasurably worse now. Probably a lot worse, but he didn't care.

"You want to keep your job, Captain Bennett, I suggest you start saying yes."

Scott laughed out loud. "Yes."

The chief sat back in his chair. "I've known you for almost a year, Scott, and that's the first time I've ever seen you look genuinely happy."

Scott shrugged. "Let's see the plans."

"They're already on your desk."

When he walked over to his office, he flipped on the aging fluorescent lights and closed the door. There was a file on his desk and a cardboard tube.

His hands were shaking. Probably because he hadn't slept in days.

And that wasn't all.

Scott popped the cap off the end of the tube and pulled out the rolled-up drawing inside. He spread it out on his desk and held the curling edges in place with his hands. Leaned closer and stared in disbelief.

He sat and looked across his desk at the empty chair Evie had almost fallen out of two months ago. The first time he'd held her in his arms.

Before he'd known how she would change his life.

IT WAS ONLY day three of her convalescence and Evie was tired of her mother fussing over her. When she'd left the hospital on Sunday afternoon, she had gone to her mother's house without objection because she was sore, exhausted and her mother's house had no steps to negotiate.

Scott had sent flowers Monday and called. He'd called again from work on Tuesday. But their conversations on the phone were guarded, reserved. He asked about her leg, her bruises, her health. But what she wanted to talk about were her feelings.

Had he meant it when he said he loved her?

Everything from that night was such a fog and she had many regrets about her actions. Especially the fact that she was spending the last week of the operating season with a cast on her lower leg.

But her biggest regret was that she had not said *I love you* back.

Why didn't Scott stop by to see her in person? She knew he was working downtown. Also knew he had approved the revised hotel plans. Not a surprise. It was exactly what he had advised from the start. Jack had been summoned to pick up the approved plans and reported to Evie that it was Scott's signature on the paperwork. Did that mean she was no longer a conflict of interest for him?

Evie was sure of one thing. She couldn't lie around on her mother's couch any longer.

"I'm going to work," she announced to Virginia on Wednesday morning. "If I can borrow your car."

She taped a trash bag over her cast, took a shower and put on her usual uniform. White blouse, navy skirt, black name tag. But only one shoe.

Her mother followed her to the car and helped shove the crutches into the backseat.

"I'd try to stop you," Virginia said. "But I think a little sunshine and activity will do you some good. Just don't overdo it."

"Thanks for taking care of me," Evie said as she eased her leg into the car and caught her breath. *Crutches are a pain.*

Virginia tucked her daughter's purse in next to her and kissed her on the cheek. "I'm your mother. It's my job. Call me if you need me."

Evie cut across Starlight Point's main parking lot without a definite plan in mind. It was a quiet morning during the last week of the season. Schools were back in session and the lot was barely one-quarter full. There would be no crowds to dodge on the midway, and it would be so nice to smell funnel cakes and hear the carousel and the coasters.

She parked in the marina lot, planning to crutch the short distance through the gate onto the midway. She'd visit Tosha for ice cream, rest on her favorite bench and maybe make her way to her office where Jack was probably eating doughnuts or gazing at the picture of his new baby.

The sun feels so nice. Evie balanced on one leg and reached into the backseat for her crutches. *So far, so good.* She simply had to pass some benches, planters and streetscaping on her way to the crossing at the outer loop road. The ticket gate was right there.

She started across the short distance, enjoying the breeze and the screams from the roller coasters. Crutch, step, crutch, step. She breathed a little heavier. Started to sweat.

Had it always been this far from the parking lot to the crossing? *Maybe I should take a break.*

She paused but resolved to keep going. When she reached the crosswalk, she was glad to have to stop and wait for five cars. It gave her a chance to catch her breath. The sound of a truck engine caught her attention. Good. She would wait for that, too. She kept her eyes on the ground, noting the ridiculous disparity between her sandal on one foot and bare toes sticking out of a cast on the other.

A truck stopped in front of her. She saw huge tires. A silver running board. Her eyes traveled up. It was the red Starlight Point fire truck.

Air brakes whooshed. A door slammed. Scott Bennett came around the truck and took her in his arms without a moment's hesitation.

She didn't need her crutches and they fell behind her to the concrete with a loud clack.

"What are you doing?" he asked.

His uniform shirt under her cheek felt so good. He smelled like fresh air and fire truck. "Going to work," she mumbled.

"Why? You're supposed to be home resting."

"I'm tired of resting," she said.

He chuckled and she laughed at the low rumble in his chest.

"Have I ever heard you laugh before?" she asked.

He drew back a little, still holding her in

his arms, and looked down at her. "I do it a lot more these days."

Car horns sounded.

"I'm blocking traffic," he said.

"You weren't heading to an emergency, I hope," Evie said. "I don't have a radio right now, so I don't know what's going on."

"You have bad luck with radios," he said, grinning. "No emergency. I was heading out to check hydrants. But I found something far more interesting to do."

"Wait a minute. Since when do you work here again?"

"Since I got my job back earlier this week." He winked. "Now, I better move this truck."

He held her with one arm, reached behind him with the other and opened the passenger door.

Evie laughed. "I don't usually take rides from strangers."

He caressed her cheek. "I don't usually pick up hitchhikers."

He helped her into the truck and she stuck her head out the open window and watched him toss her crutches somewhere in the back. He got in the driver's seat and pulled off the road behind the Silver Streak. Scott set the parking brake and killed the engine.

"You're in a fire lane," Evie said.

"I'm in a fire truck. That makes it okay." He slid across the seat, carefully avoiding her leg, put both arms around her and kissed her forehead.

"I meant what I said," he whispered. "The night of the fire."

Evie felt as if a flock of doves had been released in her chest. She threaded her arms around his hard chest and pressed her cheek to his.

"I did, too. When I said love involves risk. I watched my brother and my sister resist someone all summer and then give in before the season was over."

"The season's almost over," he said.

"I thought they were crazy until it happened to me."

"Until what happened?" he asked softly, his mouth hovering over hers.

"I fell in love."

His lips touched hers and she forgot everything but him until a seagull landed on the hood of the truck and screamed at them.

Scott laughed and tapped the windshield, scaring the bird away.

This feels so right, Evie thought. *But there are things we have to talk about.*

"When you told me about…what happened when you were young," she said. "That night. I never told you why I wanted to save money on the Lake Breeze project."

Scott smiled. "Is it the same reason you drive a car my grandmother would be ashamed of driving?"

"No. And maybe a little yes." She smiled and touched her forehead to his. "But there really was another reason. A serious one. I wanted to take the leftover money from the construction loan and use it to rebuild the employee dorm."

Scott's eyes cut to the dorm just visible near the edge of the marina property.

"The one you hate," Evie added.

"I do hate that dorm."

"See? It was a decent idea."

"Yes," he admitted. "But at least that old dorm has some fire protection—once we got the employees to stop living so dangerously."

"You mean your STRIPE classes."

"Partly," he said.

"Those nearly got me killed."

Scott's face froze and he sat back. "What are you talking about?"

"When I discovered the fire in the hotel, our department was heading out to a car fire.

I knew how to use a fire extinguisher, thanks to you, so I tried to attack the fire myself."

Scott pulled her into his arms and held her so tightly she couldn't breathe. He buried his face in her hair. "Promise me you will never ever do that again."

"With you around," she murmured, her lips against his neck, "I won't have to."

"Then I'm never leaving."

"Good." She put a hand on his chest and pushed him back so she could see his face. "In fact, I have a better offer for you. My fire chief is retiring and I need someone who's proven his loyalty to replace him."

"Do you have anyone in mind?"

She kissed him in answer.

"What do you think your brother and sister will think of that decision? Won't people say I used my influence with you to get the job?"

"My brother and sister think you're the biggest hero on the planet. At least, they do now. I had to prevent Jack from strangling you earlier this summer. But they've both learned to trust my decisions. More importantly, I've learned to trust myself."

"Just promise me you'll stick to managing money and making plans, and leave the fire-fighting to me."

"That's why I'm offering you the job. I want you by my side, Scott."

Scott swallowed hard. "I know you think I saved your life, but I have to confess something. I was the one who needed to be saved. All those years of hauling around my past nearly robbed me of my life. You gave it back to me, Evie."

"I love you," she said, her eyes stinging with tears.

He put his hands on her cheeks and kissed her lips. "And I love you, Evie."

The Silver Streak raced past with happy screams, rattling tracks and a whoosh of air.

Evie laughed. "Could I persuade you to drive me around the outer loop to my office?" she asked. "I have a major project I better get started on."

"Anything for you," he said. He kissed her one more time and then he clicked her seat belt in place, started the truck and pulled onto the loop surrounding Starlight Point.

EPILOGUE

WHITE CHAIRS LINED the boardwalk in front of the newly renovated Lake Breeze Hotel. It was the beginning of May, and the hotel and Starlight Point would open the following weekend. The Saturday afternoon was warm and sunny, promising a summer of beautiful days.

Evie wore a white-lace gown, handiwork of Gloria, who had made costumes for nearly everyone at Starlight Point. But this was her finest creation. Evie felt like a sparkling wave in the sunshine as she waited to walk down the aisle to meet Scott, who stood under a trellis at the other end. Handsome in a black tuxedo, he looked so happy to see her she thought she would burst with joy.

June and Augusta, her matrons of honor, preceded her up the aisle, along with her bridesmaid Caroline. Her mother sat in the front row with little Nora balanced on her lap. Mel sat next to her with five-month-old Abigail in his arms. Scott's parents had flown in from Arizona for the wedding and they sat in the front row on the other side.

Jack held Evie's arm as she walked down the aisle. After months of therapy, she walked steadily, without a trace of the broken bone. But she was still glad to have her brother by her side.

"Ready for this?" he asked.

"Completely," she said.

"Good. My knees are shaking. I need wedding cake."

Evie laughed. "I love you, Jack."

Firefighters in full dress uniform lined both sides of the walkway. They were members of the Bayside Fire Department, where Scott still worked a few shifts as a firefighter and kept his office hours as the local building inspector. There were also members of the Starlight Point Fire Department, where Scott would begin this season as the chief.

Year-round employees and longtime vendors Evie had known all her life smiled at her as she passed.

Evie approached the trellis and Jack kissed her cheek and did the ceremonial handoff to his soon-to-be brother-in-law. She looked into Scott's eyes and knew in her heart that she didn't need to add anything up on a spreadsheet to verify her decision. She loved him in a way that went far beyond the cautious, rational accounting that was her former passion.

As soon as their vows were said, they would go inside the rotunda and lobby where banquet tables waited with food and cake. The first event to be held in the newly renovated hotel would be a family wedding. Her wedding.

The only thing that would have made this day more perfect, Evie thought, was if her father had been there to walk her down the aisle. She thought of his name tag, pinned to the inside hem of her dress. Glanced at the beautiful façade, both old and new, of the hotel he had loved and always intended to renovate.

In her heart, she knew he was there, and she knew he would be happy.

* * * * *

LARGER-PRINT BOOKS!

GET 2 FREE LARGER-PRINT NOVELS PLUS 2 FREE MYSTERY GIFTS

Love Inspired®
SUSPENSE
RIVETING INSPIRATIONAL ROMANCE

Larger-print novels are now available...

WESTERN WP PROMISES

YES! Please send me **The Western Promises Collection** in Larger Print. This collection begins with 3 FREE books and 2 FREE gifts (gifts valued at approx. $14.00 retail) in the first shipment, along with the other first 4 books from the collection! If I do not cancel, I will receive 8 monthly shipments until I have the entire 51-book Western Promises collection. I will receive 2 or 3 FREE books in each shipment and I will pay just $4.99 US/ $5.89 CDN for each of the other four books in each shipment, plus $2.99 for shipping and handling per shipment. *If I decide to keep the entire collection, I'll have paid for only 32 books, because 19 books are FREE! I understand that accepting the 3 free books and gifts places me under no obligation to buy anything. I can always return a shipment and cancel at any time. My free books and gifts are mine to keep no matter what I decide.

272 HCN 3070 472 HCN 3070

Name	(PLEASE PRINT)
Address	Apt. #
City	State/Prov.	Zip/Postal Code

Signature (if under 18, a parent or guardian must sign)

Mail to the **Reader Service:**
IN U.S.A.: P.O. Box 1867, Buffalo, NY 14240-1867
IN CANADA: P.O. Box 609, Fort Erie, Ontario L2A 5X3

* Terms and prices subject to change without notice. Prices do not include applicable taxes. Sales tax applicable in N.Y. Canadian residents will be charged applicable taxes. This offer is limited to one order per household. All orders subject to approval. Credit or debit balances in a customer's account(s) may be offset by any other outstanding balance owed by or to the customer. Please allow 4 to 6 weeks for delivery. Offer available while quantities last. Offer not available to Quebec residents.

Your Privacy—The Reader Service is committed to protecting your privacy. Our Privacy Policy is available online at www.ReaderService.com or upon request from the Reader Service.

We make a portion of our mailing list available to reputable third parties that offer products we believe may interest you. If you prefer that we not exchange your name with third parties, or if you wish to clarify or modify your communication preferences, please visit us at www.ReaderService.com/consumerschoice or write to us at Reader Service Preference Service, P.O. Box 9062, Buffalo, NY 14240-9062. Include your complete name and address.

WPBPA16R

LARGER-PRINT BOOKS!
GET 2 FREE LARGER-PRINT NOVELS PLUS
2 FREE GIFTS!

HARLEQUIN®

super romance®

More Story...More Romance

READERSERVICE.COM

Manage your account online!

- Review your order history
- Manage your payments
- Update your address

> *We've designed the Reader Service website just for you.*

Enjoy all the features!

- Discover new series available to you, and read excerpts from any series.
- Respond to mailings and special monthly offers.
- Connect with favorite authors at the blog.
- Browse the Bonus Bucks catalog and online-only exculsives.
- Share your feedback.

Visit us at:

ReaderService.com